Love's Liberation

Book 2

Khushi T. Saha

Edited by Jessica Gang

Book production by MysticqueRose Publishing Services LLC

Acknowledgements

Writing isn't easy, but it can be cathartic. What began as a self-awareness project turned into something much bigger than I could've ever imagined. I want to thank my editor and publisher for taking the time to walk me through the process and breaking down the intricacies of working on a piece of literary fiction.

I would also like to thank my family for giving me the experiences that led me to want to put pen to paper. Most importantly, I thank my husband. Without his patience and love, I would never be who I am today. Without his encouragement, I would never believe in myself to do this. Thanks babe. You're one in a million.

Contents

Present Day,
New York City

Chapter 1

Marc opted to walk back to The Plaza, hoping the cool fall air would clear his head. He meandered his way east and north, then cut through Central Park.

He'd made a bungle of that entire situation with Simran back in her apartment. Admittedly, both rage and jealousy took over when he learned she was traveling to India to see her ex-boyfriend, even though it seemed like the last thing she wanted to do, her anger and anxiety evident. And his control, or whatever the hell that was, completely vanished in a puff of smoke as soon as he touched her, trying to comfort her. God, touching her, feeling her against him was like a drug. He wanted more, always wanted more from her. He'd felt the same way three months ago, before leaving for Vancouver, heading into unknown disasters (both with her and his business). The overwhelming sensation to be near her, with her, at all times was ever-present and he'd felt ... *scared*. Scared of something all-consuming and uncontrollable; scared of the unknown—love. Because he was absolutely certain now that the knot in his chest was linked to love.

And now...? Well *fuck*, now he was afraid that the one person he felt this way about would choose a life without him. He wasn't proud of himself. He'd thrown away what they had because of his fears, instead of jumping right in—his usual attitude with everything else in life.

He stopped in his tracks. Busy New Yorkers scurried around him, mumbling their grievances but he didn't notice. A jittery warmth washed over his body—the yearning for something so badly, but the unsurety of how to make it yours. He stared up at the sky, searching for a sign in the stars. They gave him nothing, their visibility hidden by the bright city lights. Was he … lost?

It hit him unexpectedly; the force making his heart tighten painfully as it closed off his lungs and he gulped for air.

She was it for him.

Gone was the man satisfied with an endless string of women—the sexual adventures, his pick of the day based on his whim, like choosing an elaborate treat from a box of chocolates. What a fucktard he'd been. That was an empty, cold bastard who treated women with extravagance in exchange for not giving a shit about their emotions. Was Simran right? Did some of them hold it against him that they were just the flavor of the month?

"Karma, you all-knowing bitch," he muttered, now a little winded as if he'd run miles and miles. He found an empty bench near the park's Fifth Avenue entrance and sat down. His breathing was harsh now, loud in his own ears, and he put his head in his hands, willing the sting of tears at the back of his eyes to go away. He deserved it if he'd completely fucked up with her.

He thought back hard to what happened before leaving her apartment not even an hour ago. After admitting his feelings for her, Simran stayed quiet. She nodded, only giving him a soft, "Ok,"—her only indication that she understood him, but she hadn't said anything else. Usually so effervescent and chatty, she shut down and became difficult to read. She wasn't giving him anything. Marc felt exposed, and he hated it. He usually got his way with women, got his way during business transactions; shit, he got his way with just about everything. It'd been a long time since he hadn't, but this time was different and he had no choice but to wait it out. This was trickier than anything he'd ever encountered and he didn't want to push her away. She'd already panicked at their physical connection, even though he knew she felt the familiar pull, the mutual control slipping when together— same as him—although she'd made them stop. That was like a punch to the gut, but he could tell she was feeling vulnerable and he kept his distance after that.

She'd calmly asked why then. Why he'd broken it off three months ago; what had scared him off so suddenly? Torn about not wanting to hurt or offend her again, he finally admitted it was the last party they attended together—the one where her large South Asian community hosted an annual end of summer hoopla—that had done it in for him. The ex-boyfriend, the aunties, the conversations dancing around marriage; everything had been too much. Her face had gone pale but she nodded slowly as if she'd already come to that conclusion. He tried to grasp her hand, connect with her again, explain that it hadn't been her, just the pressure of figuring out what they were doing together that had pushed him. But, it was as if he was talking to a statue. She brushed him off and stood stiffly at the door.

Her answers were clipped toward his queries about her travels to Mumbai, when she was expected back (she didn't know), and that she would try to consider the declarations of his feelings (her voice wavering at that), amongst everything else going on. There was nothing left for him to say then, and he started to leave. Somehow, though, they got into another disagreement.

"So, who was she?" she'd asked ambiguously, as he shrugged on his suit jacket, and slipped his feet into his shoes, tie in hand.

Confused, he answered, "Sweetie, I don't know what you're talking about," and he turned to her dark eyes getting big and round, with fresh fury washing over her face.

"Marc, do you think I'm dumb *and* deaf?" Her arms were crossed tightly over her chest now. "I *heard* her. I heard that bitchy bimbo in the background of your voice message." He almost broke into a smile—at least she was talking to him, even if in anger. He had to flip back through his mind, much like an old-school view master toy, because everything was a blur when all he could think about the entire time away was the woman who stood so furiously before him. Then realization dawned and without thinking—maybe it was all the anxiety, maybe it was the lack of sleep—he tipped his head back and started hooting with laughter. It was all entirely comical right now and he was convinced he was going crazy. Now he understood the racket surrounding Beyoncé—he was fucking crazy in love.

"*Seriously*, Marc? You're laughing at this?" she asked, her voice cracking in the air. It took everything in him not to reach over and grab her again. She was always so beautiful when she was mad, it was such a turn-on. Right now, she was a thunderous inferno and there were no words to describe how sexy she was with her heated cheeks and her incredible eyes trying to kill him with black daggers.

"Sorry, sorry, Sims," he said, his hands up in surrender, his chuckles subdued. "I see the confusion there. Listen, that girl was our main investor's—and I mean THE main investor's—daughter. She was visiting from who the hell knows where and accompanied us for dinner and drinks a few times. She's a sweet kid, a college student, and ..." he cleared his throat uncomfortably, "... kind of had a crush on me. I entertained her because what else was I supposed to do with my main investor's daughter, but *nothing* happened," he said emphatically. "She must've followed me outside as I was leaving that message for you." He left it there because that girl had truthfully tried more. For someone so young, she'd been extremely forward and had physically pushed herself onto him. A small part of him wanted to let it happen because he was so damn miserable and maybe he could get lost, at least for one night, in this warm body. But as soon as her lips touched his, he recoiled. She wasn't who he wanted, and even though his body needed the physical release, he couldn't imagine having sex with just anyone. He'd pushed her away as gently as he could, telling her he'd made a mistake and that she deserved better. She came on even stronger, declaring that he was dripping with a player vibe that she was more than capable of handling.

"A studly man like you *needs* varying flavors to fulfill your desires, I can tell," the girl had remarked slyly before he politely and firmly excused himself. But that last part stuck with him. He'd felt anything but a player lately. Was it a behavior so ingrained in him that *that* was how he came across all the time? He'd always been convinced that Simran overreacted to those run-ins with past lovers in London and NYC, and he'd witnessed an insecure side of her that he couldn't reconcile with the confident creature he'd first been attracted to. But the girl's words that night sealed what he knew deep down to be the reality. And fuck, he thought he was the one who should be jealous! Men were always noticing Simran, staring at her. He saw it, even though she didn't seem to notice, like at that last party they attended.

And now, standing here in front of the only woman he wanted, trying to recall what she was referring to, he couldn't even remember that girl's face, let alone her name. But her words remained with him, and he needed to do better with Simran, act better than the man he'd been previously.

Simran sighed condescendingly, blowing the bangs out of her eyes. "Fine. If you say so." And she opened the door for him to leave.

He exhaled heavily. Of course, she didn't believe him. Would she ever? He stopped in front of her at the door, staring down at her lovely face. It was stone cold, her full lips in a hard line. She wouldn't even look at him, her focus was on the hallway past his shoulder, urging him to leave. He bent his knees so he could meet her eyes with his.

"I do say so. Won't you trust me, baby?" he asked gently, hoping she would relent. She blinked a few times and then looked down at her bare toes. Her shoulders sagged and she nodded.

"Ok," she said so quietly this time, that he almost missed it. But when she looked up, he saw something bright in her eyes, something other than fury, and a tiny bubble of hope planted itself in his chest. Yes! A *point for team Lehigh, finally!*

A dog barked loudly, bringing him back to twilight in the park. He stood up from the bench and continued walking. Now it was just a waiting game. He knew she had feelings for him, even after all that went down between them, but he wasn't so sure he could stack up to her sense of duty to her father. It all seemed like a no-brainer to him. If she didn't want to do it, why was she even considering it? *Not so easy for her, you jack-ass,* he reproached himself. Her father and her culture were tied up into something more complex than he could ever understand.

Finally at the hotel, he slowed and paused. The wind whipped the flags around the triple doored entrance, while he stared up at the intricate French Renaissance architecture.

"Nothing unimportant ever happens at The Plaza," he quoted to himself, said by an unknown. "You got that right, you nameless fucker." Although tumultuous, the last few days had opened his eyes.

He bounded up the front stairs with a new determination in his step. He'd stand by her; would support her in whatever

decision she made, even if it didn't include him, because
that's what you did when you loved someone. His hands
itched to punch someone at the thought of a life without her.
He could think of no one better than the face of Anil Patel—
her ex-boyfriend—to be on the receiving end of a good face
pounding. Marc groaned audibly as he entered the hotel's
lobby.

२

Chapter 2

"Yep, Delta. I was able to get a direct flight there," Simran said over the phone to Sabine, later that evening. She was going over her flight information to India with her sister, while haphazardly packing a suitcase. She kept pushing the recent conversation with Marc out of her mind, not able to deal with his admission of love.

"So, you leave tomorrow, and just a one-way, huh?" Sabine asked, while crunching on a snack as they talked. Simran was betting it was her favorite Chana Chur Indian snack, salty and spicy, the way Sabine's personality was.

"Yeah, well, I don't know how long this is going to take, Bina."

"You actually don't know what the fuck you're going to do, do you?" Sabine asked, absolutely calling Simran out on her wishy-washy behavior when it came to matters of the heart. Sabine was referring to her one and only serious relationship—the one with Anil. It was during a very confusing point in her life. Was she the bright, independent woman she'd witnessed her university peers jumping over hurdles to achieve? Or was she the good Indian daughter, like many South Asian friends who did what they felt was life's easiest choice: honoring their parents' wishes?

When Anil had been presented to her at such an unclear time, she'd permitted her father to decide he was the one. It was just too easy to let him shoulder the burden of the heavy emotional lifting. Was it a complete mistake? Not really. After it ended, she threw herself into her career and a life in NYC, finally realizing she needed some form of freedom from under her father's thumb. What she didn't need was the whole relationship rigamarole. In fact, she decided then and there to build a tight shell around herself when it came to anything close to involving the "L-word." She'd dated sporadically after that, but those were short-lived because her partner in life was her work. When she did make time for the occasional fling (because she had physical needs she couldn't ignore, too, of course) they were cut and dry, satisfactory, and sometimes calculated with a partner who wasn't looking for more.

Marc though ... Simran stopped rummaging through the pile of colorful Indian tunics she was packing, her hands shaking. The draw to him in London had been undeniable, uncontrollable, and she had to see for herself what it was about. It was so unlike her—as if an alternate Simran took over—but she'd had the time of her life, hadn't she? Then the relationship continued when he showed up in NY, and a closeness ensued that she'd never experienced. She asked herself daily, *is this what a real relationship is?* It felt ... almost too easy with their chemistry, banter, similar interests, and not to mention incredible passion for one another. She got swept away, ignoring any warning signals whenever evidence of his playboy lifestyle presented itself. She let her tight shell crack a bit, let him inside, and then it all blew up in her face.

Should she go back to her old self and just write off love? What about obligatory marriages? She could just tell her dad that she didn't intend to marry anyone, *ever*. She sighed morosely. Her 'good Indian daughter' side would be a mopey bag of guilt for the rest of her life if she didn't address her father's wishes.

"Kiddo, this isn't the time for last-minute mental coin tosses. This is your life. Like, the rest of your *life!*" Sabine almost shouted, drawing her back to their conversation. "Remember how you just went for it with Marcus in London? Try to channel some of that 'can do' energy right now."

"Ugh, don't remind me." Did she have to bring up the a-hole who'd surprised her with his declarations of love (sweetly, too, if she really wanted to get real about it)? *He's too late,* and she shoved him from her mind again, speeches of love and all. "Why am I so torn, Bina? Why can't I just tell *Abba* to go to hell?" she asked, letting the anguish consume her as she now curled up on her bed, the pile of Indian tunics a security blanket.

"Because you're the chosen one." Sabine said it with so much conviction that they both burst into hysterical laughter. It'd always seemed comical to them, like a joke, not a serious life matter. "Seriously, kiddo, you've always been the daughter who played by his rules. Remember my goth phase in high school? Shit, I loved that phase," she said wistfully, her mind in another place. "But, I think I did myself a huge favor back then because it scared the crap out of *Abba* and he left me alone after that. Then he just naturally moved on to his next victim. Sorry about that, little sis. And when Anil slid into the picture, so far up *Abba's* ass you'd think he'd turn a shade browner, *Abba* convinced you to date him. I'm still not sure what you saw in that egotistical crap-bag, but you saw the light when he cheated on you. I guess you were young, still impressionable." Sabine continued crunching on her snack casually. It was a rote conversation and occurred every time their dad reminded Simran about family duty, while Sabine was left to explore herself. She was the self-proclaimed *sheitan* (devil) of the family and relished in it, living life by her own rules. Simran envied her to a certain degree. What she didn't covet was Sabine's strained relationship with their father. "Somehow Dad *knows* about your relationship and break-up with Marcus. Come on, did you think the gossip wouldn't reach him after you brought him to Pinky Aunty's party last summer? And now, you're at your most vulnerable and it's like he can smell it. He wants to take control again, Sima. But ask yourself, is this what you really see for your future? Don't you think it's about time you stood up to him?" She paused, and Simran could hear her licking her fingers free of the salt and spice.

"I thought you were on my side about bringing him to the party," Simran reminded her grudgingly. It'd been such a contentious decision, but she wanted Marc there with her because she'd begun to open herself up to him more.

"I was—I am," Sabine said hurriedly. "But it was super bold of you. How would *Abba* not have found out? You know Indians live off of gossip." There was an uncomfortable silence and her sister cleared her throat. "Anyway, how *did* it go with Marcus by the way?" she asked, trying to sound casual, but Simran knew she really wanted to know.

The electrically charged encounters with him over the past two days came to mind. "Well, he's still foxy as hell, and I still want to mount him if that's what you're asking," she answered, while thoughtfully fingering the soft bump on her neck where a hickey was forming. It was his favorite spot and she shivered, remembering the pleasure of him making love to that spot. It was like he'd branded her, forcing her to remember what they had between them. She had to admit that a part of her would always belong to him, even if they never worked out.

"Gross on so many levels, Sima. Aside from the attraction." Sabine made an audibly disgusted noise and continued. "How did it feel to see him? Did you tell him everything?" This was the thing about Sabine. She was a downright, cranky bag of bones at times, and yet still sensitive to people's feelings. She'd never admit it to anyone, even Simran, but deep down, she was an ooey-gooey romantic.

"He knows everything now. And, honestly, he wasn't as freaked out as I thought he would be," Simran murmured thoughtfully, recalling how he said he would have been fine having a child with her—a notion that still made her head spin.

"I *knew* it! I knew you should've told him from the get-go," Bina said victoriously. "Dude had a right to know..." And in her tone, Simran heard the judgment—that he should've been the first one to know when she found out (he was the father after all), and maybe they could've worked something out. Perhaps she wouldn't be facing this ridiculous life-altering decision in the first place.

"And how would that have changed anything? *Abba* would've still found out about me and Marc. He would've still tried to interject with my life." Simran's anger was stoked now and her ears and cheeks started to burn. Uh oh, here come the hormones. She was going to yell then go off on a crying bender—one of many emotionally linked hormonal reactions to losing the baby, which she'd done her damnedest to hide from Marc. He didn't need to witness this 'mess of a Simran.' She gripped the extra skin of her belly, still loose and flabby, while she bit her cheeks.

"Ok sure, but maybe things wouldn't have turned out like a typical Bollywood movie script," Sabine continued, blasé. "You know, the saga where the heroine is forced to marry a man she hates and has to reconcile her feelings. At least the father of your almost baby would have been in the picture, and, I don't know, maybe you could have figured things out? It's not like he's a nobody in this world—"

"DON'T YOU DARE BRING UP THE ALMOST BABY!" Simran thundered, the snot starting to run down her face, mixing with the tears that finally ran free. "I'm really trying not to hate it. If I hadn't been pregnant, I wouldn't have called him to tell him three months ago, and then he wouldn't have broken up with me ..." She stuttered then started sobbing, knowing how idiotic that line of thinking was. He would have broken up with her anyway. "And God, Bina, that baby." She wiped her face hard with the heel of her palms. She was still stunned at her own turn of feelings. After ten positive pregnancy tests, she seriously considered an abortion. After that fateful call with Marc, though, numb to everything, she'd put the decision on the back-burner, unsure of anything. But when she miscarried, her world got even darker. Dejected— not elated, as she thought she would be—that she wasn't pregnant anymore. Sometime in the months between the break-up and that defeating sonogram, she'd wanted that child with every fiber in her being.

Simran reached for a tissue and blew her nose loudly. But why for fuck's sake was her sister needling her right now?

"Shh," Sabine said soothingly. "I'm sorry. I shouldn't have brought it up—"

"I mean, this is the last thing I need right now, Bina. You're not some fucking saint you know." Her voice was shrill and she was tearful again. *Oh, sweet baby Krishna, give me the strength to tackle these hormones.*

"I never said I was," Sabine said gently. "I just never thought *you*, the chosen one, could be non-Saintly, too. It shows you have a backbone and I'm super proud of you and guess what? I really think Mom would be proud of you, too," Oh God, how she wished her mother were here so she could make it all better. "And your situation reminds me of Rani *Khala.* You remember her don't you?"

"Yeah, but what do you mean?" Simran croaked. Rani *Khala* was a beloved great-aunt of theirs who'd gone on to make something of herself in India on her own, at a time when it was still unheard of to do so. She'd thrown the typical

South Asian patriarchy out the window. Sabine had always been closer to this aunt of theirs and managed to keep in communication while Simran had lost touch.

"I talked to her recently and your situation ... it just reminds me so much of what she went through."

"She knows about me, and *everything* that happened?!"

"Not everything," Sabine said emphatically. "But she's aware of your struggles for personal independence."

"Huh." She tried to recollect the details of Rani's story, but Sabine went on, dispersing any foggy memories.

"Are you ok now? Sorry I got you all worked up." Sabine was contrite. "I can only imagine with your emotional state, that it was a fucking soap opera when you met up with Marcus. Did you talk, you know, about anything more than the pregnancy and his gallery?"

"Oh *Jeez*, Bina, just come on out and ask if we're getting back together."

"Just curious," Sabine prodded.

Simran sighed heavily, sniffling. "Dude, he told me he thinks he loves me. And that's not all, he wants me back." And holy crap what was she going to do? *Yes, yes, yes!* Her heart shrieked. *You're mental,* her brain bit back, *remember what you went through ... alone?* He was unaware of that, though, how could he be when she'd cut him off. But did she really want him back? She appreciated his honesty earlier today, but wasn't it easier to just deal with her own crazy? She'd run her own show for the past five years; been the queen of her own castle until he blew in. Was being one half of a couple, one where anonymity would cease to exist, one where developing a thicker skin was a prerequisite for handling his salacious past, really her thing? Simran realized there was a long silence on the phone and she thought the line had dropped. "*Hello?*" she asked.

"Girl, I don't know why you're tormenting yourself. *Abba* can just jack off," Sabine said passionately. This coming from the daughter who basically got to live her life the way she wanted.

Simran could only grumble at that. Then she voiced the biggest fear sitting inside her heart about Marc. "I don't know, Bina. Can I really put faith that he won't scare off again?" Her bottom lip started to quiver at the slightest inkling of going through that heartbreak again. The rip-your-heart-out kind where you couldn't simultaneously breathe or function properly.

"Sima," Sabine said firmly. "I know how hard that was. I was there, remember? To pick you up off the bathroom floor for the hundredth time and force the pint of cookies n' cream and wine from your death-like grip? The thing is, you won't know unless you try. Love's a gamble, right? And you, kiddo, love him—"

"*Give me a break—*"

"—Nope. You *do*. You wouldn't have reacted that way if you didn't, even with his dumbass behavior. I've been there, remember?" She alluded to a recent incredibly hurtful separation from her ex-girlfriend. "But look, you can't even try unless you break free from the shackles you *think* are holding you back. *Abba* doesn't have any hold over you legally. You can *actually* do what you want, you know. We're not living in India and we're definitely not in the Dark Ages. I know you're afraid to be packed in with the black sheep of the family, but he'll never learn unless you stand up for yourself. Ok, look at Rani *Khala*—how hard that must have been to decline *Abba's* help after her husband died. The fucking gossip from everyone … And look at me—coming out as a lesbian to him. He still thinks I'll 'get well' at some point then come begging him to find me a husband." She cackled. "As if … the point is we're alive and thriving, and *happy*, all things considering. It won't be easy. It goes against every grain in your body to not please him, but think about it, when has pleasing him ever made you truly happy?"

Sheesh, the black sheep had a point.

Her business degree and MBA were decisions made for her because she'd been dazed stepping out of her freshman year orientation at NYU. Instead of letting her explore her options, her father insisted that a business degree (like his own) was very respectable with innumerable possibilities for a successful future. The future he had in mind included one with his company in Mumbai. Starting her own endeavor, *Lavish Your Events*, pretty much telling him she was staying in NY for the long haul, had knocked him down a peg or two. And she'd refused his help, even though he offered financial backing numerous times. While scared in the beginning, she truly found fulfillment, with a mountain of business debt and all because it was *her* mountain of debt.

And then there was Anil. When they were together, with the prospect of marriage on the horizon, she experienced a sweet love—made more poignant by the fact that it was her first—but deep down, when it came to knock-your-socks-off passion, hadn't she felt ... nothing? The looming pressure of her guilt could've been relieved, her dad satisfied, but it was an imposter kind of love. She'd been heartbroken nonetheless. As she reflected back over the years, though, she realized something hadn't been right between them. Didn't she thank the cosmos above every day that a life with Anil Patel hadn't happened? So, what *was* she doing?!

She sighed heavily, the weight of everything almost unbearable. If she didn't do this, didn't make her voice heard, she'd regret it for the rest of her life.

"I just need to see this through, Bina. Even if it means telling *Abba* and Anil to fuck off," she said vehemently.

"Atta girl," her sister rallied. "Don't give up on yourself. And, Sima, as crazy mad as this may sound, don't give up on Marcus. I'm not gonna lie, you were the happiest I've ever seen you when you were with him. Remember, we've been living with our Indian sides our entire lives. This is all new to him. He may have run away (you know we've all wanted to more times than we can count), but he's back. And look, I'm still convinced he's a tool, but hey, you could do worse. Anil is *the* biggest tool in the shed, so, pick your torture." And with that, they said their goodbyes. Sabine told her to have a safe trip and hung up.

Well, fuck me!

Chapter 3

A FLIGHT TO INDIA

Twenty-four hours later and Simran was almost halfway to Mumbai and an unknown future. She was ensconced in her travel pod, having sprung for a business class ticket for the sixteen plus hours direct flight. With much to think about, she preferred to do so without the incessant elbowing from fellow passengers. She quickly realized though, that being alone for this long gave her a little bit *too* much time with her thoughts.

Simran reached for her laptop and popped it open. Nothing like work to take your mind off of life-altering decisions. She scrolled through her emails and to her consternation, found only two. That couldn't be right. The first one was from her new temporary hire, Mariam Abbas, who was assisting in finalizing gallery renovations and organizing the launch party. Mariam communicated that everything was taken care of, including the printer's typo on the party invitations.

The second was from her staff of three at *Lavish Your Events*. In all caps it admonished her for even opening their email, as her main goal was to recuperate. Second, it, like

Mariam's email, relayed that everything was under control, including the two fall weddings coming up and the high-profile bar mitzvah they'd somehow snagged through a client Marc had recommended her company to. He'd always been considerate of her business dealings when he schmoozed his own clients, even if she never asked for it.

And *bam*, there he was, the person her mind so wanted to dwell on. She finally gave in.

Seeing him recently—the first time in months—had been like pulling off a bandage; necessary but painful. The pent-up emotions hovered heavily in her apartment yesterday, threatening to burst free into the small space. She'd steeled herself, ready for him to arrogantly plead his case for them to be together again, as he'd done at the hotel the day before. But he'd taken her off guard, wanting to understand her father's wishes. She'd never gone into much detail with him, or anyone outside of the culture for that matter. "South Asian guilt" was a notion that many non-Asians couldn't understand, let alone perceive as an actual thing. But he genuinely listened and heard the entire distressing 'should she marry Anil' scenario. The jealousy radiating off him at the mere idea of her marrying her ex threatened to open her heart to him again, and set her libido positively racing. Never had she felt like she belonged to someone as much as she did at that moment with him. And their embrace—Holy Durga, mother of all things beautiful and destructive, that embrace. All encompassing. Familiar. She burned with need and it felt so right and so wrong at the same time. She'd wanted him, but didn't want to give herself to him. Their passion was like a third person in that room, waiting to be unleashed and reckoned with. She wanted, no needed, his large, hard body up against her, inside her, but required the distance to maintain a clear head because he made her brain, well, brainless. The remorse he felt afterward made her wish to grab him back and smother him to her again. When he'd uttered "baby" numerous times in that oh-so-sexy voice of his, she wanted to melt into him, entwine her limbs around him, with 'never letting go' the only option on the table. She sighed in resignation. To say she was still head over heels for the guy was putting it way too lightly.

And for crap-sake, the admittance of his feelings threw her. Everything she thought she knew about them was completely shaken, but not in a bad way, more like shimmering glitter in a snow globe, both fascinating, stunning. She'd known he cared for her, but never would she have thought love was on his mind. Was it possible for a person to change completely from womanizing to one-woman-loving? It was difficult to take in. Point blank, it scared her shitless—his admission of love. If he freaked out again, it would kill her. In truth, she needed this whole fiasco with Anil and her dad to win her some time so she could figure out what to do with Marc. He'd already fucked with her emotions. His break-up words still pained her if she let them replay in her mind like a janky and warped vinyl record. And unfortunately, Khans were the best grudge holders, even to their own detriment. She may never think he deserved another chance.

Just before he left, she needed to know why he'd broken it off, even if her masochistic heart already knew. Her South Asian side was complex, strong, a force to be met with head-on, and why she'd only exposed a tiny dose to him in the beginning. He was already a flight risk with his past playboy lifestyle and talks of marriage and family responsibility—the two main topics at any South Asian function—would surely make him run in the opposite direction. But she'd taken a chance and, she'd been right from the beginning about him. Sadly, if he couldn't deal with her culture—something that would always be a part of her—then he wasn't going to make it, no matter what she decided for herself.

The flight attendants were passing out dinner menus now, and Simran decided to have some wine with her meal, in the hopes it would unwind her, fully aware she'd probably regret it the next day. Alcohol and flying never did her any favors, but what the hell, she thought.

After dinner, she leaned back comfortably against the cushions, tucking the blanket around her, and scrolled through her device for some music, her mode of getting through any problem. She settled on an indie electric funk song, one that allowed her to wallow in the familiar feelings that emerged after seeing Marc again. It was the Cannon's "On Fire for You" where its upbeat dance track contrasted with the song's heartbroken words. The lead singer's wispy voice crooned gloomily, spinning a tale about her love for someone who'd left—that someone she would've died for if given the chance. After everything they'd been through, how could this person have been unaware of her feelings? Anger is what she should feel, and yet, the yearning for that someone perseveres. On and on the poetic lyrics wrapped around Simran in an ethereal quality, while her limbs ached to get up and dance. *Stupid Marc. Stupid love.*

She furiously searched for a song that matched what she should *only* be feeling right now and rugged guitar chords replaced the poppy dance track. They groaned into her ears, followed by lazy staccato drum beats. The hissing of symbols magnified the familiar angsty lament of Nirvana's "Come As You Are." She turned up the volume to Kurt Cobain's scratchy, tobacco-laden voice, as he urged her to stay true to herself. Oh, how she hoped she could once she arrived in India.

The lights were dimmed in the cabin now with most of the passengers snoozing or watching some new Bollywood flick or Hollywood hit on their private screens. Simran closed her eyes as Cobain's cracked voice continued lamenting and this ticked her off because if anyone had ever taken her for she was, it'd been Marc. How ironic that she was even considering the phony future her father laid out, instead of a future with him.

Sabine's words came back to haunt her, the ones about bringing him to that fateful party in the first place. Had she been the one who screwed up by forcing him to go?

Involuntarily, her mind skipped back to that event and what surely was the root of her current problems. It'd been a huge, Indian gathering in New Jersey where much of the community was in attendance. With their gossipy nature, the news of an unknown white man on Simran's arm must have spread quickly, all the way to Kumar Khan's ears in India, which by that point were spouting hot smoke.

So unsure of bringing him at first, they ended up having a pretty great time—with the exception of a few hiccups—followed by a night filled with newfound tenderness. Her brain skidded to a halt then and her face heated up as it always did when she recalled any sexual encounter with Marc. The familiar heaviness started to trickle down to her nether regions, and she snuggled further down into her pod. She wondered if she could relieve herself under the blanket in the flight cabin's darkness without anyone noticing.

The sex earlier in the day *before* leaving for the event had been delicious (as it always was with him), but different. It'd been a 'Marc was in complete control and she was his for the taking' kind of sex, where he hadn't used a condom, having gotten caught up in the moment. She might have become pregnant that time, or the handful of other times before he left for Vancouver when they hadn't used protection. This wasn't a new notion. It'd run through her mind countless times when her period was more than three weeks late after he left, even though she was on birth control.

And now her eyes were drooping, the wine having the desired effect. The last coherent thought she had before falling asleep was how easily mistakes could be made, and the enormous cause and effect of those tiny ripples.

Three Months Ago, New York City

8

Chapter 4

To bring him, or not to bring him? That was the question running Simran ragged for days before the annual end-of-summer bash thrown by her local South Asian community. She and Marc had been together for almost three months now, and things seemed to be going great. Granted they'd never admitted they were a real couple, but deep down that's what they were. How could they not be? They spent almost every waking hour together aside from when they were working.

This party was the event of the season, usually hosted by a great beneficiary of the community. Everyone strived to make it to close off the summer and the usual suspects of aunties, uncles, and peers she'd grown up with would be there, even those who'd moved away.

She'd wavered back and forth so many times regarding the matter of bringing him that she pretty much decided she wasn't going, worried not only about the domino effect that could result from bringing him (no one loves gossip more than an idle Indian) but that Marc would get the wrong idea. The most important obligations in life for this community—marriage and duty—would be heard from almost everyone there, and she was well aware of Marc's not so high opinion of marriage.

A long-distance call from her *abba* reminded her about her own family duty—her appearance was a must as her sister never showed up for these events. Everyone would talk if the illustrious Khan's weren't present (Kumar was a highly regarded pillar in the community). More importantly, a family friend was hosting this time and he required someone there to show support.

Loathing this kind of unwanted responsibility on her shoulders, and as a kind of "screw you" to her dad, she invited Marc last minute.

It was a childish, hasty decision, but she didn't think Marc would mind. In fact, Marc had initially been cheerful about it, under the impression that it was a small casual get-together amongst friends. But when she started feeding him details, such as more than two hundred guests attended and she'd grown up with many of them; that her dad was essentially forcing her to go because he was a beneficiary of the community; and that finally, it was in just two days, the grin on his face disappeared. In the days leading to the party, she'd catch him staring at her with that furrowed brow indicating his brain was working through intricate thoughts, but he didn't share them. It was unnerving, to say the least. *Was he mad?* Crap. She'd have to address it at some point, but for the time being, she was just glad he agreed to go.

It was full-on summer by then, the sun baking the asphalt in the concrete jungle that was NYC. The party was at a good friend of her father's home down the Jersey Shore and Simran was relieved they would be near the water in this heat. That day, she parked the white Range Rover she and her sister shared at the West Side docks parking lot and made her way over to Marc's yacht.

He was waiting for her, looking comfortable in fitted khaki pants rolled at his ankles, a white linen shirt with a few buttons opened at the top, long sleeves rolled up along his strong forearms, and tan, worn-in buck shoes. On anyone else, the look would've been ironic, but on him, it worked. Man, it always worked. He could wear a metal garbage can ala Oscar the Grouch and make it look good. His thick blond locks ruffled in the warm breeze, and he was cool and confident with his eyes behind shiny aviator sunglasses. So *hot*. She would never get used to it.

"Hi," she said as she approached him. "Damn, you look good." She was a little breathless now as his sexy scent hit her nostrils, the fresh mint and musk making her light-headed.

He reached for her, encircling her waist with his large, warm hands, looking her up and down, saying nothing, just smiling an enigmatic half-smile. She'd chosen a short, poppy printed dress in contrasting hues of sharp reds and soft pinks. The bodice was gathered and fitted, with the skirt flowing, just skimming her mid-thigh. She finished the look off with her favorite Gucci espadrille sandals that laced around her ankles and a white sheer scarf effortlessly thrown around her neck (a nod to her South Asian side).

He removed his sunglasses, tucking them into his shirt pocket then moved his hand to her hair where it was swept into a low, messy side bun. He gently fingered and tugged some loose tendrils, then tapped the Italian gold, filigreed earrings in her ears, setting them to swinging. He glided that same finger over the cap sleeves of her dress, his intent gaze watching the goosebumps appear along the wake of his touch.

"So sweet," he murmured, his low, gravelly voice holding a bit of a bite to it. Then he softly traced the neckline of her dress, his finger pads skimming over the exposed top mounds of her breasts. "So sexy." His breath was warm on her neck and more goosebumps popped up across her chest. She went weak-kneed, pure lust starting to pool into her stomach, the familiar shots of desire pummeling her insides. God, what he did to her by barely touching her. She looked up into his eyes and saw her lust mirrored back at her; his pupils dilated. But they were also squinted, his brain somewhere else. He looked … irritated.

"Marc, behave," she warned, trying to keep her own desire in check. Once they started, it was difficult to stop as they'd experienced so many times in the past; a peek inside Pandora's box that led to utter (and delicious) chaos. And she'd want it, too. But they were going to be late if they didn't get going, arriving three hours late, versus the acceptable one to two hours late, which was normal for any of these kinds of events. Especially with the early summer traffic. Now was the time for city dwellers to make the great exodus to the shore every weekend. Bumper-to-bumper traffic was the norm and a huge aggravation to Simran.

Marc had other ideas. "Don't worry, babe, we'll get to your party, I just have a few things I need to settle up," he said determinedly. He dragged her onto the boat and to the sunken sitting area. What in the world did that mean? Simran wondered. Taking a seat, he pulled her onto his lap, one large, warm hand held her waist tight and the other grabbed the nape of her neck, pulling her down for a possessive kiss, making her dizzy with want and need. He moved to graze along her jaw, licking her beauty spot on the way, then dropped open-mouthed kisses down her neck, pushing aside the material of her scarf to suck and nip his favorite vulnerable spot where her pulse beat erratically. She started to protest, not wanting a hickey for everyone to see later, but instead, a purr of pleasure emanated from her. She was totally losing out on everything, including leaving on time.

She didn't care now.

He lowered her onto her back, his warm hands skimming down her body, following to kneel in front of her. The smooth chiffon material of her white scarf slid seductively along her neck as he slowly pulled it off, dropping it in a puddle on the floor. "I like this, but it looks better off." His hands skimmed up her thighs under her skirt, and tugged forcefully at her white, lacey panties, pulling them down her legs and over her wedges, completely off. Her heart pounded so loudly in excitement she thought he must be able to hear it. He wadded them up and what he did next completely turned her on and she was lost.

He sniffed long and hard while shoving her panties up to his nose, "Mm," he growled smoothly, breathing deeply, all the while his darkened eyes held her widened ones. "Your scent always makes me so hard, baby." She exhaled loudly, not even realizing she'd been holding her breath. He tossed her underwear aside and grabbed her slender wrists in one hand, jerking them over her head. Oh God, he wasn't playing around. What was he up to? The lust was flowing like liquid lava now, below her stomach to the apex of her thighs.

"What *is* happening, babe?" she asked breathlessly, her body arching automatically to him, moisture bursting between her legs.

"Mm, just a little tit," he murmured as he fingered and cupped one breast over her dress, then moved to the other as he said, "for tat," before hooking a finger into her bodice and jerking down, exposing her matching white bra. "Sexy kitten," he said low and with approval as he took in the sight of her dark nipples showing through the scant lace. He worked the lacey cups of her bra down so her breasts spilled forward. "Mm, very nice," he growled, looking heatedly over his handy work. She moaned and arched her back again, letting him have his way with her, and she couldn't put a coherent sentence together to ask him what his 'tit for tat' comment meant.

He fondled her breasts, squeezing each with a pressure that made her hips buck. Then he licked and lavished each one, sucking hard to make her nipples stand wet and to sharp attention. He let go of her wrists as he moved his head down between her legs, spreading them with his broad shoulders. His hands glided her skirt up, bunching it around her waist as he licked and nipped the insides of her thighs, making his way up to her already moist center and she was more than happy to spread her legs even further for him, completely exposed to anyone who happened to walk past them on deck.

His mouth was on her now, nuzzling her tenderness as he spoke and tasted her.

"Such a cunt. Sweet." He licked. "Juicy." He lapped. "Salty." He sucked. Then he parted her skin to lavish her clitoris until it was swollen. She groaned in pleasure. But was he talking about her, or her actual cunt she wondered? Then those thoughts floated completely out of her head, too. She arched and bucked, her panting taking on breathless whimpers as he continued his onslaught, and her hands aimlessly grabbed above her head looking for the edge of a cushion to anchor herself with. His long fingers kept her hips from moving too wildly with his firm grip on her thighs, his palms on her ass cheeks. She felt the slip of his warm tongue enter her and she let out a high-pitched squeal of pleasure. "You like that, baby?" he asked softly, the words humming an exquisite vibration against her sensitive skin. She gasped and nodded her head. But he stopped what he was doing, leaving her wanting for more, the air a stark contrast to his warm, thick tongue. "Tell me what you want, and I'll continue," he said, his voice laden with lust, but dominating, commanding.

"Keep going ..." she pleaded, her hands reaching for his face.

"And?"

"And … and fuck me with your mouth," she panted, whiny in her need. He jerked a nod, and continued, fucking her with his tongue, muttering into her how good she tasted, how wet she was, just for him. She started losing control, her muscles quivering inside. He pulled back leaving her empty, and his three fingers filled her completely, a little brutally, moving in and out, in and out, her hips meeting the quick rhythm his hand set. His tongue returned to lavish her clit as his fingers reached further and forward to that spot that drove her wild. She didn't know what she'd done to deserve this, didn't know if she should be angry or ecstatic, but she was too far gone now, and it felt too good to complain.

She shattered inside, the blood swooshing hotly through her body and she shuddered over and over again, clenching tightly around his fingers, her body bowing up in pleasure to him and his dominant ways. Her guttural cries of, "Yes, Yes, Yes," over and over again mingled with his commanding whispers of "That's right, kitten, come for me," against her flesh, because she never wanted it to end.

Through her haze, she saw his bright eyes pinning her with a dangerous stare while she came all over his hands and lips. When he pulled back, his smug smile was glistening with her wetness.

He came up and kissed her hard and she tasted herself on him, turning her on again. He moved quickly then, unzipping his pants and pushing them with his boxer briefs down around his hips. With his large stiffened cock freed, he positioned himself on top of her. Keeping his weight on his hands on either side of her head, he thrust his full, hard as a rock, length into her, until he couldn't go any further. His groan of utter appreciation shook her to her core.

With eyes closed and face contorted into pleasure, almost pain, he could barely gasp, "So fucking tight."

She should've been outraged at no condom, but she couldn't help but keen in delight, feeling the intimate sensation of skin-to-skin contact, his naked ridges bumping and caressing every sensitive inch inside her. Her head flopped side to side as he pumped into her and she gripped his waist while she clung on to the wild ride that was sex with Marc.

It started to increase again, the pleasure, building so quickly that her thigh muscles trembled as she took him in deeply. She immediately came again, sharp cries emerging from her. She was completely unraveled, and she knew she must look like a crazed woman with a slack jaw, her eyes rolling at the intense pleasure like googly eyes in a kid's baby-doll. He continued to pound into her, his grunts becoming louder and louder, his body moving with jackhammer speed, and it was like she wasn't even there with him. He stiffened and with one final push, came into her forcefully, his grunting turning into low hissing and exhalations as he released into her, sweat from his forehead dripping onto her face as he gasped, "*Fuck, fuck, sweet fuck.*" His large body finally collapsed heavily onto her. She felt his cum as it filled her belly, warm and wet, her body suctioning around him, and holy Durga, mother of the universe, it was incredible.

"Now, this party will be filled with people I've known since I was little," she reminded him a little later in the car, flipping down the passenger side sun-visor mirror to survey what was now a rat's nest of her previous hair-do. She glanced over at his silent figure. "Remember, we need to keep the physical contact to a minimum. I don't want scandalous gossip reaching my dad." To which he looked incredulously at her while chuckling. Then catching how serious she was, he lowered his sunglasses to roll *his* eyes comically at her! Again, she noted his odd behavior, and sheesh, what was with 'the man of few words' bit?

Actually, the only words he'd uttered while they straightened their clothes a few moments ago included a sincere apology for not using a condom; he never went bareback. While pleased with his apology, she noted his usual gregarious self still missing, even after having his deliciously aggressive way with her. She remarked that thankfully she was on the pill and that he was a stickler for getting tested regularly after past partners. Trying to lighten the mood, she admitted that it had been more incredible than their typical carnal ecstasy, joking that next time he would screw her into a coma. He shot her that enigmatic half-grin again as he put his sunglasses back on. Was she just imagining it or was it like he was putting up his defenses?

When they walked to her car, he pecked her gently on the lips and nuzzled her nose with his. He asked her if she wanted him to drive. Still a little dazed and confused, while also coming down from her sex high, she agreed. He opened the passenger side door for her then went to the driver's side, getting in and adjusting the tan leather seat and mirrors.

"So, let's at least try to behave," she continued now, attempting to redo her wrecked hair-do. He chuckled again, turning the engine on. "I mean it, Marc. No canoodling in front of the *Desis*."

"On my honor, I will do my very best and *try* to behave," he said a little mockingly, with three fingers held up in a boy scout's honor salute—the same fingers that he'd so expertly fucked her with back there. Then he shook his head and muttered something under his breath, which sounded very much like an "unbelievable," to her. Whatever. She ignored it and stabbed the last bobby pin a little too sharply into her scalp as she finished touching up. Was he going to be like this all afternoon? She needed him on her side today. What would everyone say when this gorgeous non-Indian dude strolled in with her? Admittedly, the fact that they'd come this far had her stomach feeling like butterflies were hurling and attacking one another from within.

As they made their way out of NYC's crowded streets toward the Holland Tunnel she took a moment to steel herself before she turned to his handsome profile. As calmly as she could, she asked, "And ... what was that back there?" She loved it when they had dominant sex, whether he was the aggressor or it was she. But this time he'd been cold, as if he was almost not there mentally. And he hadn't used a condom which he was normally so good at. His mind was somewhere else, undoubtedly, and she wanted to clear the air before they arrived at their destination.

"Are you complaining about the fun we just had?" His voice was mild, which was a farce. Simran could read people, had always had a knack for it, and he was being a complete jack-ass right now. If he was upset about something and didn't talk about it, how was she supposed to know what was wrong? He fiddled with the satellite radio, finding the Hair Nation Station. Poison's "Nothin' But A Good Time" came blasting through the speakers. He began drumming the wheel energetically and jamming his head to the 80's rock beats.

"Did I say I was complaining?" she asked, raising her voice over the loud music as he continued rocking out. It seemed like he was going to ignore her and this topic. "Okay then," she drawled out in a huff, rolling her eyes and crossing her arms. She stared out the window with feigned interest, even though the only view at the moment was the blurred shiny, white tiles of the Holland Tunnel's interior wall.

Chapter 5

Around the time they hit the mark of crossing NY to NJ under the Hudson River, Marc finally decided to answer her. Sighing wearily, he turned down the music.

"Sims, it's ... frustrating that you invited me last minute to something that seems pretty important to you and your family. I'm happy to meet everyone but give me the courtesy of having some time to ... mentally prepare." He glanced over and saw her shapely eyebrows arch high; her mouth open in shock. "It feels like I'm only going so you can get back at your dad, too." He'd just admitted he was bothered. He never did that. He marveled at how easy it was with her, but was also a bit alarmed about how easy it was with her.

"Um, *hello* what?" Her voice was high and a little shrill, confirming he'd hit a nerve. She cleared her throat. "Marc, you spring events on me the day of all the time." She was referring to the slew of cocktail parties and charity events he'd taken her to since arriving in NY, some of which she'd dragged her heels at attending. She'd observed him converse comfortably with dozens of people, turn on the Lehigh charm, and get people to notice him, if they didn't already know who he was. Once she was done teasing him about his

Lehigh persona, she'd roll her eyes at him buttering up the guests.

He'd even been so bold as to drag her into some of his conversations, exuding her events planning talents, hoping he could boost her career because he noticed with some wonder her lack of enthusiasm at times in rubbing shoulders with NY's supremely well to-do. This confused the hell out of him. Women of his past were more than pleased at any opportunity he gave them to connect with society's influential crowd. Granted he'd only viewed her social media feeds; only caught her a handful of times up to her elbows in tulle or some other events related issue at her office, but he could spot talent a mile away and understood she was ready to reach the next tier of success. He could absolutely help her with that, so why was she always so stubborn?

"Yeah, but those are mindless socializing functions, events that I think you would enjoy with me, both entertaining, and great for networking. Not something with close family or friends, or apparently involves your father," he finished. He actually felt disappointed that she was using him this way.

They were both quiet, ruminating. He glimpsed over again and caught her fingering her gold earrings, then the diamonds studded along her lobes, lost in thought. There was a small 'v' wrinkled between her brows and he so badly wanted to reach out and smooth it away, even with his frustration with her.

She finally replied, "Mindless socializing or networking events or not, I attend with you whether I want to or not, and

I don't have a sex tantrum about it. I'd say you were more than a *little* frustrated," she said archly, referring to the incredible, bodies turned to jelly, animalistic sex they just had. He couldn't help but grin at that. He'd meant to teach her a lesson, make her beg for it until her brain exploded, but he'd been so turned on by her flirty, little outfit, by the fact that she was enjoying his "punishment" that he came so hard in her he thought his own brain ignited. And he'd forgotten to use a condom, something he usually *never* did. Thank fuck she was on birth control.

"Listen, I'm sorry," she continued haltingly. "I get that this situation is a little ... different and involves people who are like family to me. I really do want you to be there. Honestly, it started off as me wanting to get at my dad, but I think this is a good thing." She finished solemnly, her hands fidgeting in her lap.

He nodded. What he really wanted to ask was, *what is up with you and your dad?* She became a ball of nerves any time they so much as mentioned him, but he would wait until she was ready to tell him more.

"You're forgiven, baby. Now, do you need me to apologize for that exceptional fuck session back there?" he teased, hiding an uncomfortable feeling that began to creep in. Although more than satisfied with what they'd done, something grated on him about his behavior back there. Had he pushed her too far with sex?

"I wasn't complaining," she answered with a small smile. Satisfaction swelled inside him. She'd enjoyed it just as much as he had. But she continued, "Just, give me a little heads up so I can return the favor next time. I'm not a fan of using sex as a weapon." Her tone dripped with ice chips, as her head bounced back on the headrest with a resounding "thunk."

He frowned; his satisfaction deflating like a balloon with a minuscule hole in it. "I didn't realize me making you squeal with pleasure was a weapon."

She huffed, "Ok, 'weapon' was a little harsh. Just, talk to me if something's bugging you, ok?" She turned to him with beseeching, wide eyes. Now he felt like the worst human on the planet.

He grabbed her hand, rubbing his thumb over her cool palm. "I'm sorry," he said remorsefully. He *had* pushed her too far. "I would never want you to feel like you were being forced."

"You're forgiven," she said quietly. Then just to make sure she was absolutely clear, she said, "I mean I love it when you take control, just let me in on the game."

He chuckled. She liked being a little kinky with him. "Will do, baby." And he held onto her hand, continuing to rub his thumb over her palm.

They drove in comfortable silence as they headed out of Jersey City and onto the Garden State Parkway. He commented on her nice ride but wanted to know what THE DJ Sims had on her playlist and if it stacked up to his own flawless music taste.

With mock indignation, she pulled out her phone, scrolled through, and plugged in. Coldplay's "Sky Full of Stars" burst through the car. He nodded approvingly and started humming to the luminous music, singing the lyrics, feeling almost buoyant at the moment.

"Babe, I love this song. Do you know who sings it?" she asked him. *Seriously?* Did the music master in her really not know?

"Do I need to school you in music? Coldplay, obviously," he answered, shaking his head. Then went back to singing. He loved this song, too.

"Well, let's keep it that way then," she said matter-of-factly with a toothy grin. She broke into a fit of giggles when she saw his incredulous look. Marcus hadn't heard that dumb joke since high school. Simran was such a goofball sometimes. He wanted to stop the car and tickle her until they both wanted it bad again.

He cleared his throat, shifting in his seat, his dick looking for her warm, wet hole to hide in. How did a dumb kid's joke turn him on so much? Because the delivery was from a sassy, lush-lipped woman who made his tongue stick to the roof of his mouth *all the time* and she didn't care how silly she acted around him. Being with him wasn't an act, as were his past experiences. He went into those affairs aware the women were salivating over his wealth and society persona, hoping some of his success would rub off on their careers. But Simran didn't give a damn. First off, she didn't even know who he was when they'd first met. Second, she remained mostly unimpressed with his wealth and the people he knew. It wasn't that she thought she was better than all that. It was that she couldn't take the luxury he was now accustomed to, making him come down to earth with her and the other normal people. The funny thing was, *she wasn't* normal. She was genuine, and that made her special.

"You know, this song reminds me of the time we first met." And that shut her up. Her mouth was a perfect "O" in surprise.

"Really?" Her face puckered up and she looked at him like he had two heads. She didn't believe him.

"Do you remember how we met at the bar at my club in London?" She nodded. "The refrain—a sky full of stars—makes me think about when you stared up at the starlight lighting installation and we flirted, and then we had that hot make out session out on the deck. It was sexy as hell, but, and I don't know," he breathed, the tempo in his veins picking up speed at the memory, how clearly he saw the small lights dancing along her face and neck, the eagerness he felt to get to know her. "All I wanted to do was check you out all night long, maybe longer." He looked straight ahead at the road as he finished. What would her smart mouth say to that?

He'd realized early on that he was the pursuer. Deep down he understood her views of him as a player, thus, wasn't overly eager when he approached her again in NY. But he'd convinced her because she made him crave more than what he was used to. That night in London had been the start of something he never knew he wanted; not sure of it then (nor even what it was now) but he knew a fling with her was not an option anymore. More than once he'd almost told her how much he cared about her, liked having her around, but he'd catch himself, so uncertain of how to proceed with anything that resembled long-term. And, as they opened up to each other more, the giddiness of a teenage boy enamored by his first crush continued to grow. So, if now wasn't the right time, here in the car, on their way to a party that might morph what they were doing into something else, then he didn't know when was. Would she laugh in his face, or take it at face value?

She'd been silent for some time now, and his pulse raced. He couldn't remember the last time he'd felt so nervous. He glanced over to see her cheeks infused with pink, her lips curved in a silly smile. He chuckled, relieved. He loved it when he could surprise her cheekiness speechless. She met his eyes, and his heart tightened at an unspoken emotion he saw there. She looked away then, clearly overcome, mumbling something about what a softy he was turning out to be. He was still holding her hand and gently squeezed. She squeezed back. She was so adorable, so pretty. His chest swelled and it felt like it would combust.

Present Day,
New York City

Chapter 6

"Hey, Mom, it's me," Marc said when his mom picked up. It was around midnight in NY, so he could still catch her before she went to bed in California.

"Hey, 'Me'! Long time," she said affectionately. "What's up, my buttercup?" Marc smiled at her warmth and cheesiness, and it so reminded him of another woman on his mind that his smile sagged.

"Ah well, you know, this and that. Just got back from Vancouver. Left that mess in Bruce's hands ... hopefully, things turn around."

"I'm sure he'll manage. He's always so good about smoothing down ruffled feathers. Now, his smooth-talking the ladies, that's where I worry. Is he being careful? He's not doing anything he shouldn't be is he?" she asked, truly concerned. Bruce was like a second son to her, and she was familiar with his womanizing ways which had at times turned hazardous.

"Bruce is Bruce, he'll probably never change. But he's been a little lower key lately since that stunt last year. I think he's finally gotten the message that he needs to calm down."

"Mistaken marriages will do that to you, and to a South American mob boss' daughter no less. How does he get into this kind of trouble?" Marc could almost see his mom shaking her head on the other end. "Anyway, I'm happy to hear your voice!"

"You know I'm a mama's boy," he teased. "Hey, fill me in on my security detail—still giving them the silent treatment?" Last year's blackmail situation still felt all too real. Marc had someone on his payroll trailing her at all times to ensure she was safe from her slimy ex-boyfriend or anyone else who thought they could take advantage of her.

"Oh honey, yes. Brad's still following me." She was exasperated. "I understand why we have to do this, but it's unnerving. I have a right to some privacy, don't I? I guess I could just invite him in for coffee. He's quite handsome actually. Do you think he's married?" Here we go again; the romantic saga between Gail Lehigh and an unsuspecting gentleman, take four hundred. As he listened to her prattle on about finding love again, his mind couldn't help but dart back to Simran and what he was going to do.

"Honey?" Marc, lost in his own thoughts, hadn't realized his mother wasn't speaking about a romance with Brad anymore. "Ok, something is up with you. What is it?" As always, Gail Lehigh could tell if something was bothering him. The silences were a clear indication because they had a bond. For years it was just the two of them. She'd been a young mother, getting pregnant right out of high school. Her boyfriend, his father, stayed until Marc was only a few months old, then up and left, pursuing his own life with college, a career, even marriage; everything Gail had put aside to care for their son. He couldn't handle the pressure and never looked back, only offering the yearly birthday checks. Reflecting back on how things panned out, she always told Marc that she wouldn't have had it any other way. It'd truly been the most difficult thing she'd ever done in life, but she'd made it through with a little help from her parents, and a lot of gumption on her part. And she always admired the incredible human Marc turned out to be.

He cleared his throat. "Well, I'm back in New York." And that was enough to inform her what he was up to. He'd never gone into specifics about Simran, but he'd mentioned meeting someone and experiencing something new. She hadn't pushed for details but understood his need to be in NY previously had to do with this special someone. When he'd been in Vancouver, a grey cloud consistently hovering over his head, he finally confessed that things had gone south and he was trying to get through it.

"Oh, honey ..." Her voice was full of emotion. No one ever wanted their child in pain. "Do you want to talk about it?"

"Yeah, I kind of do, actually." He heard a sharp intake of breath. He so rarely surprised his mother, and he had to smile at the irony of it. This was the most miserable he'd ever been in his life (the blackmail debacle aside) and he could tell his mom was glad to be of service in the advice department.

So, he explained about Simran's pregnancy, miscarriage, and the possibility of cancer. He shared about her South Asian heritage and her American identity and how she struggled to straddle both. He told her about her Indian father who, while encouraging her to reach for the stars, was still old-fashioned and expected her to marry someone of his choosing so that she would have a secure future when he was gone. In fact, she was on her way to India at that moment to explore that future with this chosen man. Marc then expounded on what *he* saw in her: an amazingly successful, independent woman. A beautiful, smart, warm, and lively individual he couldn't get enough of; he was head over heels in love with her. He finished by admitting he was the one at fault for their break-up because he thought they needed space while he was in Vancouver. He'd been overwhelmed by his feelings for her.

There was silence on the other end. Then he heard throat-clearing simultaneously with nose blowing. *Oh, Gail.* His mom had waited so long to hear him say that he was in love. She no doubt had that tissue box waiting beside her every time he called for just this exact moment.

"Well, Marc, I think you know what you need to do," she said. "Honey," he could hear her excitement building. "You need to go *after* her!"

Marc grunted in frustration. "*Come on*, Mom, this isn't one of your romance novels. This is real life and she's an intelligent woman. She knows how I feel and will make the right decision for herself." He said this with more optimism than he felt. It wasn't just about them getting back together. No amount of pleading his case could erase the cultural expectations Simran had been living with her entire life, which she now had to face.

His patience was wearing thin at his mother's reaction, too. He should've known she would go down this path, and he wasn't so sure he was up to hear it right now. Gail Lehigh was the ultimate romantic. Case in point: her long string of boyfriends coming and going through their household while he was growing up. None of them worked out but she kept persisting. Although content now, and satisfied with herself, deep down she believed in the spark, the romance, and the happily ever after. Even though she didn't think it was in her future, she still wanted it for everyone else. The Hallmark channel was her kryptonite and was incessantly on in the background during the holidays.

"I'm not saying it is, Marcus Andrew Lehigh," she said sternly. Now he was in trouble. She almost never called him by his full name. "But sometimes the situation needs a push in the right direction. If she's already going but unsure, who knows what could turn her decision while there. You be the one to turn her decision while she's there." She waited for a beat to let that sink in. He ruminated on this. It was a good argument. "It sounds like she's still trying to figure out who she wants to be, but it also sounds like she's unhappy with the alternative to a life in NY, and possibly with you. So, go fight for her, fight for your relationship."

He let out a loud, anxious breath, a hand through his hair. "Here's the thing, I think I really screwed it up, Mom. Not only did I flip out and leave her, but I unwittingly abandoned her when she needed me the most. She didn't tell me about the pregnancy, so I should feel off the hook about that, but I don't. And you know why? Because she didn't feel like she could trust me enough to even mention she was pregnant in all those weeks apart. She cares about me, I know it. Because, how can I be the only one who feels this?" Marc knew that it had been a long time since his mom had heard this kind of raw torment in his voice, but he just couldn't hide it. "She has to be feeling this all-consuming restlessness, too, but I don't know if she'll have me back. Hell, do I even deserve her?"

Gail was silent for what felt like eons. When she spoke, it was methodically, choosing her words with care, aware that Marc had never been a believer in love. "Honey, don't you believe in second chances?"

"Mom, after everything you've been through, *why* do *you*?" His voice broke now, and not just for his own suffering but for his mother's aimless search which had produced so much heartache in the past.

"Oh, Marcus. I always will. Love deserves many chances because when you find it, nothing compares. It's the greatest gift—to feel that connection with someone that just includes the both of you. It's like your own private table of two for eternity," she teased. With no remarks from him, she went on, this time speaking to him as though he were small again, trying to understand what made the sun rise and set every day. "Honey, relationships aren't straightforward. You're not dealing with business here. This is much more delicate. Shift what you know about people. Raw, untethered emotions have no reasoning sometimes. Our actions at times *don't* define what we're thinking and Lord knows how many times in history that's happened." She guffawed. "What I'm trying to say is we aren't perfect, and we do make mistakes. I have a feeling that if she was willing to see you this last time, even after all the hurt, then there's an absolute chance at forgiveness, and even at being together." Marc turned this over but still couldn't answer, still uncertain. Gail cleared her throat. "And, Marc, there's no sugarcoating this because you need to hear the truth. You have commitment issues."

This wrangled a chuckle out of him. "What makes you think that?" he asked with gentle mockery. Of course, he had commitment issues. It was all more than clear now. His mother continued as if she hadn't heard his snide remark. "Your father left and it's affected you. Ever since college, you've woman hopped, never giving anyone a real chance. I'm not judging, honey, but when you met Bruce, it only got worse. He's a great friend, but you two took the entire UC Santa Barbara female population down with your charms, looks and who knows what else. And don't think I don't know about some of those female teaching assistants, too," she added sternly. Marc had heard this lecture before and like always he kept mum about that last part because a few of those women were lecturing professors, not TA's. "Those poor girls didn't stand a chance. As a woman myself, I completely sympathize, but as your mother, I know in my heart you were trying to figure yourself out." It was her turn to let out an uneasy sigh. "Please understand this, though, you are *not* your father. You're warm, caring, and generous. You may not believe me, but you're the kind of person that if given the chance to fall in love, you fall hard, and you stay the course. Remember your puppy Tipper?"

As she expounded about his all-consuming love for his mutt of a puppy as a kid, Marc felt a calmness envelop him for the first time in days. He hadn't realized he needed to hear those words until now; that he could be more than just the player and was deserving of love. And she was right about staying the course because he *had* fallen hard for Simran, and he would fucking persist with her, whatever it took.

"You're an amazing man, my son. I know you can do this. And, Marc ..."

"Yeah, Mom?" His mind was already formulating his next steps.

"I know it was difficult growing up without a father figure, then seeing *all* of my partners ... some not as ideal as others, come and go throughout the years. But you've never been like any of them either. I raised you right if I do say so myself. I know it took you a while; you've been scared to put yourself out there, but you've found her. She found you. Whatever happened between you two, whatever scared you, you can work through those issues, if she's worth it. Is she worth it, Marcus?"

"She's more than worth it." He breathed.

"Then don't let her slip through your fingers. What you have is so precious and the hardest treasure to find." And then she said goodnight, gave him her love, and hung up.

His heart sank as he recalled what had motivated him to end things between them. His fears had stemmed from a part of her that she could never change, and nor would he ever ask her to.

Three Months Ago, Down the Jersey Shore

9

Chapter 7

When they arrived at the beach house (more like a stately mansion) that overlooked the water, they parked the car down a few blocks behind the numerous ones already there and walked up to the house. The air thumped with upbeat Bollywood music glaring from the speakers as they reached the tall gates in front. They crossed the expansive lawn to the back of the house and the spicy aroma of curry mixed with smoky tandoori hit them, making Marc's mouth water. As they made their way in, he grabbed her hand, linking their fingers. Simran looked down at their interlocked hands and smiled.

"So, how is this supposed to go, Sims?" he asked quickly, feeling a tad out of his element, something he hadn't felt in years. She lifted her brows, surprised, then understanding hit, her eyes softening. This was one of the things he appreciated about her. She was an empath at heart and always strived to make people feel comfortable. She pulled him to her, putting her arms around his waist, not giving a damn about her earlier warning of "no canoodling in front of the *Desis*." The cool of her hands swirled circles on his lower back and he automatically relaxed.

"Oh, just some friends like I mentioned before, maybe a few old flings who have nothing on you, and a ton of Aunties," she smiled up at him. Then she explained that an Aunty was a loveable, older friend, familiar with one's family, who loved to give unsolicited advice and could kill one with their gossip. In this particular group, he would hear loud whispers of how Simran was practically the age of a grandmother at thirty-two but sadly, had no offspring to show for it. She was just plain unlucky in finding a husband, and her father would surely die of a broken heart because of it.

He chuckled. "Ok, got it. They'll be no match for my charms, babe," he said airily, the giddy feeling from before turning acrid in his stomach. What the hell was he doing here? He'd no inkling before that he'd have to fight off the topic of marriage. The word barely existed in his vocabulary, that's how much he wasn't a fan.

"*Eh*, Simran!" A few shouts greeted them and curious on-lookers started tittering amongst themselves. Simran slid her hand back into his, carefully making sure to entwine their fingers together, and pulled him along, nodding and waving as they went by. The attentive stares were clearly due to Simran showing up with an unknown man, and probably more so because he wasn't Indian. He was fine with that and smiled back. This was the twenty-first century. Interracial couples shouldn't be a shocking sight. But he also noticed some of the men's direct gazes as their eyes openly roved over her in her flirty number, and he gripped her hand a little more tightly, wanting to shield her from view. She didn't really seem to notice the attention from those men, though.

Or maybe she just ignored it, only adjusting the white scarf around her neck as she continued to wave at the well-heeled guests dressed in a combination of traditional Indian wear and American fashion. She spoke to them in what he recognized was Hindi, but what also sounded like another language.

And now Marc was utterly fascinated. He hadn't yet heard her speak her native tongue in fluent conversation and the fact that she spoke another language along with Hindi was beyond cool. Her husky voice rolling off the soft sounds was soothing poetry to his ears.

"What is that other language you're speaking?" he asked curiously.

"Oh, my other mother tongue, Bangla. Both of my parents are from West Bengal and spoke it growing up. They insisted that my sister and I speak both it and Hindi fluently." She was off-handed in her comment, and for some reason Marc wanted to haul her into the bushes and cover her trilingual mouth with his own.

"Well, *you*, baby, are turning me on so bad right now." He encircled her waist with both of his hands, pulling her body to his. Who would have thought that linguistics could give him a boner? Her mind—fuck everything about her—was so sexy.

"Marc," she hissed trying to shoo him away. They were jostled from behind suddenly. The culprit a rag tag bunch of kids. Simran's slim arms quickly snaked around his neck to steady them.

"Are you canoodling, Ms. Khan?" he teased. She looked up, and he felt like he was falling into the depths of those dark eyes.

"Oops, sorry, Sima Aunty," the kids cut in, apologizing. They shot them curious glances before running away. Simran rolled her eyes. If she kept rolling her eyes like that, they would get stuck in her head, Marc was absolutely convinced.

"Aunty? Baby, just how old *are* you?" he whispered in her ear, while taking a deep whiff of her intoxicating floral and spice scent. He closed his eyes, wanting to nuzzle his face into her neck. He heard her sharp intake of breath, then she swatted him playfully in the chest.

"Shut up," she laughed. And as he gazed down at her, that warm feeling inexplicably bloomed throughout his chest again.

"Sima, *beta* (kiddo), there you are," an elegant voice with a blend of Indian and British accents interrupted them, thankfully. The two jumped apart as a small, older Indian woman, dressed stylishly in a beige sleeveless tunic with intricate beadwork, and matching beige pants came up to greet them. Her silver hair was in a short bob and her makeup was flawless, even in the summer heat. She gave Simran an engulfing hug. "It's been so long," she said.

"Aunty, hi! *Namaste.*" Simran put her hands together in greeting then hugged her back. She leaned down to peck her on each cheek while exclaiming, "Are those this season's Prada sandals? I *love* them!" The older woman smiled, pleased at the compliment, posing her tiny feet for Simran.

"They are!" she exclaimed triumphantly. "I had them special ordered in my size. It's been two years since Tina's successful marriage, but why not still treat myself?" she said a little smugly. "And if you will just let me, I can do the same for you! I've been talking to your father, you know," she said, wagging her finger at Simran, but then she noticed Marc and curiously looked over Simran's shoulder at him with piercing eyes.

"Oh, Aunty," Simran said, shaking her head about the marriage comment. Before the older woman could continue, Simran went on, "There's someone I want you to meet by the way." She pulled Marc closer and put her arm around his waist. "This is Marcus Lehigh. He's my—" she stopped short then recovered, "—he's here with me," she said smiling adoringly up at him. She was about to say "boyfriend," Marc thought with some humor. They'd never discussed labels, but he realized she wasn't that far off. He hadn't been somebody's boyfriend since college. He tugged at the back of his collar uncomfortably, realizing it was damp with sweat, and not just because of the summer heat. He pushed his discomfort way, way down, and smiled generously at the smaller woman. "Charming" was his way of dealing with any uncomfortable moment. "Marc, this is Ms. Priya Acharya, also known as Pinky Aunty. She's the most influential Indian matchmaker this side of the globe. She's also our awesome host for today," she added, her tone a little reverent. She winked at Marc, over Pinky's head.

Marc instantly knew what he was to do here. He took Pinky Aunty's dainty, elegantly outstretched hand, bejeweled in weighty, gold rings.

"Hello, Ms. Acharya. It's really nice to meet you. I'm pleased Simran invited me. She's been talking non-stop about this party for weeks, hinting at the entertainment in store for us," he said, lying smoothly, wiggling his eyebrows slightly at Simran.

෴෴෴

Simran's eyes widened at how easily he lied, and how well he did it. They both knew she'd just told him about the damn party two days ago. Dang, the man was good.

She cleared her throat. "Yeah, Aunty, Marc is excited to try the food and see the Bollywood dancers you flew in from Houston's Rhythm India."

"Yep," he continued, "I'm just taking it all in. I love the traditional marigold decorations by the way. Are you celebrating anything in particular?" Now he was just hitting it out of the park, Simran thought.

Pinky Aunty's look darted from Simran, up to Marc, and back to Simran again. She had sharp eyes and an even sharper tongue. Simran instantly knew she would hear about this from her father at some point soon. Instead of jumpy, like a kid who knew they'd done something wrong, she was calm, almost serene at the notion. Her heart was open now, and she couldn't hide what she and Marc were doing anymore, his statement about wanting more still engulfing her warmly. She clutched his waist a little tighter, his presence here with her soothing.

Pinky Aunty's face smoothed over as she answered, "No specific celebration, except that summer is over. But what, young man, do you know about Indian traditions?" Marc went on to explain the work he did and his travels to India. He briefly talked about his time spent there, learning about some of the culture, and even having the chance to meet with Simran's father's company to help successfully open his club in Mumbai.

"*Just a minute.* Are you one of the Americans who opened Club Sundar Social?!" she clapped her hands in marvel and delight. Simran knew how she felt. When she had found out that Marc and Bruce were the brains behind Club Sundar Social—Mumbai's "It" club –she'd actually tripped on the sidewalk, almost falling headfirst into oncoming traffic before Marc pulled her back. Their club was insanely popular, with Bollywood stars flocking there to see and be seen. One could only get in if one knew the right people. "But this club is superb, so much fun, such good food and drinks, and the music selection beyond any other club!" Pinky Aunty continued.

He grinned genuinely at her reaction. "That means so much coming from you, Ms. Acharya." That beautiful smile and the appearance of his dimples made even Pinky Aunty blush a little, her hand coming to her chest. "Honestly, being in Mumbai was exceptional. Everyone was so friendly."

"*Oh,* call me Pinky Aunty, we're friends now," she said a little girlishly, looking up at him beneath her thick, false eyelashes. She linked her arm through his, pulling him away from Simran. "Sima, I'll bring him back in a few minutes. Marc, you absolutely must meet some of my friends." Simran just nodded, trying not to burst into laughter at the horrified look Marc shot her. Then, he shrugged with a "when in Rome," expression and let himself be led away.

Now, she just stood there, not sure if she should be offended. Clearly, Pinky Aunty was more interested in Marc than her. *She* hadn't been invited to chat with the "inner circle." No doubt he'd be paraded to all the other Aunties like the prized peacock that he was.

As she watched their retreating backs, she now couldn't help but openly laugh. Marc was broad and tall, his muscular arm linked with a bony one belonging to a small framed, tiny woman whom he had to continuously duck down to in order to hear. It was kind of sweet. Marc was doing her a big favor here, but it seemed like he was really enjoying himself, too. She got all warm and fuzzy inside and realized she was just standing there gawking at their retreating figures.
Her gaze swept over the crowd, hoping to spot anyone familiar whom she'd grown up with. Like Tina, many had already married and moved away, but she could usually spot a few who'd made it back between their heavy work or social schedules, usually spouse and kids in tow.

She didn't recognize anyone immediately but caught the eye of a petite woman enthralled in her subject matter, her hands flapping around to magnify the story she was telling to the women circling her. Rekha Chowdury, her childhood "mean girl." Simran quickly looked away. Rekha and her crew were faux sweet on the outside, but narcissistic in nature, continuously trying to up one another in their careers, home sizes, vacation locales, and husband's salaries. Their ears were always open wide in order to fish out the spiciest gossip to dissect so they could feel better about themselves, even though these women were successful in life. They'd grown up with everything and groomed to be the best in school. They dutifully achieved the highest marks in their studies and displayed the best tennis trophies on their mantles. They'd attended ivy league universities and thus dubbed themselves "The Ivy" whenever they were together. Here was the thing, though: they were a miserable bunch. They'd blindly followed every whim their parents desired for them, racing to what they thought was a happy future—money, marriage, and respectable titles of doctor or lawyer.

Usually able to grin and bear "The Ivy," Simran had found it more and more difficult after her failed engagement. And now, showing up with Marc ... well, she could only guess what their focus would be, whether she was present or not. She ducked and made a beeline for the bar, grabbing some freshly grilled tandoori kebabs and mini samosas from the servers passing by.

She munched on the delicious bites, shimmying her hips slightly to the music the DJ was playing. She licked her fingers of the tasty leftover oil as she watched the bartender mix drinks. *Yum*, gimlets made fresh to order. She picked one up, took a refreshing sip, and felt a hand on her lower back. Turning to smile up at Marc, she realized it wasn't him a bit too late.

"Simran, my God it's so *good* to see you," a sickly-sweet male voice dripped in her ear. "Rekha said you were over here."

Of course, she did. Rekha loved to stir up trouble.

"Oh, Dev, hey." She made no move to reciprocate as he brushed his thick lips against each of her cheeks. She could smell the beer on his breath and the sweat beneath his heavy cologne. He brushed thick black locks away from his face with an impish smile. He looked good in snug faded jeans, and a slim white polo shirt, collar tips pointed up cockily. Sweat rolled down his face, indicating that he and some of the others had been playing soccer earlier, a favored past-time at these functions. Any other time she would've found him attractive, maybe flirted a little, but not today.

"Why *so cold*, Simran? Didn't we have fun last summer?" he asked, slowly gliding a finger down her arm, taking in her curvy figure, still moving to the beat of the music, in her short dress.

Oh, last summer ... she had absolutely no regrets, but didn't need to be reminded right now. Having known Dev since they were teenagers, when his family moved from India to Connecticut, she decided to have a careless fling with him, both of them unattached at the time, and she in desperate need to drench her desolate sex life with something fun. Dev, known as the "village flirt," handsome, sweet, and overzealous in his devotion to women, had been the best choice, as they'd known each other forever and they both agreed that it was short-term. In fact, they ended it after about a month, and he, always in need of a female companion, moved on to his now fiancé. They continued to be friends after that. There were no hard feelings between them.

"I'm just trying to enjoy the party and this delicious drink, Dev." She gave him a friendly smile, realizing she was being a little rude. "How is Sheila?" she continued, referring to his fiancé who was in India now, picking out her trousseau. "The wedding is a year from now, but let me tell you, the time goes like that," she snapped a finger. "If she needs any help at all, please have her call me. The same goes for you. I hope you aren't putting all the ceremony decisions on her shoulders," she said sternly.

"I don't want to talk about Sheila. I want to talk about Simran," he pouted, his hand coming to rest beside her on the bar. His other hand was on the other side, trapping her. Oh dear, she thought. Suddenly a popular Punjabi rap and hip-hop song filled the air, making other guests exclaim and start dancing. "Simran, come, let's groove," he commanded, tugging at one of her hands while moving his slim body to Tesher's "Jalebi Baby."

"Dev, actually, I'm with someone and I said I would wait for him right here," she answered, absolutely not wanting to dance with Dev, whom she could tell had had one too many beers.

"You're here with someone?" He barely looked around at the other party-goers. "Well, where the bloody hell *is* he?" His tone was scornful. "No man would ever leave such a beauty stranded by herself. Come with me, move that bod with me," he cajoled, starting to really dance, lip-syncing Tesher's sensual words about a woman being like the candy sweet

Indian dessert, Jalebi, while bumping his body into hers. He wasn't a bad dancer by any means, but inebriated with too many beers made him clumsy. He bumped her a little too hard and her drink sloshed over onto the patio, just missing her beloved sandals.

"Dev! Sheesh, take it easy. I think you've had a little too much to drink. Let's get you some water." She turned to the bartender to grab him some when she felt him start to snuggle the back of her neck. Before she could push him off he was gone. When she turned back around, she saw Marc standing behind Dev, his hand firmly gripping Dev's shoulder, a cool smile on his lips. If she could see his eyes behind those sunglasses, she was sure they would be as cold as 'Ice, Ice, baby.'

"Hey, babe," Marc said, his voice threatening in its feigned nicety. "Introduce me to your friend."

Oh lord.

"Who the hell are you!?" Dev quipped, struggling to turn around in Marc's tight grip to face him. They were both about the same height, but where Marc was broad and had incredible muscle tone, Dev was slim and slight in comparison.

Simran hurried to make the introductions. "Marc, this is an old friend of mine, Devon Bashir. We grew up together. Dev, this is Marcus Lehigh, he's here with me." She hoped Marc would calm down. She'd never seen him act so aggressively toward someone and she hoped it wouldn't escalate into something else. Dev was no match for him and could get pounded into the pavement.

After considering Dev for a moment, Marc let go of the slight Indian and came to Simran, encircling a strong arm possessively around her waist, while pulling her up against his hard body. He leaned in and took his time to kiss her fully, lavishing her lips with his. When he tried to push his tongue into her mouth, she reluctantly pulled away before she lost control. This was too much. Marc was acting ... jealous?

He looked down at her, his jaw ticking. Then he turned to Dev. "Nice to meet you, Dev," he said finally, his voice returning to some normalcy, but that jaw still clenched. "Mm, Sims, what are we drinking?" Without waiting for an answer, he took her glass and gulped down her gimlet.

"So, *you're* here with Simran?" Dev asked accusingly. "I told her no one leaves such a woman to entertain herself. It was lucky I saw her. She loves to dance and I wanted her to join me on the dance floor," Dev continued, and then started singing the song lyrics still blaring from the speakers, "Baby let me see it ... I just wanna eat it," all while staring only at Simran. He placed his hands over his heart, doing his best impersonation of a besotted Bollywood film character, even though the lyrics were downright dirty. Simran tried unsuccessfully to keep a straight face. Here was the Dev they all knew and were used to; a bit drunk, enamored with every woman he laid eyes on, even if he was engaged to the beautiful Sheila. She glanced at Marc. His face was stony, completely unimpressed. "You know, Simran and I were a hot item last summer. I'm disappointed she's not available anymore," Dev interjected between his singing, while his arms flailed widely and his hips continued shimmying. Simran cringed.

"Is that so?" Marc turned his aviator-covered eyes onto her.

"Come on, Dev, that's all in the past. We're just friends," she spluttered, laughing uncomfortably. Shit, this was sliding out of control faster than the hundreds of DM's sliding her way from an Indian dating website Tina had signed her up for as a joke on her thirtieth birthday. And what the hell was wrong with Marc? She'd never witnessed his full-on cave-man side before. "And what about your fiancé, *hello*? Sheila?" she asked, reminding Dev of his wife-to-be. "She probably misses you like crazy right now, Dev."

"*Baby*, come on! She's just..." And in a nano-second, Marc's hands gripped Dev's shoulders again and forcefully maneuvered him through a throng of surprised party goers to the patio perimeter. He murmured some words only the astonished Indian could hear. A few seconds later, she saw Dev raise his hand to wave at her and call, "Ok, Sima, I'll see you later," all while giving her the familiar South Asian head bob, not quite a shake, and not quite an up and down nod.

"Bye, Dev," she called back, not exactly sorry to see him go.

"One of your past lovers, I presume?" Marc drawled, back at her side. Nope, his voice was definitely still not normal. She stared at the cleft in his chin.

"Yes. I told you we would probably run into a few." He was silent, that muscle continuing to clench along his jawline. "*Jeez*, Marc," she said under her breath.

"What's that, sweetcheeks, or should I call you, what was it, '*Jalebi, baby*'?" His arms were folded across his chest, and his legs widened in a battle stance.

She scoffed. "You heard me. You've met *one* of the very few from my past, and you go all ape-shit. Whereas *I* meet and greet dozens of your former harem on a weekly basis, and yet I deal with it." She shook her head and went on, preventing him from reminding her that she needed reassurance each and every time they ran into one of his past flings. His past was a lot for her to take in. "And what the freak did you say to him? He ran away with his tail between his legs. You know, he's harmless. I mean, that's just Dev. He drinks a little too much, makes a fool of himself, flirts with every woman, and we all laugh. He always goes back to Sheila, though. She's the love of his life," she explained, shrugging. "And to be honest, Sheila isn't much of a saint either. They kind of have a mutual agreement."

"So, let me get this straight, you guys laugh at a drunkard who sexually assaults women? And who's committed to someone else, I might add?" His face showed no emotion. Oh God, he was twisting her words. His moods today were driving her crazy, and not in an exactly good way.

"*Sheesh*, when you put it like that..." She didn't finish. Instead, she said, "Marc, in case you hadn't noticed, I was taking care of the situation. He's harmless," she repeated, going to take a sip of her drink and finding it empty. She turned to the bartender to order another one for herself and for Marc—he looked like he could use one—and then turned back to him as he answered.

"He was being disrespectful, and that's what I told him: if he continued disrespecting you or any other woman at this party, I would personally see to it that he wouldn't be able to show any of those slick dance moves at his wedding," he finished, his hands stuffed in his pockets now. She nodded, not saying anything as she turned back to the bar. She didn't know if she should laugh or be furious.

ↂↂↂ

Marc's eyes bore into Simran's back as she waited for their drinks while his hands balled into fists. What the hell was wrong with him? No woman had ever made him feel this unhinged. It was damn right ugly and he wasn't so sure how he felt about everything. The entire day had been one fucking emotional roller coaster and Marc hated roller coasters. He'd already swallowed the bitterness of his exhilarating high dipping into extreme low when he'd found out Simran's invitation had been last minute. It happened again when the anticipation of teaching her a lesson peaked, taking a nose dive at the realization that manhandling her made neither of them feel great. He thought he could relax after their conversation in the car, but arriving at the party had him riding full-on through stomach hurling loop-dee-loops with everyone's curious stares, the men's open (and even lewd) gazes, *all* of the aunties, and talks of marriage. And fuck, when he saw that slippery Dev guy put his face in Simran's soft neck, he felt his heart careening like he was going down another huge hill that would never end. He had to take action.

She was his. Now, he was both nauseous and dizzy. Maybe he needed to get off this insane ride for good. It couldn't be good for his health.

Simran turned around with their drinks and she seemed calmer, automatically having the same effect on him. She smiled cheekily and asked what he and the Aunties talked about. He couldn't help but grin, relaying how he'd somehow promised to take all the Aunties to Club Sundar Social, get them into the VIP room, and show them a good time. The husky laughter bubbled out of her, and Marc started chuckling, too, he couldn't help it. He was a Simran addict.

"You know, they always get what they want," she sing-songed, looking under her lashes coyly at him. Any remnants of Marc's emotional turmoil completely diminished then; jealousy and doubt receded from his veins. Simran was charming the pants off of him right now, which he didn't mind one bit (he would take his pants off for her any day). Her cheeks were flushed from the heat and the alcohol, the tip of her nose shiny, and wisps of hair pulled away from her hair-do as her body wiggled to the music (a different song, thankfully). He could tell she was getting tipsy from the strong drinks, and it was so loveable that his stomach got weighty again, but this time with a pleasant feeling. He drew her to him and started fingering the loose strands, pushing them behind her ear. All he could think was no one else but he could call her "baby." No one else but him could waltz up and be overly familiar with her.

"Baby, only I get to eat your Jalebi, got it?" *Whatever that was*, he thought. He could only assume it alluded to something sexual. Her bottom lip was tucked into her mouth trying to suppress her giggles while nodding in agreement. "Now, let's get you some food," he said, as the servers passed out yummy desserts. He took a plate loaded with colorful Indian sweets and led her to one of the many blankets spread out on the lawn. She sat down, pushing her legs to one side and smoothing her skirt down. He lay down next to her, propping himself on one elbow.

"Oh, babe, these desserts, or *mishti*, as we call them, come from the best Bengali sweet shop in Jersey. Hmm ... I don't see any Jalebi, though," she murmured, inspecting the assortment. "Those were my favorite as a kid—you know, who wouldn't love a fried sweet dipped in clarified honey?" Now the song made sense to Marc, and he sniggered to himself. Her Jalebi, was absolutely only for him to enjoy. "Here, try this one." She fed him a pale pink, crumbly bite with crushed pistachio and an edible gold leaf on top. "It's coconut flavored Burfi," she said licking her lips and fingers.

"Hm, interesting flavor." He wasn't so sure about the condensed milk taste but did enjoy the coconut.

"Ok, how about this one?" She put a large Gulab Jamon up to his mouth forcing him to take a bite. He chewed on fried dough, kind of like a funnel cake but covered with a sticky syrup and it wasn't bad. He remembered having these in India. She took a bite, too, and started licking the sauce from around her mouth.

"Here, let me help you," he said. He reached up cupping her face in one hand, and pulled her down to him, covering her sweet, full lips with his. His tongue licked the sticky syrup off, and made its way into her mouth, taking what was his and he didn't care who saw. She fully returned the kiss back, twining her tongue with his, encircling an arm around his neck to keep him close. She moaned softly and his groin tensed. They were lost in their kiss when a few guests hooted and hollered at them and broke them apart a few moments later. Simran looked down embarrassed, surprised, and smiling, tucking some loose hair behind her ear.

"Just making sure everyone knows you're here with me, ok, kitten?" Marc said gruffly, nuzzling her. She nodded and didn't complain about their canoodling, only made circles with her finger on his thigh.

That evening, back in his bed, he took his time with her, cherishing her, hoping that his tender touch reached her soul, the way he knew she was doing to him. They both came, one right after the other with so much intensity that they collapsed exhausted in each other's arms, completely spent and content. And Marc knew he'd never feel this way about another person.

He left for Vancouver just one week later.

Present Day,
A Flight to India

Chapter 8

Simran's head lurched forward making her eyes jerk open. Everything was a blur, so she attempted to go back to sleep, chasing her dream, trying to grasp at the tail end as it disappeared into that irretrievable part of her brain. Damn. No such luck and she was up now. She looked groggily around the still dim flight cabin, her head aching. The wine had definitely knocked her out. Her body lurched side to side, and she gripped the armrests tightly on either side of her. Turbulence.

The captain's calm voice spoke over the speaker, asking everyone to return to their seats as the cabin quivered high up in the air over the Atlantic. The luggage rattled overhead, like dominoes in a cup during a rousing game of backgammon. The clanking of the coffee service carts the attendants were hastily putting away, grated on her ears, making her wince. Crap. All she needed now was to go down in a burning flame. Could her life get any worse?

The collective cry from the passengers rang out as the plane lifted dangerously up, then down. Simran's stomach flipped, too. Oh God, was she about to lose her dinner? She held her belly, willing it to calm down the way she'd done when life had lived inside her briefly, and morning sickness had been more of an all-day sickness. She bit her cheeks at the memory, the longing for motherhood consuming her. With no life within her anymore, she felt like an empty, flawed vessel—a body ready to birth, but one that resisted that natural urge.

Get off it, she scolded herself. She'd have plenty of chances to have kids in the future ... wouldn't she? She was in her early thirties, at the prime for pumping kids out. Yet, when the opportunity arrived, it hadn't happened. Did she feel like a failure? Yes, in the worst possible way. And the icing on that defeating cake? The possibility of cancer. Had she been a major douche-waffle in her last life? A firm devotee of the Hindu faith she was not. But if she was, well Karma was just doing its job in inflicting these heavy aches.

She grabbed the complimentary vomit bag and dry-heaved into it. These very dark thoughts were overcrowding her already crowded mind lately. She needed to get a hold of herself.

So, what if she did marry Anil? Would that be the worst thing in the world? She dry-heaved into the bag again. Apparently, it was. A flight attendant noticed her distress and offered her a damp cloth, sparkling water, and a toothbrush/toothpaste kit. Simran nodded in thanks; her eyes watery.

After making her way to the bathroom to brush her teeth, the spearmint a thankful reprieve from the acid in her mouth, she sat back down, forcing herself to have a sliding doors moment.

So, she marries Anil and drops everything in NY—*Lavish Your Events*, friends, her life. She plays the dutiful daughter and the good wife by helping with the Khan family business, while making a beautiful home in Mumbai, with a possible vacation home somewhere else. The goal to eventually fill said homes with future kids (if her body cooperated). Simran leaned back, really letting her over-active imagination run wild. She'd murder Anil. There was no way around it. *Now there's a fabulous Bollywood film storyline for you, Bina,* she thought a little maniacally. The perfect Indian wife—the one with secret dreams for herself—heaven forbid—goes ballistic.

"*Chee, chee,*" the aunties the world over would whisper loudly in shock, while viewership would be off the charts. There had to be *many* South Asian women who privately felt trapped in their marriages; those forced into a restrictive type of life. Oh, she'd have wealth and servants—a luxurious sort of prison—but she wouldn't have what was most sacred to her: independence with a chance at self-fulfillment.

She tossed her head, a new strength starting to rise within her, a responsibility like she'd never felt before making her braver than she'd ever been. It was up to her to ensure her own happiness because when it came down to it, she actually could, unlike many other Indian daughters.

Feeling a bit calmer and stronger now, she reached for her phone, scrolling through a text exchange from before takeoff. Thank God for best friends like Tina; the ones who kept you sane and pulled you back from the ledge. She genuinely smiled for the first time in a while as she read through their conversation.

Tina: "Hey Bee-atch, where've you been!? How are your ovaries?"

Simran: "Hey, Queen. Sorry, been busy. Ovaries are cooperating for now. I'm on my way to India to see my dad, and don't freak out, but Anil, too."

Simran opted to not text Tina about her reunion (if you could even call it that) with Marc just yet. She'd already had a conniption when the whole thing blew up in Simran's face months ago, then the pregnancy, miscarriage, and cancer scare. She didn't need to feed Tina more reasons for wanting to do permanent damage to Marc. Even before the break-up, she'd taunted Simran about randomly showing up in the UK rag mags as the "mystery girl" on global playboy Marcus Lehigh's arm (he was a favorite across the pond), proclaiming that she could potentially be the laughing stock of his world when things didn't work out. Simran definitely wasn't a tabloid kind of person so was always amazed to find out she, a normal, unknown woman, would be of any interest to gossip buzz. But she did often wonder if she *had* been a laughingstock when it all ended. Tina was kind enough never to tell her.

Tina: "You a comedian now? What kind of twisted joke is this?"

No matter what Marc had done, though, Anil would always hold first place on Tina's shitlist. He was, and always would be, the dung on the bottom of any Mumbai street cleaner's shoe. Unfortunately, Marc wasn't too far off the top of Tina's shitlist either. She was thankful she had such a friend for a cheerleader, but at times, like the present, she couldn't be one hundred percent honest with her until she was clear with her own path.

Simran: "I wish. You know my *abba* wants me to get back with Anil. I need to straighten this matter out and the only way to do it is in person so that they know I mean business."

Tina: "Shit, Uncle is so radio rental."

Simran: "Um, weirdo, what?"

Tina: "Cockney rhyming slang, remember? Try to keep up, lady. I'm honing my skills to impress the other financier wives at monthly rosé all day. Kind of rubbish, but it makes my Raj look good ;p. Anyhoo, it means 'mental,' which is what Uncle is being right now. So f'ing disgusting that he thinks you'd go back to that douche. Oops, have to run. Raj and I are leaving for Singapore in a few. He has work then we're making a holiday of it."

Simran: "Sounds rough, especially the day drinking part. ☺"

Tina: "Ha! I'm dealing ☺. Look, everything seems pretty shitty right now. Kind of the story of your life lately, but it'll turn around, it always does. How about we get together in a few weeks, *nah*? We're heading to India after Singapore. Let's meet in Mumbai and hit her up after you give Anil the finger, yeah? XX"

Simran: "Sounds like a plan. Miss you and see you soon. Kisses."

Simran giggled at how English Tina was starting to sound, now that she lived her posh life over there. And her friend was accurate as usual. *Abba was* being mental. Then her heart softened as it always did when she thought about how he'd done the best he could with them without the help of their *amma* (mom). This is what he thought was best for everyone in the family—a traditional South Asian safety net in its purest form. She shook her head. Regardless, he couldn't just make this massive decision without her input. Some Indians were ok with that, even the Americanized ones, but she wasn't. She had an opinion about her own life that she needed him to hear. And shit, if her father wanted Anil so badly in their family, he could marry him himself!

ॐ

Chapter 9

NEW YORK CITY

Marc mentally went through his checklist. He'd repacked his suitcase, made sure his passport was still in his carry-on and arranged for his driver to take him to the airport.

After the conversation with his mom the previous night, he'd stayed up arranging his travel to Mumbai as quickly as he could. He checked his work calendar, canceling a whole hell of a lot of meetings, making notes to reschedule when he was back in town (whenever that may be). He moved approaching promotional follow-ups with the head of his PR, Rose, regarding the Vancouver club launch, advising her to touch base with Bruce, despite her protests that they would lose precious time. For once in his life, he didn't care. Something other than work was taking the lead.

He texted Bruce, updating him on outstanding business-related issues and his plans to leave the country. Bruce, still in Vancouver, and up late probably enjoying some female company, responded immediately.

Bruce: "Go get your princess, Prince Charming. I know you can do it."

Marc grunted and texted back a middle finger emoji.

Bruce: "Love you, too, beef-cake. Good luck."

Marc: "Thanks. I'll be in touch."

He wasn't letting on how insane he felt to his friend. Bruce already knew.

Marc's heart was continuously hammering in his chest now, fully certain that he and Simran should be together. He had to fight for their relationship. She wasn't supposed to be some little wife keeping house and tripping over herself to please her husband and her father. She was meant to be his beautiful, intelligent, and caring partner in life; *his* goddamn goddess to worship daily.

Before he left The Plaza, he headed over to the concierge desk. He had Sabine paged and waited as patiently as he could for her, his fingers drumming a fast beat on the marble countertop.

"Well, well, well, and so how was your stay this time, Mr. Lehigh? Everything satisfactory?" she asked as she came up behind him. He turned around, ready to do battle with her again, but was surprised to find a look on her face that he couldn't quite put his finger on. She was still doing her best to look down her nose at him, even though again, she was almost nose to nose with him in her lofty heels. But in this instance, she seemed to be looking at him closely with eyes slit, as if she was really looking at him for the first time.

"You know it was, Sabine. You and your staff always do an impeccable job while I stay here," he assured her, unsure of how to behave around her. She must be aware of what transpired recently between him and Simran. Must know that

Simran had left like a bat out of hell to figure out this whole Anil, marriage, and relationship with her father circumstance. But did she know that he had confessed his feelings to Simran? Were they *that* tight?

"Sabine, I have another favor to ask of you," he said, hoping she wouldn't give him the finger and leave. He was aware that he wasn't her favorite person.

"Mhm, I'm sure you do." A small, enigmatic smile lifted the corner of her lips. She was secretly pleased about something, and it made him wary.

He cleared his throat. "I need to know your father's home address in Mumbai." As he waited, he quickly came up with a dozen reasons why she should give it to him if she didn't cooperate.

Sabine stepped behind the counter wordlessly, that mysterious smile still in place, and pulled up a post-it. She scribbled something down then handed it to him.

"Here you go." Then she went over to the computer, dismissing him, seeming to go back to work.

He stood there, mouth agape. Why was she making this so easy for him? She glanced up, her eyes peering over her glasses in question. "Was there something else you needed, Mr. Lehigh?"

He pulled his jaw up from his chest and mentally gave himself a shake. Never show weakness, or fear, in the face of your enemy. Something he'd learned from his favored classic Samurai films. Be direct, he reminded himself, self-taught from his own experiences. "Please, call me Marcus. And why aren't you making this harder for me?"

She breathed in deeply, her hand fisting under her chin as she considered him, really thinking about her answer. She took her glasses off, looked for a smudge, then put them back on, stalling. "Oh, I don't think I'm quite ready to call you by your first name," she drawled. Then she sighed. "Well, I still think you're a tool." Her voice was flat and filled with so much honesty, that Marc couldn't help hoot out a laugh, trying to cover it with a cough, the sound echoing in the airy lobby. The Khan's were a bunch of fire-crackers. He wondered what their father was like. Would he have to steal himself when he came face-to-face with him, too?

She arched an eyebrow, finding this far from funny. "But most men are," she continued. "You think only with that organ between your legs. And when it's flaccid, your actual brain functions only half the time," she said, shaking her head in pity. "My baby sister seems to think you're the 'bee's knees' though, so I'm willing to give you another chance. I don't know what went on between you two and, frankly, I don't need those details. But I'm glad she told you about the pregnancy and miscarriage. You deserved to know." She came around the front of the counter, leaning her backside against it, her arms crossed.

"Well, thanks, Sabine, I appreciate you at least being on my side about that," Marc said, completely taken off guard by the direction this conversation was headed.

"I'm more on your side than you think," she responded, and she sounded surprised herself. "About second chances, though, *I'm* willing to give you a second chance, but only if Simran is, and I don't know if she will."

Marc nodded; his chest squeezing into a ball making it a little difficult for him to breathe. She definitely knew about his feelings toward Simran. "I understand. But I would be a fucking fool if I didn't try," he said as calmly as he could. He shouldn't care what Sabine thought, but he did. She nodded in agreement, her face saying he was a fool no matter what he did.

"Just remember, Mr. Lehigh, Simran has a heart of gold, twenty-four karat gold to be exact. And you know what they say about twenty-four karat gold, right?" When he didn't answer, because, honestly, he had no idea, she continued, "In the Indian culture, it's the best of the best. It's the shiniest, the brightest, but also the softest. It bends really easily, and if pushed too far, will crumble away. So far, you've bent her heart, dinged it pretty badly. It could crumble to nothing if you keep toying with her, completely irreparable. Please, don't be that asshole to her." There was an imploring quality to her speech, but her tone was laced with a sharpness. A warning, Marc realized. Without notice, his throat felt full, and his eyes pricked, moisture blurring his vision. *Shit*, was he going to cry? He blinked back the wetness as the emotion tried to overtake him, the realization that he'd almost broken the woman he loved. And, of course, now Sabine would think he was a chump. He ran his hand through his hair, trying to cover his reaction.

"Mhm," she said, nodding, her lips pressed into a straight line. Sabine saw everything. "This is love. It makes you feel full like your heart blew up ten times its size in your chest." She shook her head in wonder. "It's the most incredible feeling, nothing can top it. But then," she winced, with a voice unsteady, "it can feel like it's killing you, and you actually *want* to die because maybe everything you've tried has no sway on the other person, making you feel like the shittiest piece of shit on the face of the planet." She spoke with conviction like she had some experience in the matter. "I was there, with my last girlfriend. It leaves more than just a bruising on your entire soul," she confirmed. "You ready to take that chance?"

Chapter 10

MUMBAI, INDIA

The air was stale having been through innumerable rounds of recycling. The combination of spice and body odor hit Simran and her nostrils flared sharply in reaction. The Mumbai International Airport waited just beyond the jet bridge; she could see it from the plane. Her senses salivated for the open and airy space as she was more than ready to disembark from her long-ass journey.

She felt dehydrated and her eyes were dry, despite the massive quantity of water she guzzled throughout the entire trip. That glass of wine with dinner many hours ago had not only made her horny, sleep fitfully, but now, uber parched. And she was convinced that every time slumber overtook her, the dreams she experienced were filled with that last party she and Marc attended together, only refueling her anger toward him.

The other passengers were chatting excitedly around her and it took all her patience to not tell them to shut the hell up. She dug around in her bag for her sunglasses and put them on. She didn't give a shit if she looked like a drama queen. Her head was about to split open.

Although trying her hardest to ignore the cacophony of passenger chatter (mostly in Hindi), she could still make out some of their conversations. One guy was home for a funeral, a few were coming in preparation for *Diwali* (a major Hindu festival starting in a few weeks), and yet another passenger was heading his ass over to an *ashram* (a monastery, or sanctuary, for spiritual and religious retreats). He needed the positive energy to move his stocks in the right direction. Simran blanched and almost turned around to give the guy a piece of her mind. *Ashrams* were sacred to her and her family, at least the ones that weren't overly commercialized. It sounded like this dude was going to a fancy-dancy place with spas, massages, and five-star accommodations, not the traditional retreats that were simple and full of self-reflection. A vision of her Rani *Khala* came to mind—the aunt that Sabine had recently name dropped—and she instantly recalled this special person and her connection to an *ashram* here in India. She was someone Simran admired and put so high on a pedestal in the past, that she'd occasionally thought of her as a mystical being.

Huh, is this some sort of weird sign? Is the universe trying to tell me something?

❧❦❧❦❧

After getting off the plane, she made a mad dash for the bathroom, then stood in a long line to grab some food and *cha* (tea) from her favorite tea stall in the food court. The thought of her aunt and *ashrams* kept invading her mind above everything else going on in her world, and a plan was formulating, but was she brave enough to see it through?

Finally, at baggage claim, she saw her suitcase circling the carousel sadly with just a few bags. The bright fuchsia color and the cheesy sticker, "Work hard, travel harder," she'd slapped on years ago to make it stand out, now a moot point. She hauled it off the carousel and made her way over to Immigration, groaning audibly. She must be one of the last ones from her flight to get in line. The officers in their little booths up front weren't even visible from where she was standing. *More time to continue with planning*, she thought, trying to put a positive spin on her wait time. She plopped down on her suitcase, busting out her phone to take some notes.

An hour later, exhausted as the travel took its toll on her body, she finally exited the door for International Flight Arrivals. It was mid-morning and the weather was comfortable for the moment. But with monsoon season out of the way, she knew the day would just get hotter. She peered into the sea of other drivers, family members, and taxis, searching for her dad's familiar gold Lexus GX, with his driver Prahalad waiting. She finally spotted his slight figure in the crowd. The standard driver's uniform with the tan button-down shirt and matching pants hung loosely off his skinny frame. Shaggy black hair swung over his brows and the whites of his eyes were a stark contrast to his dark brown skin. Simran waved and he waved back hesitantly, a timid smile appearing below his mustache. He met up with her and politely asked about her flight as they walked back to the car.

He opened the door for her, then put her luggage in the trunk. She said everything was fine and asked about his family, her mind preoccupied with her quickly fangled idea.

They chatted this way, cordially but not too familiar, as Prahalad eased their way out of the busy airport. Then she threw him her curveball, asking him with feigned confidence if he knew about the additional stop she and her father had discussed last minute. He was to drive her to Lonavala first, then she would call him in a few days to pick her up to take her to her father. The mountain town she was referring to was fifty miles away, inland from where her dad lived in the upscale neighborhood of Bandra West on the coast. She looked expectantly at the back of his head, his driver's cap pushed low, hoping he wouldn't see through her lie.

Murky eyes under his disheveled hair met hers in the rearview mirror, wide with uncertainty, almost fear, conveying that these were not his orders for the day. Simran understood immediately. Her father didn't abuse his servants (quite a norm in India actually), but he would not be pleased. Prahalad's wages would be docked and his salary was crucial for his family to survive in the poor farming village they still lived in. She'd seen it happen more than once and before she knew what she was doing, she reached into her carry-on, pulling out her wallet. The wad of cash she took out was about four hundred US dollars and could easily be exchanged for rupees in the city center. She tapped his shoulder with the cash, explaining that her father must have forgotten that she wanted to stop to visit with her favorite great-aunt who lived in an *ashram* in Lonavala. She would give him half the money now, and the rest upon arrival if he took her.

Now, Prahalad was no fool. From a poor farming village, yes, but he was shrewd in money-making schemes (as a child who went hungry during some parts of the year, he had to be). He could smell a trade a mile away. The stare he gave her, squinting under his shaggy hair, was a knowing one. His head finally nodded in that familiar South Asian head bob—a silent acquiescence to her scheme—while wordlessly fisting the cash. He shifted the gears and turned the car in a different direction, acquainted with the new destination as he'd driven various family members there in the past. Whether he believed her or not would remain a mystery, though.

Simran quickly texted Sabine that she was making a detour before heading to their father's home, and not to worry about her. She was safe but needed some space to clear her head. Then she shut off her phone, wanting to remain inaccessible until she could figure her shit out.

While they headed for the hills, Simran rolled the window down and breathed in the salty air coming off the Arabian Sea. Tall coconut and palm trees whipped by as giant green blurs while Prahalad picked up speed. The sun was starting to climb in the sky, and already the air's cool undercurrent was warming up. Simran felt tranquil with her decision, though she was certain her father would throw a tantrum. But right now, she was on "Simran time," -others be damned—and she wondered why she hadn't thought of this earlier. Obviously, her brain had been too inundated to think clearly, and she sent thankful, positive vibes to that nincompoop on the plane who reminded her about *ashrams*. What she needed right now was a place to empty her mind and practice some self-care; a peaceful environment away from anything that reminded her of her current problems and would help her to hit the reset button. Who better to go to with her problems than her great-aunt, a person she always felt was wiser than anyone she knew? Someone who gave a big 'screw you' to society and made her own way to self-fulfillment. Of course, Sabine was a close second in this realm, but Rani *Khala* was like no other; a seasoned, non-worldly being who seemed to have ALL the answers to life. Heck, maybe Simran would follow in the same path and join an *ashram* like Rani. She could stay abstinent, let go of all her worldly possessions and die a nun. How great would that be not having to deal with anything but inner peace? Anything was possible at this point.

☙✸☙✸☙

LONAVALA, INDIA

The car door slammed, stirring her. Having blissfully dozed during the hour and a half trip inland toward the hills, she inched her eyes open to mist outside the car window. Frothy white was everywhere, shrouding the hills nearby and rolling over the mountains in the distance. Lush green blanketed the ground, climbing onto the rocks; a continuous carpet of emeralds as far as the eye could see. In the distance, there was the quiet 'shushing,' reminiscent of Simran's noise machine at home to drown out the loud city. Squinting into the vapor she could just make out a ridge with a waterfall above her to the left which was the bearer of that oh so soothing sound. She recalled there were multiple pools and waterfalls surrounding this serene place. It was beyond beautiful, surreal, like a poem of heaven the famous Tagore might have written.

The weather was only slightly more comfortable at this higher altitude, but the moisture fought with the cooling temperature, providing a humid quality. Simran gathered her hair into a top knot while she got out of the car, her jeans sticking to her. She stood next to Prahalad, surveying the rustic wooden fence bordering the large hill the car was parked in front of. The dusty path, beginning at the bottom, went up and beyond, in a winding trail that looked to lead nowhere. A cacophony of birds suddenly shrieked, breaking up the serenity and making Simran jump.

Prahalad grabbed her suitcase and made like he was going to take it all the way up the path to the temple entrance hidden at the pinnacle of the hill. Simran stopped him, thanking him. She took the suitcase and pressed the rest of the cash she had on her into his palm, a silent gesture for him to keep his mouth shut to her father. Then she began up the steep trail by herself. It would be challenging but she was eager. She'd start gradually at first as the pricking and pangs in her abdomen were still present from surgery. While sweat rolled into her eyes, she dragged the suitcase behind her and didn't look back when the engine started up. The car left and after a few moments, nothing but blissful silence remained.

Almost thirty minutes later, she stopped at what looked like the top of the incline. It wasn't. The path made a sharp turn left and went further up at a more gradual slant. She'd done this climb more than once as a child and was prepared. She knew there was a bench carved into the hillside one could only find if they were really looking. When she spotted it, she heaved her clammy self onto the dusty seat, dropping her carry-on next to her, leaving her suitcase in the path. She'd rolled her short sleeves up like a tank top and wished for about the thousandth time that she could peel off her sticky jeans. Her pristine knit sneakers were dusty and muddy beyond repair, and yet, she didn't care.

She took her water bottle out and chugged thirstily, also reaching for a protein bar to snack on. Suddenly a light rain started drizzling, making Simran laugh idiotically. She lifted her face to the sky, hoping the moisture would wash away her sweat and any lingering doubts she had about her future.

"If I didn't know any better, I would think you were an angel sent to visit me, *amar beta* (my kiddo)," a low voice said steadily, breaking the quietude. Simran only slightly jumped this time.

A tall figure emerged on the path heading down to where she sat, a big black umbrella opened in her hand, protecting her from the light rain. The woman had on a burnt orange *shalwar kameez*. The matching pants and knee-length tunic were a light cotton fabric, keeping the wearer cool in the humid air. Her salt and pepper hair swirled into a bun as big as a cinnamon roll at the crown of her head. A white *dupatta* (scarf) was thrown over her bun, the knotted fringe framing her face and trailing down her back and chest, mingling with the colorful beaded necklaces around her neck. Silver bangles tinkled airily like fairies on her wrists and came to silence as she stood in front of Simran.

With a weathered face still so stunning, she smiled and her oversized eyes, almost too big for her face, looked down kindly. Simran thought she might cry at seeing the familiar, beloved countenance. She wrapped her arms around her great-aunt tightly, burying her face in the soft fabric at her stomach, while smelling natural detergent and sun-dried cotton. She managed to mumble a "*Namaste*," against her aunt's waist before becoming completely overcome with emotion.

"Ki (what), Sima?" And she put one long arm around Simran's shoulders and held her, letting her just be.

"*Bar Khala* (great-aunt)," Simran finally managed to choke out. "I'm just so relieved to see you," she said, finally looking up at her.

Her great-aunt gave an elegant nod of her head. "*Asa* (come), let's go up to the temple. Get you settled. This is a surprise, seeing you here. You look so much like your mother, I thought I saw a ghost." She smiled tenderly. She explained that one of the other attendees had seen a bedraggled person struggling up the path, suitcase in tow, so she'd come down to investigate, thinking it was a wayward guest.

Her great-aunt was also named Simran, but everyone called her Rani. Simran was actually named for her, as this aunt had been a favorite of her mother's. Rani was a little taller than Simran with a willowy body, wide shoulders, and hips. She had a graceful, gentle demeanor, but commanded respect wherever she went. Without children, she always considered the next generation of kids in the family as her own. She welcomed them to visit the *Antarik Shanti Ashram*, which she founded almost forty years ago. And when they did, more often when Simran was little and her mother was alive, she let the children run wild in the waterfalls and pools, showed them the silence caves and the proper behavior when seeking meditation, and put them to work feeding the farm animals. She doted on all her great-nieces and nephews and did her best to instill in them that any serenity found through self-reflection was not freedom from the storm, but peace amid the storm. If one didn't possess inner harmony, there was no way to make it through life's ups and downs.

They walked up the path in comfortable silence, the light rain beginning to wane. The older woman closed the umbrella with a soft click, and as she linked her arm through Simran's, she asked why she was here.

"Oh, where do I begin? I'm not at peace with myself. I'm actually really confused. I was supposed to go to *Abba's* house, but … just couldn't," she said haltingly.

"*Thicke ache* (all right). Going to Kumar's house would have been the opposite of peace," Rani chuckled softly as they arrived at the temple. Her relationship with Simran's father was not a close one. The two butted heads every time they saw each other (which was rare now), both having such strong, dueling personalities. Rani was also one who broke the traditional mold, and it scared Kumar. She left the family and used her own resources as a wealthy widow to start her own private practice. It was a place where only a select few friends and clients could attend. Simran's father had been dead set against the idea, wanting Rani to live with them at the time. As his wife's favorite maternal aunt, he felt responsible for her. Rani had other ideas of what constituted her own happiness, and she went for it.

She steered them into the ornately carved entrance onto the property and continued, "*Beta*, you know you are welcome anytime and for however long you need." She paused, then went on, "Does this have anything to do with a *bishesh* (special) American?" she asked curiously.

Simran's eyes went wide. Holy sacred cow, the lady wasn't going to beat around the bushes.

She gulped. "*Jee*. It does." How much had Sabine told her?

Rani sensed Simran's discomfort and turned to face her, putting her hands reassuringly on her shoulders.

"*Beta*, you and Sabine are like my own daughters and linked to my heart by your *amma*," she said reassuringly. "You know you can tell me anything, *heh*?" Simran only nodded. "Now, rest a little. My meditation ceremony will begin soon and then we will eat a late lunch after. Join us for the meal in the dining hall, *atcha* (ok)?" Again, Simran could only nod.

Rani led her to the temple building, which was a large, white stucco manor with red clay shingles reminiscent of an Italian villa. Simran paused to take in the surroundings, memories flooding back to her of shrieking kids playing tag on the grounds, kicking up the dust, and scaring the wild peacocks. What she didn't notice then, she noticed now which was that the location of *Antarik Shanti Ashram* was ideal. At the top of a hill, it was offset by a lovely, lush mountain-scape in the background; the perfect setup to get away from it all.

Upon entering the enormous double front doors carved with images of Hindu deities, they were met with one of the servants. He and Rani chatted and Simran took in the central, open-air courtyard. Not much had changed and it was comforting. The airy space had natural orange stone tiles underfoot and a lovely fountain in the shape of a lotus blossom in the center. The trickling water mingled with the rustling windchimes and strings of bells, which jangled merrily, almost too pleasantly to ward off evil spirits, which were the main purpose for these charms, or bell *totas*. Everything orchestrated together created a lulling lullaby, and all Simran wanted to do was sleep now.

The servant came to take Simran's suitcase and she followed him up to the second-floor landing to one of the unoccupied guest rooms. Once ensconced in the sparse, but cozy room, Simran kicked off her shoes, peeled off her dusty, muddy clothes, and fell back onto the bed with a giant exhale of relief.

Chapter 11

MUMBAI, INDIA

Marc was hellbent on remaining composed as his driver drove to Kumar Khan's home in Mumbai. The travel to India hadn't started exactly as planned. Just as they stood on the tarmac in preparations for take-off, a last-minute check discovered a faulty engine on the company's private jet. It would be out of commission for a few days, so Marc immediately started looking at commercial flights as plan B.

"What do you mean there are *no* direct flights today or tomorrow to India?" Marc almost shouted, wanting to reach over and shake the coolly collected airline employee across the counter.

"Sir," the man said calmly, "*Diwali* starts in India soon. Many are flying back in preparation for the five-day festival of lights and to celebrate with their families and loved ones."

"I have a loved one I need to see asap." Marc tapped hard on the counter with his pointer finger.

"Sir, I can check with other airlines." The attendant looked down to his monitor while clicking away on his keyboard. "And yes, there's nothing until the day after tomorrow." He looked up to Marc's retreating back as he stomped away.

After that, he called his personal assistant to help him charter a private plane. Luckily, he secured one by throwing an obscene amount of money at the charter company. The departure time was later in the evening and, unfortunately, hopping on a last-minute charter meant he had to ride the first route already booked for Zurich, then head to India from there. So, in all, he'd lost over an entire day and never had he wanted to get somewhere as fast as he could, making him a goddamn beast the entire time, his usual Lehigh charm missing in action. He snapped at anyone who crossed his path, namely a flight attendant who served him the wrong drink and tried to get out of her mistake by flirting with him.

He didn't even attempt to work or listen to music. Nothing could help him relax right now because all he could do was think about her. *Her. Jesus, was he obsessed?* She was it for him and he wasn't sure what he would do if she rejected him. He didn't know why he hadn't seen it earlier. And damn, that wasn't even the truth. He'd been aware of his feelings before he left for Vancouver but didn't want to face them, not fully comprehending what they were. Everything had felt too enormous. Why couldn't he have explained it all to her back then? She'd made it clear on multiple occasions that he should try to talk with her if something was bothering him. The stress about the Vancouver project had consumed him and the all too familiar need to squash anything interfering with his business trajectories came crashing back. He didn't think he could manage it all *and* his feelings for her. It'd felt like he needed to choose one or the other. Focus on work was difficult to nail down and everything had felt dire with the possibility that the club wouldn't even open. And then, ironically, after ending it with her, things were much worse, his concentration shot during crucial investor meetings. Bruce always picked up the slack with his boyish humor, making excuses for Marc.

His behavior had been arrogant, bordering on immaturity, with a good dose of asshole thrown in when he tried to end things back then. Wasn't he the one who'd dragged her back into their relationship in the first place, following her to NY like a dog in heat, as Bruce so eloquently put it? Then he tossed it all aside when it got too tough for him. And for what? A damn club opening? There would be plenty of business opportunities for *LC Enterprises*. There was only one Simran Khan.

What in the fuck had he been thinking?

He hoped when he did reach her, that he didn't come off as demanding, like her father, but that she realized, just like him, that they belonged together. They needed another shot.

Having never done this before, and up against the unchartered territories of love, both the heat of that incredible feeling oozed into his chest simultaneously with the chill of defeat. The dueling feelings vacillated within him throughout the entire flight. *Get your shit together, Lehigh, you can do this.*

Grimacing, he recalled that fateful conversation months ago. It'd been over the phone, even though he was a firm believer that personal matters should be taken care of in person. He hadn't even given her that courtesy.

TWO AND HALF MONTHS AGO

"Hey, babe! Jeez, I'm glad we caught each other. We're like two ships, aren't we?" Simran's sweet laughter made Marc's chest expand, then tighten. "So, um, you may need to sit down and brace yourself," she said nervously. "I have some ... really big news for you." Her voice was high and squeaky as she cleared her throat. "But first, how are you?"

How was he? He felt like shit with his mind in overdrive. They'd been playing phone tag the entire two weeks he'd been in Vancouver and it was ridiculous. His day consisted of back-to-back meetings with investors, vendors, and builders, while she was hair-brained with wedding after wedding all over the Hamptons and Jersey Shore. They were both living and breathing their work at the moment. The difference was the joy in her voice contradicted the pressure he was feeling. Marc could tell she felt alive by her busiest work season. His problem was that they were facing a number of unforeseeable snags in their newest club venture and he hated that they weren't on top of their game. Combine that with his brain continuously fuzzy from missing Simran like hell, and he wasn't on point at this crucial moment with *LC Enterprises*. It was a pivotal moment for them. Their investment group was discussing the opening of a chain of clubs across Canada, the one in Vancouver being the launching off point.

"Sims, hey," he finally said, somber.

"Marc, you don't sound great. Is everything ok?"

"Not really. We have major issues. The bulk of our last shipment of building supplies is delayed. Half are stuck in customs, and the other half washed away in a fucking typhoon—swooped out to sea and lost for good—just like that." He shook his head in disbelief. It was one thing after another, and no one could foresee natural disasters in business timelines. He was also more than pissed that they were behind schedule. There was no way they were opening in two weeks.

"Holy crap! I'm sorry to hear that," she said sincerely, but he could tell she was distracted. "Hold on, Marc, I have a call on the other line." She switched over before he could say anything. She came back a few minutes later, and in that time, Marc became more resolved in this conversation and what he had in mind. "Sorry! I'm so sorry. Catering issues ... again." He could almost see her rolling her eyes. "You were saying, a typhoon, building supplies lost at sea. Babe, don't forget I'm from India. I get it. So, what's the backup plan? Need me to brainstorm with you?"

He'd like nothing more than to kick around alternative ideas with her. He'd learned while in NY that she was extremely creative at problem-solving when it came to last-minute disasters, her reason for being so good at what she did. But he deflected. He needed to stay on topic. "Sims, I don't have much time. I have a lunch meeting in a few but I need to talk to you."

"Oh..." she hesitated. "What's up?"

"Listen, I've been doing some thinking. We're both busy and stressed right now. We can barely get a hold of each other. Maybe we should take a bit of space from this. Truthfully, I don't know how long I'll be here. I thought two, maybe three weeks tops, but now, I just can't say. It's not fair to you, to us." He sighed raggedly. "And, I'm having a hard time focusing on work. It's like I need you with me at all times." He did need her at all times, but she wasn't available right now. And in truth, he wasn't so sure he *wanted* to need her all the time.

"Are you saying you miss me, Mr. Lehigh?" She laughed sweetly again.

"Yeah, I fucking miss you," he almost growled over the phone. "But I think we need some space," he reiterated.

"Okaaaay," she said a little tartly, her reaction to his grouchiness. "Hm." Now she was thoughtful, and he knew she was trying to process this new information. "Well, I'm right here, sweetie. I know we aren't together physically, but you can always text me or try to call. I'll be done in a few weeks and can come to you. I miss you and need you, too." He remained silent and she continued. "So, are you saying you want some space so you can focus?" And by God how he really cared for this woman. She got him and was trying to understand. Was he making the right decision here? "How long? A month?" Her tone bright. "I mean, I guess I could do that. I won't like it, but I understand if the situation requires your undivided attention there."

Fuck. He cleared his throat. "It may be longer. I've had ventures launch six to twelve months after projected opening dates. I'll be real here—our London club took almost six months longer than anticipated for us to open its doors. We're trying to get better with our timelines, but sometimes there are unforeseeable roadblocks." He knew he was rambling. *Hell,* get to the point, Lehigh.

"That was delayed by six months? Huh, I guess in the grand scheme of business that doesn't matter, but," and her voice caught, "six months to a year in a relationship? You can't be serious, Marc."

"Well, we left things pretty intense back in NY, and now it feels like we're back at level one with long-distance. Maybe we just go with it."

"Levels? Sounds like one of my cousin's dumb video games when you put it like that," she snorted, and her giggles were starting to sound squeaky and nervous. Then she went silent. When she finally spoke, the dawning and hurt in her voice was unmistakable. "Were we just a game to you, Marc?"

How had she gone there!? "No! God no, Sims. You know I care about you, but I'm having a fucking difficult time with this long-distance crap."

"Oh, God. Look, I get it," she snapped. "But you don't just say we go from something intense to nothing in only two weeks. It's not black-and-white like that. We may not be fucking around like bunnies, but it's not just about the sex, is it? We have feelings for each other, don't we?" He was silent.

The physical aspect was a huge part of their relationship, and right now, its absence was only amplified with their lack of phone time, too. "Don't we?" she asked again, this time faintly. She waited for a beat. "You don't, do you?"

"Yes, of course," he said testily, running a hand through his hair. This conversation was getting too difficult. He just wanted to put a pause on what they were doing, even though he didn't have a concrete timeline in mind. He knew letting her go would not be easy, but he also knew his focus had to be on work at the moment. *LC Enterprises* was his own blood, sweat, and tears, and he needed to see it through. Right out of college, the drive to succeed, and do it well, was always his top priority and something that completed him. He'd never let anything get in the way of that in the past. *She* of all people should understand this. And yet, the roiling in the pit of his stomach was very real now that they were actually having this conversation. It truthfully didn't seem as cut and dry as he first imagined. But he had to admit that throwing himself back into work would bring back the familiar contentment he was so used to, the determination to concentrate on only business, especially with the unfamiliar emotions emerging for her that he wasn't so sure he wanted to face.

Her voice pulled him back. "So, tell me, because I'm super curious to know, what am I supposed to do in that time without you, Marc? Do I sit with my thumb up my ass waiting for you to come back? What if you change your mind in twelve months, and I waste a whole damn year of my life?" She scoffed. "Or maybe, I try to date or screw other men to try to get over you, get over us?" Fury was igniting her tone, making her voice louder. The thing he knew about Simran was she was understanding, caring, and loyal to a fault, but if pushed too far her anger consumed her, making it hard for her to see straight until she calmed down.

He physically blanched at the thought of her with any other man but himself between her glorious legs, touching what was meant only for him. His hands curled, the knuckles cracking under the pressure. If he didn't relax, he would crush the phone he was holding. No way did he want her with someone else. *Selfish fucker.* He couldn't ask that of her. She should be able to move on with her life, even though he was in a holding pattern of emotions.

"Sims I—" He blew out a frustrated breath, resentful of a non-existent new lover. "I can't ask you to wait for me. That wouldn't be fair." *Fuck, don't date anyone else, baby.* "And, I don't mean a year, but maybe give it a few months, see how we do apart. Look, you're not seeing the forest for the trees. I think you'll better understand when we've had some space from each other. You'll realize that what we're doing right now is too fucking hard. It shouldn't be this tough."

☙☙☙☙

Simran thought her heart might have stopped. Breathing became impossible with her head swimming. She knew it for what it was: a heart attack of the emotional kind. Marc was asking for space, but it sounded more like a break-up. A few months, a year?! How would that even work? Tears started to sting the back of her eyes and she mentally told them to fuck off. She needed to think clearly right now. There would be time for tears later, so much time. Had this really all been one big game to this jerk? No. Deep down she knew it wasn't like that for him. But right now, his self-serving attitude didn't even involve her anymore. And she couldn't believe how easy it was for him to just cast her aside.

"I can't believe you just used that idiotic idiom. It's such a cliché, and really the dumbest thing I've ever heard. I'm living in the moment, in the details because I *am* living, you moron," she fumed. What she really wanted to do was call him the fucking asshole he was.

She heard him gasp, incredulous. "Come on, Sims, it's true, don't you think? This is too tough. Don't we deserve a break from it?"

"*Oh no*, a relationship is hard. Somebody call the village elders!" Her voice was dripping with sarcasm. Sometimes she forgot that Marc was still a newbie, this having been the longest and most involved he'd ever been with someone. Not that she was the ultimate relationship guru, but she did have more experience. *Great.* Now the next woman would reap the benefits from everything she'd taught him, and get the best of Marcus Lehigh, courtesy of "Khan's Relationship Training Program." Shit, were they really breaking up? "This is really what you want?" she asked softly, trying to reign her temper back and think with some clarity. "It just seems so sudden. What about me? Don't I get a say in the matter?"

He sighed long and loud, making her pull the phone away from her ear. *He* was annoyed with *her*? How dare he!

"I've put some thought into this and it's for the best in our scenario. If two people aren't on the same page, then it's not going to work. Think of this like a business partnership. The results won't be ideal if the vision isn't the same." And Simran wished she was there in person to strangle him and his stupid patronizing tone. He was using a business analogy, just like he had when they first met? She'd fallen all over that shit and he got her to sleep with him. Now, he was cut and dry, a little cold when he said it, and she felt a little nauseous, and not just from the big news she'd wanted to share with him, which she absolutely couldn't now. He continued, "And, Simran, it's not what I want, but we'll both be able to focus on work better—"

"Except that this isn't a business partnership is it?" She reminded him, the heat in her tone rising again. She took a deep breath. "And, um, for your information, *Marcus*, I'm doing just fine with work. I've never been better," she said truthfully. For her, knowing she had Marc with her, on her side, made her happier, even more self-assured in her work. Ignorance was bliss, wasn't it? How wrong had *she* been in thinking they were ok these past few weeks? "Marc, everything you're feeling, I completely empathize, please don't think I don't. But, honestly, I'm not experiencing the same thing. I know you're not asking me to wait for you, but the possibility there's a future for us when you're ready, well, I would think you knew me by now ... I *wouldn't* be able to date anyone else. I *would* wait for you. It's pretty unfair, actually. In my opinion, you're either all in, or you're all out. People shouldn't be left to dangle." She paused, searching for the right words. "Look, it's hard right now, but it won't always be this way. Work won't always be a constant barrier..." Now she was pleading, and she hated that it had come to this. And, sheesh, talk about not being able to see the forest for the trees. He needed to take a good long look at what he was asking.

"So, what you're saying is it *is* actually black and white," he countered evenly with an audible sigh of relief.

"Oh my God. That's not—what I meant." Jeez, no wonder he was a super successful businessman. The guy was shrewd and could twist anyone's words around. "You were talking 'feelings' before, which can range a ton throughout any relationship. But what makes or breaks a relationship is that 'all in' or 'all out' status." She heard him blow out a frustrated breath, and she knew she was losing his attention, and possibly more. "Look, we still have some feelings for each other, right? And you're saying you possibly want a chance in the future, yes? Well, ok, then we're sort of 'in' something together—not 'all in,' but as soon as you start adding other people to the mix, things get hairy. I personally wouldn't even be able to date anyone else in that scenario ... would you? Do you see what I mean, now?" Did *she*? It felt like she was speaking in tongues. Maybe she was the only one who felt this way. Was there someone over there who'd sparked his interest and he wanted to make a move on? Her body shook from the sudden jealousy sweeping through her. She had to remember that he'd proven time and again that he wasn't like that, even though his past told her otherwise, and she continued to have a niggling of doubt.

He was slow to answer, but when he did, chunks of her heart crumbled. "You're absolutely right. I can't keep you dangling. I'm sorry, but I *do* need the space," he said deliberately, his voice both firm and quiet. He was only thinking about himself right now, so what more could she say? She'd been in this scenario before. When one party didn't want the same as the other, what was the use in arguing? It only led to bleeding out slowly which was agonizing. Her brain made her breaking heart keep quiet to any more pleading. His stupid business analogy was spot on. *Fucking smart-ass.*

He cleared his throat. "So, you said you had some news for me? Is this about The Knot spring publication? Did you make it on their 'Best of' vendor list?" His tone was soothing, soft-spoken with the sudden change in topic, and she wondered how he did it. How did he just shut her down and out of his life, but expect to be able to continue to know about what was happening with her? Well, she couldn't do just friends with him, and that's what it seemed like he wanted.

"Uh, *no*, actually that wasn't the news," she laughed harshly. "But you know what, you're super busy. Don't even sweat it." She was acting childish. But what she had to tell him, on the heels of his admission to her just now, would blow his mind out of the water, so she kept mum. He didn't need to know more about her personal life anymore. They were through, weren't they? "So, if this is it, I guess I should go. We're done talking?" The words were a knife to her, her face crumpling, but she kept her tone steady so he wouldn't know the pain he was inflicting. How did they get from being intimate in body and mind only a few moments ago to this, where she felt like she didn't know him at all, wasn't allowed to know him like that anymore?

"*Jesus*, Sims, you can still tell me things. We can still talk and keep a line of communication open." He sounded fazed, finally. Good. He was so naïve when it came to this stuff, she couldn't even believe it. Or maybe it was just the male brain's way of dealing with emotional hardships, with compartmentalization a built-in program from birth.

"Oh, you mean be friends? So, I can hear about your most recent sex-capades with some leggy twat or another? So, I can pat you on the back and say, 'Well done, friend, go get some more of that pussy,' when what I really want is for *us* to be screwing each other's brains out. Huh?" she said pretending to give it some thought. "Nah, I'm good." *Yeah, now you can go fuck around to your heart's content.* To think she thought she could ever hold him, the world's biggest player, with more than sexual chemistry. *Duh, dumbass.* Of course, he would want to sample all that Canada had to offer, and it wouldn't be too difficult, would it? He was gorgeous, held that incredible sexual charisma ... every beaver would scurry to mount his log.

"That's the furthest thing—"

She didn't want to hear it, interrupting him, "Don't worry, I won't fuck up your gallery project. I'm committed to it and it's too positive of a vision for me to want to mess with. I'll keep you posted somehow, maybe I'll send you a smoke signal or something." She laughed drily. So, this *was* really happening. *Fuck me, I can't believe I didn't see this coming.* It felt all too familiar. How did that saying go? Fool me once...?

"Sims—"

"Stop. Calling. Me. That," she bit out haltingly between a jaw so clenched, she thought her teeth would shatter.

"Ok, *Simran*," he replied, stunned. This was too much. The dam was about to blow and she needed them to finish so she could get off the phone and collapse into the heap of chaos and depression she knew was mounting. "I appreciate you continuing to offer your help. You're so good at what you do. And I know you won't mess up *our* gallery project, you could never do that. You don't have a mean bone in your body," he said softly. *Damn the egotistical bastard.* He knew her so well. Now she really was going to throw up.

"Oh," she laughed viciously. "I can be mean. You want to *hear* mean? Go fuck yourself, Marcus Lehigh. You're an epic asshole. Don't you *ever* fucking call me again," she shouted hotly, and hung up as the dam burst, her ears and cheeks scalding in humiliation as the bile rose in her throat.

Marc leaned his head back, closing his eyes in agony as the car went over a series of potholes, thrusting him back to the present. He'd punished himself by replaying that conversation over and over again during his hours in the sky, and now on land. He deserved it. It wasn't just his own pain that gutted him from that conversation. He was aware of the immense hurt he inflicted on her during and after that call.

She avoided him from then on, unresponsive to any voice messages or texts. He'd wondered if she'd blocked him on her phone or changed her number, all of his communication going into an unknown digital vortex. Now he knew she'd been inundated with the pregnancy and her health. She didn't have the brain space to give him another thought.

But, after almost ten agonizing weeks of silence, her text popped up on his screen. He'd been in the middle of an important work dinner and felt his phone vibrate. When he saw her number, he fumbled to read it immediately, almost dropping his phone in the process. Bruce had given him a sympathetic look, nodding for him to move outside. He called her back right away, hoping to catch her, hear her husky voice, even if she was still mad at him. But she didn't pick up and he decided right then and there to go back to NY. He didn't realize the investor's daughter, what's her name, had followed him outside and was talking in the background. They'd kissed then, his mind and emotions a mess still, and then he pushed her away. *God-fucking-damn it.* The thought of that kiss with the unknown girl still haunted and disgusted him. He was the epic asshole Simran had called him, only looking to lose his sorrows in any available warm flesh. He had to make it up to her some way; he'd fucking grovel if he had to.

ᘇᓂᘇᓂᘇᓂ

He warily eyed the large, stucco home as his driver turned the car through the tall metal gates standing open. The gravel crunched under the wheels as they pulled into the large circular driveway.

Kumar Khan's home was located in a well-to-do neighborhood off of Mumbai's south coast dotted with large, gated homes and well-kept landscapes. Kumar's home was a vast, peach structure made-up of modern columns and porticos, with metal bars on the outside of all the windows; more of a beautiful fortress than a home. It sat on two acres of rich, green land scattered with large banyan trees and what looked like a mango grove. There was a manmade lake to the right of the home, with bright pink flamingos languishing, as a fountain of Ganesh joyfully spouted water from his trunk.

He took a deep breath as he got out of the car, looking up at the rows and rows of windows. Which one was Simran's? Was she inside or was she out of the house visiting friends, family, or even meeting with Anil and his parents? Jealousy seethed inside him. *Stop. Just get inside. Just get to her.*

Chapter 12

LONAVALA, INDIA

The smell of incense and smoke wafted through the air, the sandalwood and vetiver tickling her nose. Simran had napped for a good hour and now she got up, muddled, her dreams all Marc shaped. *The man was with her wherever she went.* She mindfully pushed the thoughts aside. There was a porcelain basin on the teak dresser holding freshly boiled water and she cleaned off the travel dust with a cool sponge bath then searched her suitcase for something to wear. She found a rose-colored long tunic, the hem reaching just below her knees, and threw some leggings on underneath before heading downstairs to lunch, feeling more energized.

Her bare feet slapped the hard, smooth stairs, as the custom was no shoes inside to keep the sanctuary clean and pure. Reaching the bottom, she stood and watched the end of the meditation ceremony. Numerous votive candles flickered along the courtyard perimeter and incense smoke made curly half circles up and out through the open roof, the culprit for the intoxicating fumes she'd smelled earlier. The wind chimes and fountain continued their humming, a mellow soundtrack in the background

There were eight guests in total, the lucky number Rani followed based on her last astrological reading many years ago when her husband died. The *ashram* could definitely host more, but Rani always refused. The number eight was her sweet spot where she could bestow undivided attention to her participants and guide them back to feeling whole again. She was trained in ayurvedic healing practices along with meditation from some of the most distinguished gurus in India, and her main focus was devoted to helping lost souls When she'd started out many years ago, only a few friends attended her retreat, those who had been friends of her deceased diplomat husband. Her following grew through word of mouth after that, and here she was, decades later with a successful, exclusive, almost traditional *ashram*—it wasn't a place for religious learning and guidance as Rani believed that wasn't the root of people's problems.

Right now, all eight guests were strewn randomly around the spacious courtyard, sitting on matching jute mats with crossed legs. *Criss-cross apple sauce*, Simran thought humorously, remembering again when she, Sabine, and her cousins would visit as kids and Rani would try to get them to sit still for at least ten minutes daily for some kind of self-reflection. No easy task with wild and crazy city kids, but Rani managed. One withering look down her nose quelled them into submission.

As the ceremony wound down, Rani pulled out her *harmonium*, her long fingers pumping the boxy instrument and plucking the piano like keys. The reedy sounds broke the peaceful hum and Rani's low voice rang out, bringing everyone back to the present, singing Sanskrit words of encouragement, spirituality, and light. Simran closed her eyes to the entrancing sound accompanied by the wind instrument. Her tone was low and comforting, pleasing to the ear and so different from the popular singing voices which were high-pitched and sometimes too nasally for Simran's tastes.

Afterward, they all sat down in the dining hall toward the back of the house to eat a delicious mid-day meal of sauteed local vegetables, roast chicken in an aromatic gravy (for the non-vegetarians), and *dahl* served over basmati rice, the traditional way to eat the lentils stewed in a fragrantly spiced broth. All had been cooked by the in-house chef, but all prep work was done by the guests. The intention was to take pride in what one was eating by understanding how and where their food came from.

After the meal, Rani took Simran outside to talk privately. They strolled over to one of the old fortress structures still standing on the property, a reminder of a prominent, ruthless ruler from the seventeenth century. Meditatively circling around the only surviving piece, a huge crumbling tower with vibrant green moss spilling from the cracks, Rani pulled out what was bothering Simran. It was a simple but effective technique, forcing the truth out while one's body was in a rhythmic-like trance as they went around and around the building.

"So, this American. Do you love him, Sima?" she asked directly, breaking their silence as they circled the tower for about the tenth time. Rani never shied away from getting to the point. Why waste time dancing around the topic when you could pursue living it, or in this case, pursue loving him.

"Without a doubt, *Khala*," Simran answered, and then she stiffened at her own admission, a little horrified. It was true, she did love Marc. *Damn, the woman was good.* Simran peered at the older woman in awe. She'd come to find a little peace for herself, maybe get some direction on which path to take, but she realized that Rani could help her with more if she let her.

"*Amar beta*, then why are you here?" Rani asked nonchalantly, her body intent on making its way around the broken stones, not even pausing to glance down at her great-niece. "You are not running away from your problems, are you?"

"No!" But she kind of was. "I mean, it was too much. I needed space to figure it out." Rani was silent, her hands clasped behind her back as she strolled, giving Simran the opportunity to air her grievances. So, she went on. "This guy—Marc—he ... he hurt me. I don't think I can trust him again," Simran finished frankly, curious to see if Rani had the same opinion as Sabine, or if she thought what Simran did at times—to screw him and move on.

They continued walking in silence. Simran stopped to watch a peacock fan its glorious blue feathers before it darted away. When she looked back at her aunt, she spied the tall figure slipping into the fortress and she hurried to follow her inside. Rani stood staring up at a decrepit carving of a man in profile. The namesake of the fortress no doubt.

"Trust is a hard thing to find and keep," Rani said nodding in agreement, still staring at the profile as if she were talking to it. "But love is rare. Some people never experience it in a lifetime. Not even once, Sima," she said emphatically.

"But, he *hurt* me. He left me when I thought things were going so well. He didn't trust me enough to talk to me about his fears in the first place. Now he comes back and tells me he messed up and wants another chance. What if it happens again? How can I ever trust him? And then I have *Abba* pushing me to marry Anil, ugh!" She moaned in frustration, slumping down onto a moss-covered boulder.

"Sima, I understand the need to respect your elders. I admire you for wanting to consider Kumar's wishes because you know how I feel about him. But *mama-nee* (little one), when someone does not respect you, why do you still feel the need to give and give and give?" She turned her oversized eyes to Simran, looking into her soul.

Simran straightened up, startled. She'd never heard anyone say her father didn't respect her. "He respects me, *Khala.* He loves me and wants me taken care of." She defended him because that's what she always did. "He's just doing what he knows, and I owe so much to him. He put me through college, pushed me to get my MBA. I'd never be where I am today without him. I mean, he never fails to remind me that he's done everything for his children's happiness, sure, but I want to make him happy, too. He did it all without *Amma's* help. Don't I owe it to him to consider his wishes?"

"*Heh* (yes). Have you considered them?" She eyed her great-niece, coming to sit next to her. Simran nodded. "So, you have given him that. Now, consider what *you* want to do." Rani's thick brows furrowed. "I never had my own children. But if I did, I would not expect anything in return for giving them life and helping to find their full potential. Well, let me rephrase; I *would* expect some things like love, the gift to see them live their life as the remarkable person I raised ... and maybe a few grandchildren." Her face crinkled as she laughed heartily. "But, *beta*, a child should not be seen as a puppet to fulfill one's own destiny. Do you understand?" Was Rani, an actual elder, tearing down the unspoken, all-time notion of South Asian guilt? The guilt that many South Asian kids faced to follow through with ideals not necessarily their own in order to please their parents?

She shook her head, feeling a little winded about Rani's revelation, slowly acknowledging everything. "I never looked at it like that. I just assumed it was the way things were always done in our culture ... I never really got anything else from *Abba*..."

"It *is* how things are still done, but not all the time and not in every situation. You are not a child anymore, Sima. You have every opportunity to continue to be happy on your own terms with your independent American life and your successful business." Her aunt's eyes shined with pride and encouragement, and she draped a long arm across Simran's shoulder bringing her in close for a hug. "You did that on your own, without your father. You know you get that from our side of the family." Her shoulders wiggled girlishly. Simran smiled, knowing her aunt couldn't resist tooting her own horn and dumping on Kumar. "So, what are you afraid of?"

"Disappointing *Abba* and losing his love for starters."

"*Atcha.* So, you would rather forego the possibility of true love in your future—a chance at your own happiness—in order to keep your father's love, by marrying someone you do not love?" Her aunt snorted, not even trying to hide it. "*Beta,* do you really think any good can come from that? You would resent Kumar for the rest of your life. How do I know this? Because we are having this conversation in the first place. I know you do not want Anil. And really, who would?" she said, this last part under her breath. It seemed like everyone still thought Anil Patel was a crapbag. Poor Anil. "Now, if your *abba* truly loves you, he will come around to the idea that *you* chose your own future, not him. It may take some time. Nobody holds a grudge better than an arrogant Indian man whose wishes are not met. And there will be gossip," she said knowingly. "But, really listen to your heart, sometimes it sees more than the brain."

Simran's heart was beating so fiercely like it was agreeing strongly with everything Rani said. She thought it would burst out of her. Was it really that simple? There was still a nagging doubt, though.

"But what about trusting Marc?"

Rani sighed, getting up. She turned to face Simran and waved her arm in a large, flourished wave. "What about it? No love is perfect. Mistakes will be made—and many of them along the way, all looking very differently. We are not saints after all. You have to see past those mistakes to the truth.

With that truth comes understanding and then forgiveness. But you have to *want* to accept that truth and *want* to understand it, then you can grow together. Have you never made a mistake before, needing the other party's forgiveness?" Her huge eyes were poised on Simran, a world of knowledge behind them as if she knew all her secrets. *Holy baby Krishna!* Rani knew about the pregnancy, and how she hadn't revealed it to Marc. Oh, she'd give Sabine a piece of her mind when she spoke to her again. At least the older woman wasn't judging her about premarital sex. Instead, she was opening Simran's eyes, and admittedly she felt better than she had in days.

They continued talking as they walked back to the house. Simran was certain she knew what she wanted her future to look like now. She just needed a few more days in this quiet sanctuary to unwind, build her fortitude, and let go of her past anger.

Chapter 13

MUMBAI, INDIA

amn it! Marc slammed the heavy door behind him, jogging down the front stairs. As he got into his waiting car, his driver, Akash darted over, having been idly chatting, and smoking with someone across the courtyard. An employee of Kumar's presumably. Akash quickly crushed the butt of his cigarette under his shoe, then slipped into the driver's seat, peering at him in the rearview mirror. He was waiting for instructions on where to go. Marc was momentarily at a loss. He leaned his head back forcefully on the seat behind him, closing his eyes. *Now what?*

Yet again, it hadn't gone according to plan. After ringing the gong of a bell at the front door, Marc was shown into the vaulted foyer of Kumar's home by a servant who looked him up and down with interested eyes. Marc knew he appeared shabby and travel-weary in his favorite beat-up jeans, worn in ULTRA Music Festival t-shirt, and comfy loafers, no socks. He asked for Simran anyway, she wouldn't give a shit what he looked like, and hopefully he wouldn't run into her father. He was told without a hint of emotion that Simran wasn't there. Confusion mixed with anxiety rippled through him as he was asked to wait. He stood, taking in the marbled high ceilings, the enormous staircase that split toward opposite corridors at the top, and the oversized crystal chandelier hanging from the ceiling. It was all so non-personal. How did one live in this fortress comfortably?

"Marcus Lehigh, I presume. And what brings you to my home?" The loud booming voice came from the level above. "Would this have anything to do with the fact that my daughter is missing?!" the voice crescendo 'ed, echoing off the walls. Marc heard a gasp and turned around to see the servant from before look down and scurry away. The hell?! Simran wasn't here?

For such a loud voice, the person who owned it was fairly small. The quick tap, tap, tap of his shiny toffee colored penny loafers reverberated in the entryway as Kumar rushed down the stairs, the off-white silk kurta tunic he wore and matching pants billowing behind him. He looked like he was in a hurry and on his way out to some function or other as he fiddled with the thick gold watch around his wrist. He came to a stop a few feet away and Marc saw that Simran's father was many inches shorter than him, about the same height as her actually.

He stepped forward, hand outstretched, "Mr. Khan. It's nice to finally meet you. I don't know if you remember but—"

"Yes, yes, Club Sundar Social. I know who you are," Kumar interrupted, irritation sweeping over his countenance, waving a hand in Marc's general direction. He actually ignored his extended hand altogether and Marc was momentarily stunned. It'd been a hell of a long time since he'd been spoken to with such dismissiveness and with so little regard. He stood up straighter to his full six-foot, three inches, staring down at Kumar.

"Simran isn't here?" he asked quizzically, one eyebrow raised as he gave his iciest stare to the shorter man. Was this a ruse to get him to go, leaving Simran and her life alone?

While he studied her father, he tried to discern some resemblance of the woman he loved in the haughty expression of this man, but it was difficult. Gold chains roped around his short neck. A full head of silver-flecked black hair was swept over in an exaggerated side part, with a thick layer of gel holding the style in place, giving him a debonair, aging Bollywood actor quality. A silver beard covered the bottom part of his face and Marc could make out the high cheekbones that Simran had inherited. He had the same full lips, too, but Kumar's were curled back in something trying to mimic a smile. A long round nose, slightly bulbous and tinged pink, hinted at his possible reliance on alcohol (maybe a bit too much). As he squinted up with eyes caramel in hue, the glare piercing like a tiger viewing its prey, Marc immediately recognized the Khan countenance. But the sassiness he loved so much in Simran was translated into hotheadedness with her father.

"Come," the smaller man finally said, apparently remembering his manners. "Join me in the sitting room. I have a function I must leave for, but I can spare a few minutes. Kulsom!" he barked. A middle-aged woman in a simple azure blue and white sari appeared from nowhere. "Cha (tea) and snacks please," he ordered.

Without waiting for Marc, he entered an arched doorway into an adjoining room, his shoes now quiet on the thick Persian rug covering the marble floor. This room was also enormous in size, with overstuffed burgundy and gold chairs and matching sofas strewn about the richly decorated room. It was very Louis XIV in its ornate extravagance; a poor rendition of Versailles, Marc thought and tried to hide his distaste for the overly showy décor.

"Please, have a seat," Kumar said, hitching the fabric of his pants up slightly to sit comfortably, crossing one leg over the other. He leaned back and surveyed Marc as he took a seat on the other side of the ornate coffee table.

The woman, Kulsom, bustled in pushing a teacart. She placed two cups of steaming tea in front of each man. The fragrant cardamom and other spices tantalized Marc's nose and he realized he hadn't eaten in hours, right before landing. She placed an assortment of snacks including different flavored digestive biscuits, a spiced kind of trail mix, and some dry Indian sweets on the table between them then left.

"Please," Kumar said again, extending his hand over the snacks and tea, then started to serve himself. "My household staff really does know how to make the best cha in Mumbai. Every time I go to one party or another, I always end up coming home and asking for a cup of homemade cha followed by my favorite scotch," he said smiling over his cup of tea as he took a long, loud slurp.

Marc took a nice mouthful of the milky, sweet tea and closed his eyes. It tasted like the nectar of gods. He took a few biscuits and downed each one in two bites, not caring about the flavor, just trying to ease the growling in his stomach.

"So, which is your favorite?" he asked, over a particularly tasty pistachio biscuit. Kumar gave him a confused smile, tilting his head to the side. Marc continued, "Scotch whiskey? I prefer the Glenlivet, aged twenty-one years versus the twenty-five years. Interestingly, I find it smoother, but it still has a nice peaty undertone and some of the recognizable smokiness." His aim was to make friends with Simran's father before jumping into dangerous territory about her.

Kumar leaned forward, his eyes brightening in comprehension. "Ah. I just purchased a case of the twenty-five; travelled directly to Scotland for it actually. But, this is good to know." His head nodding in agreement. He cleared his throat. "I have a bottle open. Would you like a taste? We may need more than just sweet tea and snacks for this discussion."

Marc agreed, admiring the older man's forthright attitude. They chatted idly about Scotland and the distillery, the best time to visit, and when was the last time each had been there while Kulsom brought them their drinks.

When they were each settled with tumblers of the rich, amber liquid, they both took inquisitive sips and let the alcohol relax them for what was no doubt about to be a difficult conversation.

Marc started first. "So, Simran isn't here, Mr. Khan. Do you know where she is?" He may have looked calm, sitting back in the plush cushions, one ankle crossed over a knee, but his heart was beating in his ears. Where was she?

"Well, Marcus, I was hoping you could answer that question for me. I assumed when she never arrived two days ago that she was somewhere country hopping with you," he said mildly, a far cry from what Marc had expected, given how he'd greeted him earlier. Kumar continued after taking another nice long sip of whiskey, draining the glass, the large pink jewel on his pointer finger winking in the light. "And, do not think for one minute that I am unaware of your reputation, young man. I will have you know I am not in agreement with my Simran being with a person like you."

Marc had to keep calm and maintain some respect toward this man if he was going to get anywhere with him. "Mr. Khan, first of all, I'm just as confused as you are. Obviously, she's not with me. We haven't been together for months. I really thought she would be here: that's why I came. Secondly, I know what my reputation was, but that's all in the past now. Ever since meeting your daughter, she's all I want for good," he said with honesty, his chest expanding at the truth and the low, heavy feeling settling in his stomach comfortably at that statement.

"My boy, she is already spoken for," Kumar said with a sympathetic laugh. He quickly glanced at his watch and his eyebrows shot up. He reminded Marc of the erratic white rabbit from Alice in Wonderland.

He chose to ignore Kumar's need to rush out the door. "With all due respect, she is not spoken for. We talked a few days ago and she told me she was unsure of her decision, but not exactly happy at the prospect that awaited her here. In fact, she was coming to figure it all out. Now, if you're telling me she never arrived," and he had to catch his breath at the fact that no one really knew where she was, "then her decision is still up in the air, am I not correct?"

Kumar leaned forward, putting his glass down with a resounding clank on the table's glass surface, missing the coaster altogether. He squinted at Marc, trying to really see him for who he was, or, to discern if the younger man was hiding something from him.

Reading his mind, Marc jumped in, his hands up. "I swear, Mr. Khan, I have no idea where she is either. But are you sure you can think of nowhere she might be?"

Kumar stood up and sighed. "I spoke with her sister and she assured me that Simran was fine, but needed some space." He looked up at the ceiling shaking his head. "My children have become so Americanized," he mumbled. "Sabine would tell me nothing else, as is her usual way. I swear on my beloved wife's grave, I have no idea where I went wrong with that one." He frowned, his face a splotchy red now, just mentioning his other daughter. "But I give you my word, I am unaware of her whereabouts, and she could be anywhere. I am extremely anxious about all of this. My driver said she never arrived. He waited for over three hours for her at the airport." He sucked his teeth in frustration, wagging that jeweled pointer finger at Marc. "I blame this on you,

Marcus Lehigh. This is not how we do things in this country. My Simran had her head on straight before she met you. Now, she questions my best interests for her, disappears without telling anyone where she is ..." He sucked his teeth again and slit his eyes with annoyed anger. "I must go. I need to meet with the prospective in-laws," he said meaningfully. "But please, stay, have some more refreshments," he offered, ever the generous host. He stood up and this time extended a hand out to Marc.

Marc got up, finally feeling somewhat at ease knowing Simran was safe. He took Kumar's hand and firmly shook it. Before letting go he leaned down to say definitively, "Mr. Khan, I gladly take full responsibility for Simran's behavior. Meeting me only made her absolutely sure of what won't make her happy. And I'm extremely fortunate that Simran lives in America, and is American. She doesn't live in this country." And he grinned down at the slack jaw in Kumar's dumbfounded face. "It's been a real pleasure meeting you and thank you for the refreshments. I'm pretty sure you'll be seeing more of me in the future." Then he turned and left, rushing down the front steps and jabbing the air with a fist pump, feeling buoyant, until he slipped into the car that is.

Now, as he met his driver's expectant gaze in the rearview mirror, uncertainty snuck back in. He took a shot in the dark and swiped her number on his phone and quickly texted her.

Marc: "Simran, did you land safely? I haven't heard from you ..."

Minutes passed, and he knew she wasn't going to respond. He tried calling her but it went straight to voicemail.

Damn it, woman. She really had him on a wild, fucking goose chase. He was exasperated, but also slightly exhilarated, and a dopey grin appeared on his face. She hadn't seen her father or her old boyfriend. Concerned about her whereabouts, absolutely, but he was ecstatic that she hadn't made any decisions yet. There was a chance her heart might return to him.

Then he recalled her anger when they met to discuss the gallery project. She'd been caught off guard by his determination to be together again and she'd rebuffed him. What if she wasn't keen on seeing him here, in India? Something made him feel more confident than before that she would be; just a gut feeling he had (or possibly foolish and wishful thinking), as he thought back—for about the hundredth time—to that hot embrace in her apartment. He hadn't meant for it to get out of hand but it spiraled quickly from innocent to sexually charged. Despite her protests, she needed him as much as he needed her and his blood started pounding in his chest just thinking about holding her like that again. He fucking dreamt about it every night, thrusting him back into wet dream territory which he hadn't experienced since puberty.

And if she decided after everything that she still didn't want him, well, he had to remind himself to be selfless. His goal was to encourage her to be honest with herself, no matter what choice she made. If she really didn't want to be with him, he could live with that, even if it would take until the day he died to get over her.

"Mr. Lehigh, sir. Excuse me," Akash interrupted his train of thought and turned around in the driver's seat.

"What is it, Akash?" he asked curtly, not looking at him, his eyes still staring aimlessly at the ceiling of the car. He would need to contact Sabine and beg for information on Simran's whereabouts. Did she know where she was?

"I have some interesting information."

Marc stared at Akash's grinning face. "Well, what is it?"

"Sir, this household's driver had a very amusing story." He nodded his chin in the direction toward the side of the house where the lanky figure from before had retreated. "He boasted that he just came into a good amount of cash, around four hundred American dollars." Akash's brow danced up and down in eagerness.

"And?" Marc dead-panned. What the hell was he getting at?

"Mr. Lehigh, he said the madam of the house gave it to him to take her to a location in the hills, one that most people don't know about, at least those not of a certain class."

Now they were getting somewhere.

"Wait a minute? When?" So, she'd landed, but hadn't come here first.

"Two days ago. He was inquiring about a reputable place to trade in dollars for rupees, and it all just sounded so interesting, that I got him to continue talking." Marc thanked the stars above for Akash's wily nature. His driver didn't know Marc's business entirely but was just doing what most Indians loved best, extracting gossip—something that he and Bruce experienced years ago while there for business, and which

Simran had offhandedly commented on when they were together.

"Good man, Akash. This is very helpful. Do you know what hill town?"

"Yes, sir. Lonavala."

"Ok. But where in Lonavala?"

"I know this, too." Akash grinned at him, giving his head that peculiar side bobble combined with a nod. Then he turned back around, opening up the driver-side window to light up another cigarette.

Marc leaned forward and clapped his driver on the shoulder gratefully. "Change of plans, Akash. Take me there immediately. I know it's getting late, and I apologize, but I'll double your pay for today," he replied firmly, beating Akash to any haggling for more payment. The man could be sly, but he was a damn good driver; one who kept his employer's business under wraps, given he was monetarily provided for. Akash shucked his cigarette and immediately programmed the address into the navigation system. He maneuvered the car out of Kumar's home and toward their next destination.

As Marc rested back, the jitteriness from the past few days started to quiet itself within him. The exhilaration from before was becoming a hope that he could actually taste. He searched his bag for his device, suddenly in the mood for some music. It was at the bottom of his carry-on; a pleasure forgotten in his anxiety. He put his earbuds in and scrolled through. There it was, his favored playlist dubbed 'Simmarc'; a combination of music he and Simran had enjoyed together. He sunk back further, shutting his eyes as he listened to the hypnotic strains of Jaymes Young's, 'Infinity.' The indie alternative pop music was quasi electronic, and written by a popular, newish artist Simran had shared with him as Marc's tastes ran more old-school and underground. The song was, in a way, a message to Simran. Without a doubt, he could reach her before she decided anything, but no matter how things unfolded, their love would never die. Fate wasn't something Marc held dear but what they had was fate if ever there was "a meant to be." She must feel it, too, given her change of plans. Their love was unquestionably for infinity.

58

Chapter 14

LONAVALA, INDIA

It was dark by the time they arrived. *Where the hell were they?* Marc could only make out that their direction turned inland about an hour ago, and they'd gone higher up into the mountains. The air was slightly cooler and smelled earthier, but there was a dampness that permeated.

"Mr. Lehigh, this is it." Akash got out of the car to survey the area, leaving the headlights on so they could make out their surroundings.

"Do you know what this place is, Akash?" Marc asked, getting out of the car, too. They were facing a huge hill—almost like a small mountain. He saw a path, illuminated by garden lamps close to the ground, snaking up so high he couldn't see the end destination. A scraggly wooden fence was at the bottom, and Marc could only assume it encircled the entire wide hill's circumference. He heard the ripples of water coming from somewhere beyond but other than that, it was a stark yet calming atmosphere.

"Yes. I have only heard of this place," he replied in awe. "The *Antarik Shanti Ashram*. A very exclusive place for relaxation and only for well-to-do sort of people," he continued excitedly. "Sir, I'm surprised you've never heard of it." Akash lit up a cigarette, the light from his lighter making his face a little ghoulish in the dark.

"Hm. Interesting," Marc commented, taking in the unadorned look of the place. He'd never heard of it, so it must be extremely selective. Did people really pay a fortune for this kind of stark retreat and locale? He'd seen and experienced crazier ways for the uber-wealthy to spend their money, so he shouldn't be shocked. But he found it unlikely that Simran was really here, given that she would never spend an exorbitant amount of money on a simple relaxation retreat, even if she could. He sighed. Was this another dead end?

"Ok, Akash. This is where you leave me." He reached for his suitcase as Akash opened the trunk and headed toward the uphill trail.

The car pulled away, the headlights and engine receding. Marc was left in the moonlight with just the echoes of nature to keep him company. He hurriedly made his way up the path, the garden lanterns dim, but throwing enough light to show the way, and thankfully so, since the path was steeper than he initially thought.

Twenty minutes later, having mistaken about ten minutes back what he thought was the top, he finally arrived at what looked like a Mediterranean Villa. The white stucco gleamed under the shining half-moon and even in the dark, he could tell the place was somehow special, reverent. He entered through the ornate arch in front, looking up at the house more closely, and saw few lights on. He picked up the heavy brass knocker, shaped like a lotus leaf, and let it drop. The loud clang resounded in the quiet surroundings, and he hoped he hadn't awakened the entire household. He waited a few minutes, thinking to knock this time, but the door opened, the brass hinges barely squeaking.

A small, wrinkled man wearing what looked like a long black and white sarong and an undershirt stared up at him. Without a word, he opened the door wider, stepping back for Marc to enter. He probably assumed he was a guest. Marc followed the little man into an open courtyard lit up by electric lanterns lining the corridor on the level above.

The man moved to take his suitcase, but Marc waved him away. The smaller man put his gnarled hands up in question, looking at him curiously.

"Is Simran here?" Marc asked. The man gazed at him for a moment, then motioned him to stay there.

Again, Marc waited, but looked around with interest. It was a simple, but beautiful place. There were large potted trees dotting the courtyard, their small leaves dancing in the breeze, appearing like polished silver coins in the moonlight. They clicked softly and mingled with the tinkle of wind chimes creating a comforting, meditative essence. Marc knew instantly that Simran was here. She'd always talked about needing peace from her crazy life, a reason she'd been in London in the first place, even though she admitted sheepishly that *that* had been the opposite of relaxation after all the partying she'd done, and then of course, meeting him. Had she ever mentioned an *ashram*? He couldn't remember.

"May I help you?" a low, steady voice came from behind him. Marc turned around to a graceful and agile woman approaching him. She was barefoot, and as she stood in front of him he realized she was inches shorter than him, but she carried herself as if she were ten feet tall. Up close he saw the lines on an attractive face, revealing she was not as young as she looked from a distance, even though she had a litheness that belied her age. Her black and white hair was gathered in a low ponytail at the nape of her neck, the ends reaching the bottom of her waist. She wore a long, white tunic and matching pants, the material light and airy.

"Hello. I'm sorry to bother you, but I'm looking for someone. I wonder if you can help me," Marc said awkwardly, while also trying to hide his frustration. "Her name is Simran—"

The woman held up hand, stopping him.

"I am Simran," she said with a warm smile.

Marc stuttered, "Oh. I apologize. I meant, a different Simran. Her last name is Khan." *What the hell was going on? Who was this woman? Where was his Simran?*

"Ah," she said with understanding, her large eyes shining. "My name is Simran Singh. I preside over this *ashram*. What is it that you want with this ... other Simran?" she asked, her head bent to one side inquisitively.

"I was told she was here, and I need to speak with her. I need—" he abruptly stopped. He didn't know this woman. Why was he telling her his business? She continued studying him and he realized there was a guilelessness about her that made him want to unleash his problems, tell her everything that was troubling him.

"It looks like you have been traveling for quite some time," she said breaking the silence. "Would you like to sit down, have some refreshments?" Her arm extended toward the back of the courtyard. "Follow me," she said, not waiting for an answer, turning to go. Marc followed her back to a dining hall. She sat with him at the long table and bench, while the little man came back. She requested water and some food from dinner. Marc looked at her gratefully. He needed a real meal.

When it came, he washed his hands in the bowl of warm water, knowing the customs from his travels before, then dug into the *dahl*, rice, and tasty vegetables. The older woman sat and watched him, a small smile playing on her lips. "I was not sure of your dietary restrictions. We do have some chicken and goat ...?"

Marc swallowed a delicious bite, answering, "This is perfect, thank you."

As he finished, he asked her about the *ashram* and what exactly she did there.

She leaned her arms comfortably on the table as she spoke. "I founded this sanctuary almost forty years ago when I was looking for a place to heal. And now, my purpose is to instill peace unto others," she said simply. "I guide meditation, yoga, hiking, and ayurvedic healing treatments for one's body and soul."

"It's an incredible place. I would love to find out more, maybe partake in some healing activities, but first, I need to find Simran Khan. She must be a guest here. Do you know who I'm talking about?" he asked her before taking a long drink of the cool water.

"Yes, I know her quite well, actually. But before I go on, please, tell me why you are here to see her. This is a place of quietude and harmony. My guests come for solace and healing, not only physically, but emotionally. While here, they are under my care and I cannot have any of them harmed in any way," she said steadily, keeping her eyes directly on his.

Marc nodded in understanding. "I'm here, Ms. Singh—"

"Please, call me Rani *Khala*," she interrupted.

"I'm here, Rani *Khala*," he continued, "because I need ... I need her. We have ... a past, one that was amazing, fulfilling, and which I stupidly screwed up. We aren't together anymore because of me. But I would like her to be a part of my life again because, without her, I can't seem to function properly. And I want her to be my future," he said hopefully, imploring his case. He was mystified again by how open he felt with this person. With any luck, she would feel some pity and tell him Simran's whereabouts.

Rani *Khala* nodded. "I understand." She stood up. "You may see my great-niece, but you *must* promise to not distress her. She is asleep right now and has had a troubling journey both of body and mind. But you know this, young man. You may wait until tomorrow to speak with her," she said, grinning widely as she looked down at him.

Great-niece?! Marc couldn't hide the amazement on his face and Rani *Khala* started laughing, a low husky sound similar to his Simran's but a few octaves lower. His worry released at the knowledge that his Sims was certainly here. All of a sudden, he felt a bone-deep weariness and his eyes drooped as he stifled a yawn.

Rani Khala called the little man, Gopal, back and asked that he take Marc up to a spare room on the second floor. Marc followed him up with his luggage, settling into the cozy room. Hope radiated from his chest as he tugged his clothes off. He fell into the downy mattress and right away a deep slumber overtook him.

Chapter 15

Still suffering jet lag and the time difference, Simran was up before dawn. She lay in bed while listening to the odd bird calls and the rushing waters in the distance. She knew she wouldn't be able to go back to sleep and she kicked off the comforter as excitement bubbled within her. Her mind was too active with the knowledge that her future was her own to make. She wanted to explore the peaceful quietude; thank it for the service it bestowed in helping to restore her confidence.

Throwing on another lightweight, cotton tunic (a soft yellow one with white embroidery bordering the edges) she also donned some comfy black leggings. She left her room, grabbing the towel from the hook on the back of the door last minute. Today she was visiting a hidden pool; a place that held many special memories.

As she bounded down the stairs, she spied one of the guests already up in the half-light, and moving through sun salutations by herself in the courtyard, as if coaxing the sun to rise fully.

"Hi, Raquel," she called softly to her new friend as she passed by on her way to the front doors. Raquel bowed a *namaste* to her and continued with her practice. Simran thought back to the previous day, thankful that she'd met this woman, and grateful for Rani Khala's chance introduction between the two women at breakfast.

It was in fact not just any arbitrary meeting, though. Rani *Khala* was no fool when it came to dealing with an individual's complex pain and innately understood that Simran was dealing with an ache which needed proper guidance for her healing process. She planned the two to meet and get acquainted while breaking their fast.

In the short time from meeting at breakfast to the hike up together to one of the silence caves on Rani's property, Simran learned that Raquel, a woman in her mid-forties, had struggled significantly to conceive a child. She'd lost baby after baby early on in each of her thirteen pregnancies, finally conceiving years later when she stopped fixating on 'the getting pregnant' part and focused on herself and her relationship with her husband. The candid way she spoke about her devastating experiences made Simran feel a little less like a failure. Her argument that it was society's norm to hush up miscarriages, making women feel even more guilty about what they couldn't control, was kind of a mind-bender to Simran. But she saw it for the truth that it was.

They continued to whisper as they'd rolled out their jute mats on the rough stone floor within the silence cave and lay down. Simran closed her eyes, and her thoughts wavered between the sense of loss she still felt from her miscarriage, the guilt, and the contentment in finally acknowledging the love she felt in her life. Even if she and Marc tried again, she was pretty sure that the sense of loss wouldn't go away. She really did need this time to focus on how to heal that part of her heart. That's when her brain shut off and she fell asleep. Her friend, Raquel, gently awoke her around lunch time and they walked back to the *ashram* together.

So today, she was visiting a happy place by herself. It was a reminder of a simpler time in her life; a place where she knew she could be joyful and carefree. She'd visited this special hidden pool many times in the past with her sister and mother. Although the trek down to its location was somewhat difficult, it was well worth it because it was high up on her list as one of her most favored places in the entire world.

Her arms reached up to stretch overhead languidly while she stepped outside. As she sat on the porch to put on her sneakers, she noticed the sun starting to peak up behind the mountains. It would eventually push aside the heavy mist still surrounding the distant hills, creating a humid warmth. But it was going to be a good day; she could feel it.

Leaving the arched entryway, she popped in her earbuds. It was time. The moment had finally arrived for her preferred brand of drug. She needed some "Marc music." She'd sworn off everything about him, including all of his favorite bands and music genres in the past months (no easy task as music was her everything). But the reminders were too painful as she'd been desperate to get over him. That was far from what she wanted now. She wanted and needed to revel in him.

She turned on her phone and immediately saw a text and missed call from him, making her heart beat wildly. *Speak of the devil.* He asked if she'd landed safely. She quickly texted back a thumbs up to him. Then her phone beeped with twenty new voice messages, all from her dad. She ignored them. First, she needed to focus on herself.

She shuffled the music on her phone and a classic, well-known guitar riff sputtered into her ears with an addictive rockabilly-esque motif. Led Zeppelin's "Whole Lotta Love" filled her head and she started humming the tune. Even though she was a lover of all things classic rock, she'd never gotten into this band and Marc had been aghast. He couldn't believe that a self-proclaimed DJ, with her own small, but dedicated following, knew nothing about "The Led." He'd gleefully taken it upon himself to school her in the utter genius of one of his favorite groups. It'd been annoyingly adorable.

Now, as she made her way down into the morning mist, listening to the erotically aggressive words, she couldn't help but think that it mirrored what she and Marc felt for each other. Robert Plant was singing about giving it to a woman because she needed it badly (Simran could totally relate), but his words were almost lovingly poetic. He sang about 'learnin' and 'yearnin' and when all's said and done, both parties collide together, needing "a whole lotta love" from each other, and only each other. For her, the song wasn't just about hot sex, but the yearning to be the other person's everything.

Before she knew it, she was upon the path she remembered. It curved behind the house, down and around the chartreuse hued hill. She descended comfortably for a few minutes before the path turned into a steep incline. Slowing her pace, she sidled up the side of the hill and grabbed onto the thick rope that was attached sturdily along the stone siding for just this purpose. The sound of rushing water became louder as she inched further down and she finally came to the bottom of a small canyon. It was hidden, surrounded by electric green and emerald moss-covered stone walls that made up part of the hill, and it was glorious. Translucent water pooled out calmly in front of her, a few mere steps away. Further back, a good-sized waterfall arced into that pool, splashing foam at the bottom. The noise was loud but heavenly.

Simran snapped her towel open, smoothing it flat on the soft patch of grass nearby, and kicked off her shoes. She took out her earbuds and put her phone down. Then she walked into the cool, clear water, the grey pebbles at the bottom visible as she waded in. She kept going until her shoulders were below the surface and taking a huge breath, she dunked her head, feeling the currents swirling around her. She came up for air and lay weightlessly on her back, staring at the sky as it awoke for the day, the color turning from orangish pink to a hazy powder blue. Her hair floated around her, and she splayed her arms wide, just like she'd done when she was a kid in this exact pool. She could stay here all day, watching the clouds move lazily in the sky, letting the water clog her ears and muffle the sound of the waterfall.

She finally rolled onto her stomach and swam back to the tiny shore where she came out to dry off with the towel. Then she spread it on the grass again and lay down. Flipping her "Marc music" back on, she drank it in while watching the clouds form shapes that she tried to make out in the sky.

The quiet in his small room was deafening, making Marc forget where he was. He rolled over, trying to open his eyes, but the sleep crust was laid on thick and he had to wipe it off to fully move his lids.

Yesterday's adventure suddenly came rushing back to him. He got up and threw the window slats open and the mountain view covered in thick mist greeted him. He breathed in deeply, stretching hard as wonderment filled him up. It was all absolutely breathtaking. Everything as far as the eye could see was covered in thick green and it smelled of fresh earth and nature. The day was sunny with big fluffy clouds softening the rays; a hint at some rain to come later.

Marc found a pitcher of fresh water next to a basin on the dresser and washed up, brushed his teeth with the bottled water sitting on the nightstand, and got dressed in lightweight khakis and a white t-shirt. He grabbed his loafers and headed to the shared toilet on the same floor. Then he went downstairs, an eagerness in his step. The other guests were already up and he checked the time on his phone as 7:45 am, also noticing a thumbs-up sign in a reply text from Simran. It came a little over an hour ago and just that little bit of communication had his hopes floating.

He saw that the others were already eating and chatting quietly in the dining hall. Marc smiled a greeting at their interested stares, searching through the faces for Simran. He didn't find her but turned to see Rani *Khala* enter the room with a small backpack.

"How did you sleep, Marcus?" she asked approaching him. He couldn't remember if he'd told her his name or not last night, but right now, nothing could surprise him and his head was filled with someone else.

"Very well, thank you." He looked around, distracted.

Rani *Khala* gave him a lop-sided grin, handing over a small backpack. "Here, take this. It's filled with some bottled waters, bananas, freshly cut mango, and some boiled eggs fresh from our chickens here. You will need it. Go find her. She is at her favorite swimming hole." And she explained to him how to get down to the private natural pool at the back of the hill. It was a bit treacherous at some points so he should be careful. Marc took the bag thanking the older woman, and went outside. He slipped into his shoes and swung on the backpack.

As he started downward on the path behind the house, it wasn't lost on him that this was monumental. This particular path would lead him to his future, whether it was everything he sought out or not. It was riskier than any commercial venture he'd ever taken before; risker even than that first opportunity when he'd nervously signed his name on the dotted line for his first business loan many, many years ago.

But this involved something he desperately craved with every fiber within him—mind, body and soul. This involved *her*. He became euphoric just thinking about her. *You're a sap, Lehigh.* If that made him a sap, then he would be the best damn sap there was out there. He was always good at what he did, he smirked to himself.

After taking the steep part carefully, grasping the rope tightly so he didn't slip on the moist stones in his loafers, he came to a stop at the bottom, just taking in the view. If he thought the mountainside was breathtaking, then he had absolutely no words for this scene. The clear water shimmered in the sun, and the waterfall was almost deafening as it shot over the ridge—a ribbon unspooling forcefully—into the pool, echoing off the moss-covered stone walls.

His breath hitched as he spied a figure laid out on a towel on the grass, clearly lost in her own world. Her arms were snaking above her in rhythmic movement and as he moved closer to her, he saw she had her earbuds in listening to something. She must have already taken a dip in the water, as her black hair was damp and splayed about her, starting to curl thickly as it dried. Her yellow tunic clung to her coppery skin, doing absolutely nothing in the modesty department, the main function of its loose style. Her curves were on full display, and he could make out a black bra and black leggings underneath. Lust hit him forcefully. That physical want, added to his already elated state, made the blood pulse in his veins, straight down to his groin.

All right, horndog, keep your pants on.

He inched nearer, not wanting to frighten her, and laid the backpack down, then took his shoes off. He was even closer now, but she still didn't notice him. He smiled, watching as her slim arms moved hypnotically. What was she listening to that had her so entranced? Goddamn, what a gorgeously, sexy sight. He could stand there drinking her in all day. But that wouldn't get them anywhere, and it was kind of creepy. He leaned his head into her vision, just shy of her waving arms.

"What are you listening to, beautiful?" he asked, trying to keep his voice light, while a massive smile cracked his face. It felt like comets were streaking through his chest and pummeling his heart. There was no other way to describe it except that he was fucking thrilled about seeing her again.

Chapter 16

Simran was lost in her thoughts, drunk on her music, when suddenly a shadow fell over her. A head appeared above, blocking out the sun, the face overshadowed by the brightness behind. She let out a scream of terror, the high pitch bouncing off the stone walls. She scrambled to sit up, grabbing the towel's edge and pulling it up to her chest. *Who the fuck was this!?* Some crazy pervert following her? As the figure stepped back, she blinked up and had to rub her eyes. Was she dreaming? A familiar handsome face looked down at her, an enormous grin under a short beard. And holy facial hair, he was hotter than ever. Dark and light blond locks tousled back off his forehead, with a few strays falling into his ice blue eyes which were so warm and intense. He broke into deep laughter at her confusion. *What a freak of nature!* And she told him so.

"Seriously, Marc, are you *insane*!? You can't scare a person like that. I almost had a heart attack." And her heart was indeed galloping out of control by the initial terror. She put a hand over her chest to calm herself. But it continued at its rapid pace by the realization that he was actually standing in front of her, here, in India, in a private sanctuary not many knew about. *How the freak did he know she'd be here?* And crap she wasn't really complaining because he was utterly delectable. He was still grinning his perfectly beautiful smile, dimples, eye crinkles and all. His shirt stuck to him in the moist air and she could make out every defined muscle of his wide chest and abs, along with his happy trail that led down to a very happy place. Her body started to tingle and a warmth snaked down to her core. She averted her eyes embarrassed, the heat coming to her cheeks. "You're lucky I didn't use my self-defense skills on you," she said, trying to shake off her sudden arousal. "You would've been so sorry."

She heard him continue to chuckle as he sat down so near to her that the heat from his body made goosebumps jump up all over her skin. "I didn't mean to scare you," he said low, his voice gravelly. The shivers inevitably came in response—they always did—running up and down her spine. He tilted her chin back toward him with long, warm fingers, looking into her eyes. "I'm already defense-less when it comes to you, Simran. That wouldn't have been a fair fight." His stare continued searching over her face, seeing her, as he said this.

Her breath jammed in her lungs and she coughed trying to clear it. "Are you a stalker now?" she asked when she recovered, confusion both joyful and irritated already budding inside her. She'd missed him, was finally coming to a conclusion about him, and now he was actually here, in one of her favorite places in the entire world. But what in the *hell* was he actually doing here? This was *her* time and space to clear her mind. "Or were there issues to deal with at Club Sundar Social?" she asked archly. That had to be the reason he was in India, then he somehow found out where she was and made a detour. Did he talk to Sabine? She must have worked it out and told him...

"Both options sound really crappy," he said, his voice careful and a little restrained. He leaned back on his elbows while his long legs splayed out in front of him. She couldn't help staring at his long toes, the curve of the high arches on his feet, and then his ankles with golden springy hair starting to crawl up under the cuffs of his rolled pants. Even his feet and ankles were attractive. "You seem to think that everything I do involves work." This time she detected a hint of hurt in his tone.

"What else am I supposed to think? Our first encounter was in London where you happened to be for your club opening. Then," she ticked off on her fingers, "you came to New York for investor meetings. You found me, I get it, but would you have really come if you didn't have work there? And let's not get into how you traveled to Vancouver for that project and what happened then..." She tucked her hair behind her ears, trying to maintain some control of the rising anger, and the tell-tale pricking at the back of her eyes. *Steady on, Simran. Let him explain himself.*

He sighed. "I'm not stalking, I promise. It's more like I'm drawn to something I can't control, nor do I ever want to try to control it again." He crossed one ankle over the other. He said it with an openness that was rare in their initial relationship, making only a few heart-felt cameos toward the end, and surprisingly debuting as a full-on leading role before she left for India. She wanted to believe he'd changed, but how?

Her gaze moved up from his feet, past his muscular legs encased in khakis, and the sticky shirt clinging to his chest, finally to his face. His eyes were probing her. She had to glance away, gulping with difficulty. What she saw there was a look of such tenderness, that she knew he was here for her, for them. She thought she needed more time to figure this out, but in reality, she was more than ready.

"This is a beautiful place. I can see why you would want to return here," he continued, changing the subject, and curiously looking around.

Simran nodded, and leaned back on her elbows, mimicking his relaxed posture. "I used to visit here when I was little. My mom and Sabine and I used to swim and play in this exact pool. My mom taught us how to do handstands in the water right over there." She pointed to a particular spot, the memory making her smile widely. She felt his hand closest to her inch over and his fingers touched her own. A fiery spark quivered up her arm, and she didn't move away.

"I hope to see those handstands one day."

"Do you? What makes you think you deserve to see them?" She didn't look at him, pushing her feet into the neon green grass, her toes curling at the soft petal-like texture. She was trying to keep her nervousness at bay because now he was making her all mushy and gushy, with a need almost consuming her to feel him on her again. But she required their words to play out. They could only move forward if they were on the same page.

His sigh was shaky. "Simran, you're not wrong. I know our first encounter started in London because of my club. And when that investment meeting came up for my Vancouver project, I chose it in New York so I could see you again. But I think the stars bestowed luck upon me because I was fated to be in your sphere each time. I swear, though, now I'm here because of you, and only you." He was talking stars and fate, and her own fingers involuntarily grazed his back, needing to feel him again.

"How did you know where to find me?"

"A man will do a lot of crazy things to get back the love of his life, even meet head-on with her sister who hates him, then scour for clues about your whereabouts when no one knows where you've headed." Simran nodded, trying her hardest to remain serene at the "love of his life" part of his speech. So, Sabine hadn't known where she ended up.

"But how—"

"Let's just say my driver loves gossip and finds curious stories about fellow drivers who are looking to exchange a big sum of US dollars into rupees intriguing."

Simran fidgeted with her tunic. *Great.* If Marc's driver knew about her father's driver and how she'd bribed him, would Prahalad get into trouble with her father? She'd have to fix that.

"So how did your driver know?"

"What does it matter, Simran?"

"Just tell me," she said anxiously. She didn't want to get an innocent man fired.

"All right. Well, when I went to your father's house first—"

"Wait, you went to my father's house?" Her pulse was beating in her ears. Had she heard correctly?

"Yeah. And that's where my driver, Akash, happened to be chatting up with your father's driver and found this out. I don't think he knew it meant anything but shared it with me because he thought it was interesting and that's why we came here."

Simran let out the breath she was holding. Ok, so Marc and her father hadn't met. It also seemed like bribing Prahalad wouldn't get back to her dad, and she could do some damage control if it did. "Ok go on," she said, encouragingly.

"With which part?" he asked humorously. She started to chuckle, too.

"You were giving me your speech about stars and fate, and wanting to be here because of only me. I would like to hear the rest of it, if you have more that is," she said, a little embarrassed.

He scooted closer to her, but still didn't touch her. "All right," he said again, his acquiescence a little unnerving. Usually, by this point, they were either squabbling, or in the midst of a rousing game of sexual pursuit by banter that would turn into a hot and heavy winning streak for the both of them. "Simran," he continued, "I'm sorry about everything. I know I hurt you. There are no words to express how sorry I am, and if I could take back the hurt you felt—feel—I would in a heartbeat. It kills me to know I was the one who caused you that pain. You're the most generous, warm, beautiful person; you always put others before you, and I was the dick who couldn't see that. I fucked it up with you." From the corner of her eye, she caught him running his hand through his hair and over his face. He was anxious. "You were all I had on my mind those first weeks in Vancouver, and I was pissed at myself because I couldn't focus on the shit show that was happening there. I thought ending it with you would do me some good, and eventually you, too. What we had was so unfamiliar to me, and well, it messed with my head. I'd never experienced that kind of connection before, and fuck, Simran, I got scared. I got scared shitless like a stupid ass. I thought I could go back to the person I was before you, but, God, it was so much worse, Simran, way worse." His voice caught and her glance swiftly went to him. His eyes were closed, and his face was contorted as he remembered how it felt to be without her. "I couldn't concentrate on a damn thing—ask Bruce. He'll happily tell you what a bumbling doofus I was reduced to in meetings because you were all I had on my mind and I completely blew it." He forced out a huge breath, blowing the locks that had fallen into his eyes again. "But, I couldn't go back to the man I was before because you changed me. And I'm not blaming you, I'm glad for the change. I want to care about that someone who is meant for me. I want to *be* with that someone who is meant for me." Simran could only nod. All words escaped her. "Baby, I love you." He sat up, as she looked away again, and he tried to catch her eye. "You're it for me, Sims." She took a moment to calm her furiously pounding heart. When she finally met his eyes, she was pulled into their bright depths with a look so tender and she recognized it as one she'd recently tried to ignore days ago.

"If you think you can give us another chance, I can prove to you I'm here for you. I'll always be here for you."

The tears were starting to pool in her eyes, and she couldn't stand the distance anymore. She rolled over onto him, craving to feel the connection, making them both flop onto the ground. Her hands were folded between her chest and his, but his hands remained at his sides, unsure of what was happening. His brows went high as his eyes widened, searching her own back and forth.

"You're an idiot," she said, nose to nose with him, her tears splashing onto his face.

"I know," he breathed, his hands coming up to wipe away her tears. "I think the exact, perfect word was 'asshole.'"

"Epic," she added.

"Epic." He nodded in agreement; his eyes still wide. "Will you take me back, Simran? My life isn't the same without you." And that was all she needed. She crashed her lips onto his, hungry for his taste and it was everything she remembered and more. Minty and musky ... and familiar. His hands cupped her face as his tongue swept between her lips to tangle with her own. This was pure, unfettered Marc and she trembled at how much she missed him and missed this with him.

Their kiss went on, for how long, she didn't know, but his lips were loving, and firm and soft over hers, gently sucking on her bottom lip. Her hands had twined into his thick hair, holding them together, her body conforming into his hard one underneath and nothing had felt so perfect; two puzzle pieces that fit intrinsically together.

Her smell was all around him, and he was dizzy with bliss just being with her, feeling her soft form on his, claiming her as his own again. But she hadn't agreed to anything. Before they lost control—like they did every damn time—he needed to hear her say it.

He reluctantly broke their kiss, both of them panting and out of breath. His hands were tangled in her curls and he wanted to tug back and expose her beautiful neck to himself so he could lavish it with kisses. But he stared into her eyes and saw liquid black. Tears spilled onto him again, and he reached up to wipe them away, a little concerned.

"Baby, making you cry was the last thing I came here to do." She nodded wordlessly and then gulped air, hiccupping in the process. Now he was anxious. "What's wrong?" Did she not want him back? Was she going to tell him to fuck off again? He didn't know if he could handle a repeat of that kind of rejection, especially if she decided she wanted to uphold her family duty and marry Anil. His jaw gritted in frustration, but she rolled off of him onto her side, clutching his shirt, making him roll onto his side to face her.

"I love you, *too*," she said finally, her words watery through her tears as she blustered and teared up again. There were those comets, pelting his heart again, but Marc needed to remain grounded, though her words made him want to jump up and shout their love to the world. His grin was wide, too, and surely that of a madman. She continued crying at her admission, though, and an uneasy feeling slid up his spine. Why would loving him cause her distress?

"Simran, you love me?" He hadn't meant for it to be a question, but this was all so new to him. He'd never heard of a woman crying her eyes out, and miserably so, when they told someone they loved them back. She nodded, her face a crumpled version of itself. He grimaced, not sure if he should be happy or sad now. "Simran, help me out here." He was kind of losing his hold on the situation. He pulled her into him, his beacon of safety, and the one person who always made him feel calm, but the one person who could cast him away and make him lose his mind.

She huffed and huffed, and he felt her body rise and fall with her breaths until she was calmer. He cradled her, reminding himself, *be selfless, Lehigh.* If she chose another path, other than him, he would support her.

"I'm sorry, *too!*" she finally wailed into his shirt, as a fresh wave of tears streamed down. He was at a loss for words. Not only was she a broken fountain, but she was apologizing? He needed to get to the bottom of this.

He lifted her chin again and reached for her lips with his own, kissing her—the only thing he knew would make either of them feel better right now. He tasted the salt on her full lips, licked the wetness off, and replaced it with his own. He peppered kisses along her cheeks, wiping the tears as he went. He made his way along her jaw, kissing her beauty spot reverently just above the corner of her lip, before reaching her ear where he whispered comforting words like, "Please don't be sad." "Tell me what I can do." "Please tell me you forgive me, the biggest dick out there." She giggled weakly at that, her frown finally turning into a soggy smile. He pushed her hair behind her ears, drinking in that soggy smile. "Sweetie," he said as gently as he could, "what do you have to be sorry for?"

"I'm sorry about never telling you about our baby," she whispered.

He sat back shocked. It'd never occurred to him that he should feel anything close to needing an apology for that. But he listened intently.

"If it had lived, you would've been involved, no matter what happened between us. I would never force you to be like your father, someone who doesn't know their child. That would be cruel." All he could do was nod because his own eyes sprang with wetness that he blinked back. Never had anyone read him so thoroughly until Simran. She was aware that no matter how much he acted like he didn't care about his father's uninterest in wanting to know him, deep down, it still bothered him.

"Thank you," he said quietly. "I love you so much, Simran," he said simply, staring into the deep, dark pools of her eyes. What more could he say? This woman saw him, and they were made for each other.

"I love you, too, more than I ever thought I could love someone," she replied, as she held his gaze. There it was again, but only part one of the two-parter he wanted to hear from her. He felt warm and fuzzy as he leaned in to nuzzle her nose, rubbing his lips over her full ones again. His hands moved from her hair down her back, and finally one rested on her abdomen, which still had a slight swell to it. She let him and she rested her head against his chest. "I feel better knowing you were as miserable as I was. But," she pulled away and sat up, the air that replaced her felt cold in the warm heat, "you broke my heart, Marc." She looked away from him. "I mean, you're here now, but nothing can erase how shattering that period was. I may need some time to trust you again."

Marc sat up, too, careful to keep his distance, worried that whatever trajectory her mind was on, would go in a direction away from him if he tried anything. "I wasn't there for you when you needed me the most. Never again, Sims," he said vehemently.

She shook her head and wrapped her arms around herself. "The time for needing someone the most isn't completely over, yet. I still have to hear back from my doctor about my test results." He'd forgotten about her cancer scare temporarily in the moment of trying to win her back.

The possibility that he could lose her for good was horrifying. His voice cracked on his words and he tried to remain strong, anything to not fold over and howl like a baby. "I'm here for you no matter what. As much or as little as you need me. If it's cancer, even if we aren't together," his breath caught, but he continued, "I'll stand by you, I won't disappear. I'll fly the best doctors to New York to treat you. Fuck, I'll be your friend through all of this, if that's all you want..." Was he sounding desperate to her, because he absolutely was to his own ears? She needed to trust him again, and if she just wanted to start off again as friends, he'd do it, just to be near her.

"Marc, I can't just 'be friends' with you. I already told you that." She rolled her eyes trying to ease the tension. "What we have is an only-in-the-movies kind of connection." She'd said something like that back when they'd broken up and he now knew what she meant. It was all or nothing between them.

"Marc." She covered her face with her hands. "God, I—I hate you so much. Believe me, I wanted to get over you … you've always been on my mind, though, and I knew in my heart I never would. But I need to work through some of these personal ugly feelings I have. Everything is a big confusion inside me—my heart wants us back, but it's wounded because of losing you and then the baby. I don't know if you noticed back there but my emotions are a wreck." She inhaled through her nose, then deeply out of her mouth. She did it a few more times before finally stating, "Everything feels too much right now." And her bottom lip started quivering. She tucked it in between her teeth to keep from crumpling. She was pushing him away, protecting herself.

"So," he gulped hard again, his chest feeling like it was caving in, trying one more time, "I can't be around you and help you if you're sick or upset? Simran, I love you. You love me. Life is too short to not spend as much time together as we can. I can't even be your friend?" he whispered, pleading with her. They sat in silence for what seemed like an eternity, as she pulled out blades of grass mindlessly, her thoughts adrift.

She started to speak, but he grabbed her hands and hauled her onto his lap, not giving a shit about keeping his distance anymore. This is where they were the best, when they were in each other's spheres, when he could coax her with his touch, and she would do the same in return.

"Simran—"

Her hand was on his chest, tracing his nipples and she put the other one up to cover his mouth from saying anything further. "No," she said firmly. Before he could even comprehend what was happening, she pulled his face down to hers and murmured, "I can't do this." She breathed out shakily and his first thought was that he'd lost her for good. "I'm still a mess," she continued, "but I've decided I need all of you. I *want* all of you. Your friendship, your partnership, your love … ALL of you." She nipped his bottom lip sharply, then sucked it with a pressure that softened where she'd bitten. "You're mine, Marcus Lehigh. I claim you as all mine."

59

Chapter 17

She was snuggling into him, practically burrowing into his chest. Her face was in his neck, and she heard him inhale deeply. She'd finally crossed that hump, finally told him and herself that he was hers and even though there was an unbelievable amount of worry in her life at the moment, she felt whole. She needed him by her side as she dealt with everything. If she knew anything about Marc, he would help her through all of it, support her, and more, because when he cared about something, he put everything into it.

After she'd told him she wanted him back, his whoop of joy resounded in the canyon, even breaking through the deafening waterfall, and terrifying a few resting birds in the tree boughs above. They took flight, affronted.

"Suck it, Anil Patel!" he shouted victoriously, up on his knees to anyone who would listen. And she was completely taken aback. Had he been worried she would choose Anil as her future? Men really were so bullheaded.

"Ok, big guy. I didn't choose you over Anil. I already decided that I wasn't going to choose that path on my flight here. You were an entirely different matter."

He turned a completely ecstatic face to her, his bright eyes lit up almost blindingly. "Yeah, well, Sims, back at your apartment, you seemed so unsure. I wanted to make sure you were honest with yourself."

"Did you now?" She couldn't help it. She was starting to fume again. Who the hell did this guy think he was?! As if it was his duty, his right, to make sure she was happy. "I think I can make my own decisions for myself, thank you very much." But could she? Hadn't she been waffling back and forth so blindly that even Sabine wanted to smack her upside the head? She'd been clouded by her emotions, recuperating from surgery, and finally overcome by seeing this handsome beast again.

"Sims," he said gently, crawling back to her. "Please don't be angry." Oh, how he knew her well. "After seeing you again, I knew that I had to make sure you were happy, no matter what your choice was. Even if you didn't take me back, I wanted to ensure that you choosing Anil, and more importantly, what your father wanted, was the right choice for you because, baby, you were fuming over it. I could see it in every fiber of you." He was nodding his head enthusiastically, a bobblehead going crazy. "I wasn't lying when I said everything you do will always matter to me."

"You're a self-centered dolt, Marc. It's not your responsibility to see me happy. I might be changing my mind about wanting to be with you," she muttered.

"Am I self-centered?" He was astonished. "I only wanted what was best for you."

"Yeah and that best thing apparently serviced you, too." She crossed her arms over her chest, and lifted her chin, looking up at the sky, willing herself to just shut up. What in the Goddess Durga was wrong with her?

He came up, putting his arms around her. "Simran," he said, as if talking to a small child having a tantrum over something senseless, which, let's face it, she kind of was. "Isn't this the best thing for both of us?" He seemed to genuinely want an answer from her. "The way we can finally be together is for you to see that you should be with me." God, he was so arrogant. "And I with you. You see me as no one has ever seen me before. And correct me if I'm wrong, I see you better than anyone has before me. You belong in New York, you belong with your friends, you belong at the helm of *Lavish Your Events*. And fuck it, if I sound egotistical, so sue me," he muttered. "But you belong with me." He finished firmly, crossing his arms across his chest now.

"Sue you. As if I have that kind of money…" she scoffed. The man had a point, he always had a good point or a dozen. She sighed, conceding. "Marc, I do want to be with you. But understand this, you are a choice I've thought long and hard about. Something separate from deciding that what my father wanted wasn't right for me."

He stood and pulled her up to standing. "Let me see those handstands in the water now."

"Say what?" What had just happened?

"You win. I am a separate entity from your father's decision. Although, I think your father would beg to differ." He pulled on her curling strands, entranced by the bounce back.

"What do you know about my father?"

"Well, when I talked to him, back at his house, he seemed to think it was either Anil or me—"

"Wait, I thought you only went to his house and asked the servants about me. You didn't mention my dad *being* there." Her breathing was becoming laborious.

"Sims," he uttered in disbelief. "Come on, I assumed you knew your dad was there—"

"You *assumed*?! I'm not a freaking mind reader!" she huffed, her cheeks on fire. "So, my dad *was* there? You met him?" Her heart rate was rising again and she stepped back blindly.

"Well, of course." He shrugged, his hands reaching out, trying to steady her.

Now she was going to hyperventilate. She took large gulps of air, but they just didn't seem big enough. She bent over and put her hands on her knees "Did he freak out? Did he have a stroke? Oh my God, I think I'm about to have a stroke, too."

"Relax," he said softly. "Sims." He stood over her, his hands on his hips. When she didn't answer, he rubbed her back. "I don't see what the problem is. Your dad is a good man. He's definitely set in his ways," he chuckled, "but I got the impression that he's wrapping his head around how American you are now ... and that maybe you won't always need him to guide you." He continued rubbing her back in calming circles. "I think he and I are more alike than you think." He sounded like he'd just made this revelation himself.

Even folded over, upside down and catching her breath, she could see the confusion on his face. The man really didn't know, did he? "Um, duh, Marc. He's full of himself and so are you." She slowly stood up, regaining some semblance. "He's an incredible businessman and so are you. Some of your strongest qualities are a few of the things I noticed in you from the get-go and why I was drawn to you in the first place." She flipped her hair over her shoulders as she shrugged them, her eyes rolling of their own volition.

He was on her in a nanosecond, tickling her under her armpits and when she thought she was going to collapse from laughter, he pulled her into him, reached behind to her uber sensitive spot above her ass, and lightly glided his fingers over, tickling her some more.

"Marc!" she choked, the squeals peeling out of her. His hands slowed and he reached down to cup her ass. "Marc," she sighed, resting her head on his thudding heart, a place she'd missed dearly. The heat of his body almost burned through the thin cotton of her tunic, setting her skin on fire. She turned her face up to receive his kiss, which started gentle but quickly turned passionate, his mouth possessing hers like she was a fountain to quench his thirst.

"I want to make love to you, sweet Simran," he murmured against her. Oh, baby Krishna and his squishable cheeks, this man had it all, including the way he could sweet-talk her. She swore her ovaries clenched right before she felt a burst of warm moisture between her legs.

"Marc, we can't." He'd angled her jaw so he could reach down to his favorite vulnerable spot on her neck. He sucked it gently, alternating between kisses and licks. It sent tremors through her entire body, knowing what that mouth could do to her.

"Why not, sweetcheeks?" His hands squeezed her ass in just the right way, making her knees buckle. She grabbed onto his solid biceps, holding tightly. "No one will see us, except maybe those angry birds." His hands were skimming up her hips, raising her tunic as he went. He groaned as his fingers felt the bare skin of her waist.

She smiled, shaking her head. "That's not it, baby. I'm not fully healed from my surgery." And she pushed him away, denying her body what it so craved. She wrapped her arms around herself again.

Marc stood staring at her with his brow creased, his jaw tightened. "All right. We'll just have to wait for me to make love to you then." He took her hand and pulled her to the water. She hid her goofy smile. They'd never mastered the art of making love. When the time did come, they would attack each other and eventually burst into passionate flames with lightning speed. "Let's take a swim. I think we both need to cool off." His devilish look raked over her body, and she couldn't help noticing the bulge in his pants.

"One cool dip it is," she agreed breathlessly, trying to temper down her own desire as she followed him in.

After splashing and swimming, dunking, and many, many handstands later, they dried off and sat down to eat Rani's prepared breakfast. The juicy mango dribbled down their chins as they devoured them along with the eggs and bananas. Making up is hard work and they were ravenous.

Then they lay together on Simran's towel and dozed as she burrowed into him.

Around lunchtime, they finally packed up to leave the beautiful spot that was so special to both of them now. Halfway back, it started to rain a fine mist and they laughed and hurried back to the *ashram*. By the time they entered, completely soaked, the rain had stopped, and the clouds broke with the sun shining again. They both went to their respective rooms to change before looking for Rani *Khala*.

Later, both refreshed, they sought out the older woman to thank her for bringing them back together. She shook her head, smiling. "My *betas*, I was only helping you along to your destiny with each other. Now I think, you both feel whole again, and are at peace, *nah*?" she asked. She only nodded, confirming she was right when she saw them staring tenderly at each other, holding hands. "*Atcha.* I think your time here is coming to an end. Go back to living your lives. Love each other fully and see how much your cup will overflow."

ೞೞೞೞ

The loud bang in the quietude of the temple's open courtyard surely would have woken up every revered spirit or deity, if not the entire household. Marc held his knee, whispering angrily every curse word he knew, and making a few up in the process. He heard giggles from the other side of the thick wooden door, signifying that Simran heard his entire litany of hate at the foul door frame which he'd bumped his knee loudly on in the dim lighting.

He finally entered her cozy room, an exact replica of his own, just down the hall. She was on her knees on the bed, clearly waiting for her late evening rendezvous with him. Her hands were covering her mouth, trying not to burst into further giggles. She was in a short, loose white nightgown, her shiny black hair tousled and a mess, her coppery skin glinting in the moonlight from the one shutter she left half open, and she was perfection. *Cuddling, snuggling and no more*, he reminded himself. Simran needed to heal physically before they could be together like that. He could do this. He pulled off his shirt and shucked off his pants. In just his black boxer briefs, he came to the bed and pulled her soft, warm body to his, rolling them onto the bed so that her back was toward him. He curved his arm possessively around her waist as he held her close.

They lay there for a few minutes, listening to each other breathe, and the silence that was periodically broken up by animal and bird calls in the night. It was paradise. He nuzzled into her, wanting to get drunk off her scent, and then because he couldn't resist, he pushed her hair aside and started trailing kisses down the velvety skin on the back of her neck. She shivered, holding his arm tighter, and moving her backside into him.

"Marc," she sighed. His name on her lips when she was tiredly pleased was the sexiest thing ever. "We can't, remember?" He remembered. And he'd have a fucking case of painful blue balls until he could have her. But this wasn't about him. He knew she needed him.

He rolled over her, and she was on her back now, her eyes half open, the straps of her nightgown askew and slipping off. She was the goddess of his heart. "Will you let me help you?" he asked, leaning down to nuzzle her nose, then capture her upper lip, sucking playfully, covering her mouth in a kiss that he knew would drive her into delirium. Who was he kidding? He was driving himself into a delirium, too.

She wrapped her arms around his neck, holding him to her. Did she know her knees had fallen apart, and her legs had widened so that he fully rested between them, his pelvis to hers? She bucked her hips up slightly. She knew. She was his naughty kitten.

"What did you have in mind, baby?" she asked huskily, a little hesitant.

He kissed down her neck, onto the swells of her breasts. Fuck, he missed this body.

"I want you to take what you need," he said and started grinding slowly into her softness. She moaned sweetly. "Shh. We don't want anyone to hear us," he said. Imagine if Rani *Khala* found out he was in her great-niece's bed pleasuring her right now?

"We're sneaking around. It feels so bad." She giggled between her quiet moans. "What about you?" she panted, arching herself up into him as her hips started flexing him more deeply, rubbing her softness onto him. He hissed, trying to control himself. She would make him lose it right there in his boxer briefs if he didn't focus.

"All I want," he murmured, as his lips captured hers again, and his hand sought out her breasts to fondle those full globes, squeezing them, and plucking her hardened nipples, "is to please you right now." He groaned. Fuck her tits were made to be worshipped.

"Oh, Marc," she panted and that was it, she was gone. She rubbed herself in a frenzy against him, and she lifted her knees and angled her hips in such a way that her eyes rolled into the back of her head while she keened loudly. He covered her mouth with his, swallowing her cries as her body shuddered, and he had to feel it as well as see it, so he pushed his hand down her underwear and palmed her moist pussy. He could almost feel her outer lips pulsing. Oh, how he would do anything to push his fingers into her tight opening, feel her clench him, but he knew he couldn't. So, he pressed the heel of his hand down on the pad of skin hiding her clitoris and started massaging, knowing it would push her over again. And over she went once more, tearing her mouth away from his and yelping, "Marc, yes!" before he could cover her mouth with his again, chuckling at his passionate little kitten.

He continued massaging as her body trembled, one long finger gliding between her slick folds to find her swollen clitoris, and gently stroking as she rode out her waves of pleasure. And as he pulled back to watch her calm down, satiated, all he could think was that he couldn't wait to taste every inch of her.

Her cheeks were flushed, and her eyes were open now, glassy with pleasure, gazing up at him. A dreamy smile slowly widened on her face, and it was everything he wanted to see in her, witness in her tonight.

"You are so fucking beautiful, Simran. I've watched you come so many times in my memories and my dreams, but nothing is like the real thing. *Nothing.*" He leaned down to kiss her tenderly, his chest on hers, feeling her heart beating quickly against him.

"You're a pervert," she teased lovingly against his lips, cupping his face. She ran her fingers through the prickly hair of his beard. "You always know what I need," she sighed sleepily. "I owe you big time, babe."

"Shh. No, you don't. This isn't a trade-off, baby. I just want to be here for you and take care of you." She sighed, content.

"That you did, my love, that you did." She pulled him down so she could snuggle facing him, wrapping a smooth leg over him.

Her love. That had the best fucking ring to it. He fell into a deep sleep with the biggest grin on his face, her love surrounding him.

Chapter 18

MUMBAI, INDIA

"**I** don't know, chick, but does it scream 'bang me in the coat closet?" Her best friend, Tina, scrutinized the snug teal catsuit Simran wore. "I mean, your ass looks phenomenal." She made a square with her hands, examining through like a camera shot. "And your boobs, well, if he's not salivating I don't know what's wrong with him." She waved a hand and crossed one long leg over the other, leaning back on the pink velvet divan inside the dressing room to get another perspective. They were in a well-known boutique in order to outfit Simran in something spectacular for the night out Marc had planned at Club Sundar Social the following evening.

At first, almost enraged that Simran was back with Marc, "the slimiest player ever," as she'd deemed him, Tina had refused to help. She finally calmed down when all was explained to her; especially the part about Simran not taking him back immediately. Hearing that he'd come to India to profess his love made Tina thaw. She gave Simran an A+ for punishing him, and she could think of no better way for him to spend his pile of money than to chase after the best thing to ever enter his life. Her only warning was that he better spoil the crap out of Simran.

"I'm not going for that kind of look, Tins, remember? I need something sexy, sophisticated, and more importantly screams 'don't even *think* about thinking about my man,' to all the other women."

"And some men, too, I'm sure," Tina murmured. "Are you sure you don't want to be banged in the coat closet? Girl, you're practically gaga over him. I could call him now and get him to bang you right here, right now in the dressing room, if you like." She held up her phone, shaking it at Simran.

"Don't be *sthool* (gross), Tina. Why is your mind always so garbage?"

"Don't you Bangla me!" she said a little affronted (Tina spoke Hindi and understood only a little Bangla). "I know my mind can be garbage sometimes, Sima, and let's be honest, you need a garbage-minded friend to tell you how it is at times ... but, seriously, *I'm* being gross?!" She snorted and chortled. "I'm not the one who said she needed to be bent over the car and taken immediately this morning while watching her hunky man's fine ass walk away." Her head shook in her feminine version of the South Asian head bob, her chin length shiny hair floating around her face.

"I know, I'm totally gaga over him, and I needed it like, yesterday." Simran admitted not even embarrassed one bit by it.

"Are you sure you're ready?" Tina asked, her filthy mind on the back-burner now, as her concern for her friend, and everything she'd been through, took over.

"I'm more than ready, Tins. I've felt the need to mount him since we got back from Lonavala."

"I know. I think my eyes are permanently damaged from catching you two dry-humping," Tina said, making a gagging noise. It was all Simran could talk about since Tina had arrived from Singapore the previous day. She'd even caught them making out hot and heavy on the living room couch in their hotel suite when they thought she and Raj were still outside on their balcony admiring the stunning Mumbai coastline at sunset. "How about we go to that adorable lingerie shop I like once we're done here? Then you can really give him something special tonight?" Her eyebrow wagged and she shook her shoulders coquettishly

"Oh, I like that idea." Simran started to peel off the catsuit. "Can we be done here? I'll just borrow something from you, Tins."

"Um, I don't think so, love. Your boobs are bigger than mine, and I definitely don't want any sex juices as a reminder. Believe me, I'm glad you're getting banged, but I don't need the evidence."

"Oh my God, Tina. As *if!*" she said horrified, before they both burst into laughter.

After calming down, Tina checked the time on her phone. "Ok, let's hurry this up. That stomach of yours will start whining soon. You know what, before that even happens, here." She rummaged around in her Hermes satchel and tossed Simran a packet of peanut M&M's. "Don't ever say I wasn't there for you." She winked at her. "I'll be right back. I'm going to find Riya and see if I can't get into some of the newer pieces that are still in boxes." She tossed her phone into her bag while unfolding herself from the deep cushions and disappearing out of the dressing room area on a clear mission.

Tina was a regular at these high-end boutiques. A fashion mecca for well-heeled Indians, Bollywood actresses, and models, this was her domain, and she knew all of the salespeople's names by heart (they definitely knew hers; she provided a huge commission for them every time she was in Mumbai).

Simran sat down on the lounge her friend just vacated, and tore open the bag of candy, grateful for Tina's "maternal instincts." The woman was a contradiction at times, she ruminated, smiling to herself. As she crunched loudly, her mind went back to Marc, making her chomp a little more enthusiastically. Her back arched at the mere thought of him and the week they had spent together, not having sex.

He'd been an absolute gentleman, sweet and attentive, respecting her space and not pushing her physically. They snuggled on the couch catching up while listening to music. They held long embraces as they took meandering strolls around some of Mumbai's beautiful gardens and visited famous sites. It was romantic.

His fingers did begin to stray a little, grazing her ass, her breasts, but only because she was teasing him first, her own hands not able to keep away from his incredible butt and solid chest. Her body always seemed to find a way to be up against his; his magnetic hold on her unstoppable. And apparently, her eyes were trying to have sex with him, as

Marc put it, when he caught her multiple times staring at him longingly. But how could she not? The knowledge of his genuine love and respect for her, and his caring attitude, made her senses more heightened. In fact, it was one little question he asked her, while Raj and Tina had visited them yesterday, that made Simran jump him on the couch. He'd squatted down in front of her where she was sitting, taking her hands in his, and asked if she was feeling better after her headache earlier. His sexy musk and mint scent filled her nostrils and a tidal wave of lust rolled through her body. She'd startled him by grabbing him by the collar, and pulling him to her, attacking his lips, as his large body toppled over hers. She writhed under him, needing to feel him against her like that. And he didn't complain, groaning and taking control of her mouth, rolling them so he could pull her roughly to him. A loud "ahem" from both of their guests interrupted them. But Marc whispered wickedly in her ear that they would have their evening of beautiful love-making, followed by a night of incredible fucking very soon. It was up to her to name the date.

She'd been wet all evening, fidgeting in her chair at dinner while trying to catch up with Raj and Tina, Marc's arm around her shoulders, his fingers teasing her bare skin.

So, tonight would definitely be the night. And now her panties were soaking in anticipation as she sat in the dressing room. She rolled her eyes at herself, and shifted in her seat, as she munched hard on those M&M's.

Her phone pinged and she pulled it out of her purse, grinning from ear to ear. It was from Sexy Fox, her nickname for Marc in her phone.

Sexy Fox: "Hey, Beautiful. How're you feeling?"

Ever since Marc had found out back at the waterfall that she fell into moments of melancholy, he'd been tentative to her moods. He didn't want her unhappy, becoming almost a churlish child himself when it would happen. He was in "fix-it" mode, even calling his mother to get advice when he didn't think Simran was listening. It was just another aspect of his sweet nature that made Simran fall more deeply in love with him every day.

Simran: "I'm fine, I promise."

She was. She hadn't broken into an uncontainable fountain of tears once that day … yet. She'd been too busy to think about her sadness, in the hopes of finding something to wear. Plus, being with Tina always lifted her mood.

Sexy Fox: "So, how's shopping? Miss me yet?"

Simran: "Always."

She couldn't think of anything smooth to say back because she did always miss him.

Simran: "I'm sitting here naked in the dressing room REALLY missing you. I had to change my underwear already."

She hit 'Send,' stifling her bubbling giggles.

Sexy Fox: "Text me your coordinates NOW. I'll be there in ten. Save some of that for me. That's an order."

And now Simran laughed out loud, her back arching involuntarily again. God, he made her wild.

Simran: "You know Mumbai traffic. You'll be here in ten hours."

Sexy Fox: "Damn. You're right."

She could almost hear him groaning over there, see him running his hands through his hair.

Simran: "So, what are you up to, besides thinking about me😊?"

Sexy Fox: "Went for a much-needed run, showered, now catching up on work. Have you thought about what we talked about on the drive back from the *ashram*?"

Simran audibly grumbled. Why was he such a good man?

Simran: "Not quite there, yet."

Sexy Fox: "Maybe pass it by Tina for another weigh-in, that is if she's past wanting to scratch my eyes out. I'll let you get back to the important task of making yourself even sexier for me, though I doubt you could. And please save some of your juiciness for me later 😊. I love you, sweetcheeks. XX"

She chuckled, and heat bloomed in her cheeks, dripped into her chest, and warmed her heart, as her pulse raced. As if she could stay dry now. Yep, tonight, was definitely the night.

Simran: "I love you, too, Sexy Fox. XOXO."

Simran leaned back in the chair as that conversation came back to her from a few days ago during their travels back from Lonavala.

࿇

Chapter 19

FIVE DAYS AGO

Simran had fallen asleep again. It was a running joke that she could sleep anywhere, and in a bumpy car ride back to Mumbai, no less. Her eyes fluttered open to catch hazes of green whipping by; her confusion starting to wear off. Her dream had been emotional and although she couldn't remember the details, all she knew was she was about to start crying again. She blinked back the tears threatening to spill over.

"Hey," Marc whispered into her hair. "You sleep ok?"

"Mm," was all she could muster, relief taking over that she was safely in Marc's arms, nestled into his heat, to the point where she was almost on top of him in the roomy car. He didn't seem to mind and his tender smile down at her made her levitate. Did she look like she had stars in her eyes, too? She reached up, pushing back the hair that persisted in flopping over his brow, then ran her palm over the spiky hair of his beard, still fascinated with the soft prickling on her skin.

"Don't look at me like that, kitten. I'll have Akash stop the car and leave us alone if you keep it up." She giggled at that.

"And I won't need that much time either, just a good five minutes, maybe six," he whispered low and gravelly in her ear.

She turned her smile downward, and scrunched her brows low over her eyes. "Is this better?" she asked innocently, her frown difficult to hold.

"You know it's not," he replied dryly, referencing how turned on he became when she was pouty and angry. He took her hand and placed it over his groin. She sighed, feeling him already stiff beneath the coarse fabric of his black jeans. Marc shifted in his seat. "Akash, do you think we could stop to get some air and move our legs around?" He glanced down as she widened her eyes. "Relax, babe. I'm respecting your space. I really do need to stretch my legs, and maybe get a little room from your hot body which is doing things to me I'm having a hard time controlling." An eyebrow was raised as he flicked his gaze down to his groin, then back at her. Simran pursed her lips, nodding.

They stopped at a rest area, got out to stretch, and drink some water, while Akash grabbed a smoke. They left him leaning against the car as they strolled up a little nature trail, holding hands.

The tall banyan trees swayed gently above them, creaking lightly. Marc stopped in the path, squinting up at the long branches with their wide reach, and the thick bundles of vines extending from them, just sweeping the ground.

"Sims, did you check to see if you got your test results back?" he asked mildly. This was the fourth time he'd inquired since their reunion back at the waterfall yesterday. Despite his tone, it was clearly driving him crazy not knowing, and also because he was used to having answers immediately. She reminded him each time that her lab results were waiting dutifully in line until it was her turn. She didn't have preferential treatment over this, or just about anything in her life the way he was accustomed to. In truth, she hadn't checked her email in days because she was so afraid of the results.

She sighed, pulling her phone out of her back pocket. Time to face it. "Let me check." She scrolled through her inbox and saw one from her doctor. Her pulse began racing double-time as she glanced up at Marc, not able to keep the alarm from her demeanor.

"Do you want me to read it?" His concern made his voice rough as he reached for her phone.

She shook her head and clicked it open. She read it, then she read it again and her nerves began to calm down.

"Jesus, Sims," Marc muttered, pacing back and forth with his hands stuffed into his pockets.

The grin she gave him felt like she was radiating sunbeams of relief. He immediately understood and swooped her into his arms. She relaxed, letting him hold most of her weight, their deep breaths matching, in sync with the reprieve they both felt from this stressor.

"Christ, Simran. I'm so relieved." His voice shook, his deep exhales blowing her hair.

"Me, too," she admitted. She remembered the pain of her mother's illness. The cancer was more than just a vice in her body killing her. It also affected everyone around her. When she died, a piece of everybody died, too. Her father especially felt wounded and misplaced for a long time. There was no way she would want that inflicted on Marc, or the rest of her family and friends. "Now that's something I don't have to tell my dad about."

She was muffled in his embrace and felt his chest rumble in response against her cheek. "About your father, are you going to tell him about us this time? This is your choice, and you are happy with it. It should come from your mouth, don't you think?"

Simran tensed. "Sheesh, why are you so noble?" she asked, pulling back to stare hard at his muscular chest under his fitted t-shirt.

☙☙☙☙

He liked the sound of that. Was he noble? He just wanted her to do the right thing here and told her so. What came out of her mouth next surprised him, but he understood her hesitation.

She started to finger his chest mindlessly, tickling him. "I'm afraid, Marc. I know it sounds silly because I'm a grown woman. I have my own life and created my own career, but he's always made me feel like I'm still a child in some ways, and that I owe him something for everything he's done for me. He tried with Sabine first, but he stopped years ago when she didn't engage and now their relationship is strained—something that continuously hurts him." She paused trying to articulate this difficult topic, and Marc covered her hands with his own. "I don't expect you to understand, but it's this guilt I've felt my entire life. Remember I told you about it back in New York, the 'South Asian guilt'?" He nodded. "I've had a responsibility rooted in me ever since I can remember to please him with whatever choices I make. It's kind of like an exchange for everything he's done as a parent to raise me, us." She sighed. "Part of it extends to ensuring he's happy in his old age," she continued, "and I'm not the only Indian who feels like this, by the way. After college, Tina was so confused, and she couldn't lock down a career. Her parents went from cloud nine with a daughter who graduated with *all* the academic honors from NYU, to disappointment. Totally unfair, don't you think? How does one really know what they want for themselves when they're only twenty-two years old? Whatever." She shook her head, her lip curling in disgust. "On a whim, she decided to meet the man they were looking into as an eligible husband for her. She had no idea what would happen, she just caved to their incessant disappointment with her. It was something she never wanted to do—the whole arranged marriage thing. But it ended up working because the chemistry was there between her and Raj. And, don't get me started on all the others I grew up with in my Connecticut South Asian community. To make it as a doctor, or a lawyer, or any kind of success with money was, and still is, a pressure cooker of another level. And then to achieve marriage, hopefully with an Indian or another South Asian, and dutifully provide grand babies ... I kind of thought I had it easy, until recently..." She trailed off. It all sounded so old-fashioned, but who was he to judge how other cultures did things?

Marc tipped her chin so he could look into her dark eyes. "Nothing you've said about this part of your life sounds silly or easy. I can't imagine going through early adulthood feeling that way, especially if it was expected of me while I was raised in the US where personal freedom is a right, not a luxury. I'm glad you had others to commiserate with." He held her close again. "Simran, I'm really fucking over the moon that you decided *not* to take the path your father laid out for you. He's not the one living your life, you are. I'm proud of you, but more than anything, you should be proud of yourself. You don't need others to give you that sense of fulfillment. I want to because I love you, but I hope you see that everything you've accomplished in your life is because of you." He poked her in the chest, trying to drive home these facts that she couldn't seem to see for herself.

Her eyes filled with tears and her mouth wobbled between a smile and a frown.

"Hey now." His hands came up to stop her tears, his thumbs wiping the wet streaks over and over again, but they continued. "Sims?"

"I'm sorry. I can't stop." She buried her face into his chest, and he continued holding her, the two of them standing in the middle of a trail in a rest area somewhere between Lonavala and Mumbai, while she sobbed into him. And not quiet sniffles, but big, huffy, shoulder-wracking sobs that shook her entire frame. Marc could only rub her back in comfort.

"Sims," he said again, now wary. He shook her a little. "Talk to me."

She finally pulled back from him as her hands covered her face in awkwardness. "I think I completely soaked your shirt," she mumbled. He pulled her hands away to find her face splotchy with eyes swollen and red. "Marc I ... I didn't accomplish everything. The baby ..." she trailed off and her hand fisted at her mouth as her eyes welled up again. "I lost it," she whispered almost inaudibly.

Comprehension made Marc reel back almost physically. He was such a fucking idiot. Of course, she would be feeling like this. She was an empath at heart, a sensitive soul. The baby loss would absolutely take a toll on her. To be honest, he knew nothing about it, but a woman suffering a miscarriage must go through some kind of mourning period. Shit. He would need to call an expert on this. He'd give his mom a call that evening for starters, when he knew Simran was asleep so as not to embarrass her.

"Sweetie." He wrapped his arm around her shoulders and pulled her into him again. "That wasn't your fault. It happens all the time." He hoped he was quoting some medical journal correctly.

"How do you know?" she said into his shoulder. "Wait a minute, have you gotten other women pregnant before?" she asked suspiciously, her melancholy starting to turn fiery. Shit, her emotions were a pendulum swinging back and forth. He'd get dizzy if he didn't work with her on this.

"I don't think so—"

"Wrong answer." Her fingers found his nipple and twisted, hard. He grabbed her hand to stop the painful tweaking.

"What I meant to say is, no woman has ever come to me claiming that I was the father of their child—"

"But it's possible?" She was scowling now, with her hands on her hips, and her dark eyes were trying to hurl black flames at him. Was he getting turned on? Maybe, just a little. He urged his inner horndog to put on a muzzle.

"Sims, for the love of God. That's not the point. The point is you're hurting, and I can't stand it. I don't like it. Let me help you, whatever that may be." His hands sought her out again, needing to feel her against him. She let him drag her to him once more.

"Fine. But I'm not ready to get into it, even if I do want your help." She was surly now. "Jeez, you're so persistent. I guess I should consider myself lucky. First, you came to me in New York, then you came here to India for me, and now..."

"Sims, we'll have to talk about it at some point." She was trying to skirt the topic like she always did when they forayed into uncomfortable territory. He continued before she could start arguing, "And I'd say I'm the lucky one. I didn't think it was possible to ever find that special someone who you want to fight for and cherish, who you need in your life to feel whole." He put his chin on top of her head. "I do think I'm being rather selfish here. I would do anything and everything in my power to make sure you're happy, because it makes me happy." He felt the puff of warm breath against his neck as she sighed sweetly. He took her hand and continued up the path. "So, that being said." He cleared his throat. "You should speak to your father while you're here."

"*Crap-freaking-ola!* You and your persistent ways!" She spit out, trying to tug away, but he held on tight. "Seriously, Marc?"

"Seriously, Sims. You just said yesterday you didn't ever want to put me in a position where I'm like my father—a person who never knows their child. But isn't this the same thing? You not speaking to your father, not being able to communicate to him about your chosen path will hurt him and he'll never have the chance to really know you. I've been on the receiving end of that kind of hurt, and I would never want anyone to experience it."

She nodded, kicking some dirt with her heel. "I see your point. It wouldn't be fair to my dad if I kept our relationship from him again. He'd find out through gossip like before and that didn't go over so well then. Plus, it's not fair to you. If I respect you and what we're doing, then I should grow some balls and tell my dad about us." She took a deep breath. "Let me at least think about it. We're here, or at least I'm here, for an extended period of time. I didn't buy a flight back yet."

He pushed some hair behind her ear, looking into her lovely face. Didn't she get that they were in this together?

"Hey, you're here for an extended period of time, then so am I. If you want, I can come with you to speak with your father. I want you to be brave, but I would never make you do this on your own. Plus, there's only room for one pair of balls in this relationship," he continued matter-of-factly as she guffawed and rolled her eyes. "And, when we're ready to leave for New York, you can be my special, one and only flight companion on my jet."

"Oh, sheesh, you and your jet. I don't think I'll ever get comfortable with your wealth." And here was one of the reasons Marc loved Simran so much. She was always herself and would never be impressed with his money. It was something he noticed in the very beginning about her and was so unlike the women he'd encountered since he'd first made it big.

"If it makes you feel any better, it's not *my* jet, but the company jet. You have a company van, remember?"

She snorted. "Yeah, sure because my company van is just like your company jet."

He chuckled as they turned around and headed back to the car. Akash must be wondering where they were.

"Mr. Lehigh," she suddenly quipped, her tone flirty. "You're very presumptuous by the way."

"Am I now?"

"I'll bet you want me to join the mile-high club with you." Marc chuckled. Oh, she had no idea the many things they could do miles up in the air in that regard. "I mean, is there some kind of mile-high membership card? Do you get a punch on it for every sex-capade in the bathroom?" She looked at him sideways as they walked, peering at him from under her lashes. "What kind of prize do you get if you fill in all the boxes?"

Marc hooted out a laugh, making her chuckle in return. Oh, she really had no idea. "Baby, we don't have to do it in the bathroom. There *is* a bedroom on my jet." He wiggled his eyebrows at her as her own reached her hairline. "But seriously, you'll love it ... the ride on my jet, I mean."

"Oh yeah? The ride on your jet, or the *ride* on your jet?" she asked innocently.

He exhaled, trying not to get turned on by the way this conversation was heading. "What I mean is you will enjoy the flight from Mumbai to JFK in your own seat." She started laughing huskily. He leaned down to whisper in her ear, "You, my little kitten, have a very, *very* filthy and perverted mind, which I adore." He felt her shiver. "As far as I'm concerned, I already have the best prize there is, by the way." His hand involuntarily slipped down to the curve of her round ass, and he squeezed slowly. "I'd be more than happy to induct you into the club, though. I've a feeling you'd be an enthusiastic member." He bent down to capture her mouth with his own. He was content, complete, relaxing with her in his arms. With everything that happened between them, he was still wrapping his head around the fact that she was his again. He knew without a doubt that he had always been hers from the moment their eyes connected back in London. He held her tight before returning to the car.

20

Chapter 20

The sharp rap on the dressing room door interrupted her train of thought and Tina bustled in with an armful of new outfits.

"Ok, we need to tackle the holy trifecta here—tits, ass, legs." She fingered off on her hands. "Lucky for you, chick, you're already stacked in those categories." Her voice boomed loud enough for the entire shop to hear. She eyed Simran's breasts with envy. "I really do wish my jubblies were so big…" She looked down at her own chest, then kept gazing back at Simran's.

Simran rolled her eyes. "Here, give me." She held her hand out expectantly.

"I think this number will do the trick." Tina handed her a racy, black mini dress. It had long sleeves, with dainty puffed shoulders. The material had some stretch, with a fine sheen to it, and would show every line and curve, including the extra skin on her belly which was finally starting to look normal again. Simran shooed Tina out and wriggled into the dress. She turned every which way to make sure she liked what she saw. It was a simple design, but in its simplicity, it offered everything she was looking for in the "make your jaw drop" category. The high neckline went straight across her clavicle in front, but the back was the "wow" factor. It was a deep open "V" with the bottom point just skimming right above her tailbone. The whole look was very 1980s rocker-chic and she loved it. Tina really was a magician. This *was* the dress.

After trying on the perfect heels to go with the black number, Simran made her purchases, and they headed to Tina's favorite lingerie shop where she picked out a few options for that evening. Then they went on to take care of more urgent matters; a much-needed lunch break at their favorite snack shop.

They over ordered as usual, and ooh'ed and ahh'ed as the assortment of tasty food arrived at their table which included *Kathi* rolls (egg with spiced vegetables wrapped in flaky flatbread), *samosa chaat* (fried potato dumpling drizzled in yogurt, chutneys, and spices), and *pani puri* (crispy dough balls filled with spiced chickpeas and served with a tangy sauce). They attacked everything with fervor both groaning and moaning at the delicious decadence.

Simran leaned back in her chair, patting her belly. "Dude, we always get way too much. Ugh, now I'm stuffed." She took a gulp of water, watching Tina continue to eat and take large swigs of her mango juice. She didn't know where the woman put it. Both of her long slim legs must be hollow.

When Tina finally finished up, she daintily picked up her napkin and tried to quietly belch into it. She leaned her long, thin form back against the chair, her usual non-existent belly rounded out a bit. "Ah yes, my buddha belly," she chuckled and rubbed her barely-there stomach. "Damn, Sima, why do you let me eat so much?" She hiccupped another burp out.

Simran snorted. "As if I could stop you. You're like a freight train when it comes to delicious fried foods. Anyone caught in your way would get seriously injured!"

"Well, now I need a fucking nap like an old Aunty." She took a sip of water. "This baby needs digesting," she chuckled, patting her stomach again, then realized the error of her words. "Oh my God, sorry, soz! Sima—"

"It's ok," Simran said, chuckling at the British slang Tina mindlessly sprinkled into conversation now.

"No, it's not. I need to be more aware and shut my fat mouth." Simran cocked her head, looking at her best friend curiously. Tina always told it like it was. Her friend continued, "Your sis called me and warned me about your mood swings. She said I needed to watch it so I wouldn't set you off." Her light brown eyes looked down at the table, and truth be told, Simran hadn't seen Tina this remorseful in a long time. "How are you doing with all of it by the way?" She sat up, reaching for Simran's hand, squeezing comfortingly.

Simran smiled reassuringly at her. "I'm ok, really. I mean, I have my moments. You should've seen me with Marc a few days ago. I couldn't stop crying. He must have thought he signed up for the wrong Simran. I wouldn't be surprised if he considers checking me into a loony bin."

"Chick, you're already loony, so I'm sure he knew what he was in for." Tina patted her hand. "Seriously, though, if you need some help … I don't know, with mental stuff … I can try to find a good therapist. Mental health is nothing to laugh about," she said firmly.

"You're right." Simran sighed. "I'll think about it. Marc is worried, too."

Tina nodded. "And if I put my big foot in my mouth, you'll tell me, yeah? You know I don't mean it—"

"Tina, we've known each other since we were little. I know you. You would never deliberately hurt me."

"Ok then. So ... how are things going with you and the player, anyway?"

Simran smiled gratefully at the change in topic. She didn't want to delve into "sad Simran," either.

"Don't call him that, Tina. He's changed. He told me so, and I believe him." She leaned her chin in her hand on the table. "I'm so in love with him, it's almost stupid," she said wistfully.

"Oh God, there you go getting all moon-faced again. Well, I'm happy for you. If you can take him back after what he did—"

"Tina," Simran warned.

She threw her hands up in defeat. "All right, already. I'm glad you're happy, but I'm going to err on the side of caution for the both of us, *nah*?" She shook her head. "Someone has to. You're so clouded right now." She flipped her hand, the giant diamond on her ring finger almost blinding Simran.

"Ok fine. Whatever," Simran said, now wanting to drop the subject. "Can I get your advice on something?"

"Bring it," Tina said, while taking her phone out of her bag to text her driver to come and get them.

"Should I tell *Abba* about me and Marc? It's for real now. We've *actually* put a label on it. We're together officially."

"So, he's your boyfriend and you're his girlfriend now," Tina said looking up curiously with a raised eyebrow. "THE Marcus Lehigh has committed for reals to a girlfriend?"

Simran chuckled. "Yeah, I'm his freaking girlfriend." She felt warm and fuzzy inside.

"I say tell Uncle then. He's going to find out one way or another. Either you never show up to your "wedding" to wanker face Anil, or you can just get it out of the way now. Just put your big girl panties on and be upfront about it. I know he can be over-bearing, but Uncle loves you and he deserves to know that you're happy, and in love," she said with conviction.

"See, Marc knew I should ask you. He thought you would have some excellent advice on the matter," Simran grinned, nodding at Tina.

"Huh, he said that, did he? He just moved up in my book," Tina chuckled.

Chapter 21

Marc entered the private elevator and took it up to his penthouse suite in Mumbai's lavish Four Season's hotel. While Simran had been busy all-day shopping, he'd visited Club Sundar Social for an update on how the place was running. He already knew the establishment was financially lucrative, but he wanted to ensure the physical space was up to standards. After catching up with his GM over lunch, sampling some of the innovative dishes the chef had come up with, and tasting the new drinks the mixologist had created, Marc was more than satisfied. He couldn't wait to show Simran and her friends a good time tomorrow evening.

He entered the spacious living room and was greeted with a spectacular view of the coast under the Indian sunset shining through the large picture windows. The haze mingled with the waning sun's rays and the city's bright lights, creating a surreal, pastel-like quality. It was breathtaking, and it beckoned to him.

He dropped his suitcase and left his phone on the charger. Loosening his tie and tossing his business jacket off, he headed to the glass doors. From up on the twenty-fifth floor, it was their own private haven; the traffic and pedestrians from below were an entire world away. He opened the balcony doors and walked out onto the large patio, outfitted with chaise lounges, potted palms offering privacy, and a bistro table and chairs where he and Simran had been having their breakfast every morning since arriving here. He smiled. It'd been wonderful waking up to her every day and breaking their fast together. His smile wavered at the thought of returning to NY and how she would stay at her place, and he at his. Sleepovers would happen—like before, but it wasn't enough for him. What was the solution here? There was only one. He would think of a way to ask her to move in with him when they returned.

"Is that you, babe?" she called from the living room.

"Who else would it be, sweetie?" Marc teased, laying his palms on the warm concrete balustrade and soaking in the view.

"Maybe my *other* boyfriend," she taunted sweetly, now behind him. Marc smirked, as her arms wound around him from the back. He heard music coming from the surround sound inside; a quirky, sexy synthesizer, while a deep bass filled the air, almost addictive in tempo, and a female singer's sensual voice singing, "Boy you make me float ... Boy you get me high..."

He turned around in her arms, and his breath lodged in his throat. Gorgeous didn't even come close to describing her, with full, curly hair in disarray around her shoulders— just the way he liked it—and a long black satin robe hugging her form, and black stilettos on her feet. She started to finger his loosened tie, humming to the song, "Baby, now hold me close ... Let's take this overboard now..."

Blood started to thrum in Marc's veins and his dick flexed.

"You're digging in the catacombs for this one," he teased, his hands gripping her waist tightly as guitar chords bounced alluringly, and the bass beats filled his body. He started moving with the music, his tempo matching Simran's as she danced against him.

"Aaliyah's 'Rock the Boat' is hardly an oldie, but you're right, it's a classic," she said huskily, then started singing the lyrics, "Rock the boat … Rock the boat … Work the middle…" Holy hell. He'd been thinking about her all afternoon, ever since she'd mentioned over text how horny she was. The last few days had been utter torture, but was tonight finally the night they were going to make love?

His hands slid down from her waist, feeling the smooth, silky material warmed by her skin underneath, and grasped her swaying hips. Her scent filled his nostrils, making them flare, and his dick started to harden, his breathing becoming heavier as he felt her softness.

"I've wanted to have sex to this song ever since I can remember," she breathed staring into his eyes, her breasts just feathering against his chest. "You're actually a really good dancer, Marc. I wish you would dance more with me," she coo 'ed, her cool hands sliding down his chest.

"For your eyes only, baby," Marc said softly, his heart racing, realizing his own pelvis unconsciously moved side to side with hers. "So, what's underneath here?" He reached for her robe tie. She stepped out of his reach, holding on to the end of his tie, and tugged him with it, like a dog on a leash.

And that's what he was at that moment, a dog salivating happily at his master.

"Mm, you'll have to wait and see," she murmured, leading him toward one of the chaise loungers, behind the wall of potted palms that obstructed anyone from viewing them. She pushed him down and leaned over him to undo his tie, her cleavage just inches from him. Too quickly, she stood back up, dragging his tie from around his neck and tossing it on the floor as she circled behind him. Her robe followed suit, landing in a pile of black satin at his feet. Her hands caressed his shoulders as her hair tickled his cheek while she bent in close, repeating after Aaliyah's words, "You going to stroke it? Stroke it for me? Will you work my middle?" The energy in the air turned heavy, and he could almost envision the raw, erotic promise.

"What are we up to right now, baby?" He was trying not to sound overly excited. Sex was definitely on the menu tonight, but she was in the mood to play first. He undid the top few buttons of his dress shirt and unclasped his belt buckle, leaning back into the cushions to get more comfortable. He only hoped he could hold out on what she had planned and not end up with an embarrassing accident in his pants. He'd been patient, waiting these past few days for her to properly heal, not only physically, but mentally. Sure, he'd relieved himself in the shower daily (sometimes more than once), but any hint of getting into bed with her was absolutely going to make him lose it faster than he wanted.

She strutted out from behind, twirling in between, the material on her outfit fluttering in a flirty attitude. And, he was speechless, finally seeing what was under that robe. He'd dreamt of making love to her so many times these past few days, and now it seemed like she was ready to be fucked … *thoroughly*. The sheer, wine-red teddy, just skimmed the tops of her thighs. Her large, perfect tits were barely covered by the lacy bodice, her dark nipples just peeping out, the deep cleavage the perfect cleft to lavish with his tongue. She had on a tiny matching thong, with a garter belt attached to black sheer stockings, which encased each of her incredibly toned legs. Those black stilettos finished off the look.

"*Fuck*, baby. That better not be for your other boyfriend," he said gruffly. He was fully aroused now, his blood pumping through his veins, his cock completely hardened. Her skin was smooth and coppery in the fading sun, and her eyes were so dark, almost black, shining with excitement. She put both hands on his legs and jerked them apart, coming to stand in between his thighs.

"Here, let me," she said smoothly, as she slowly slid, then jerked his belt off. His hands skimmed over her hips down the sides of her legs as he looked up at his sexy goddess. He had no words as he gazed at this beautiful woman.

"You know," she continued, dropping the belt on the floor, and sensually moving her hips side to side, increasingly exaggerating her movements until her body was low to the ground, then she rolled back up, her hands in her hair tousling the waves even more. "You've earned some TLC, baby. You've been so patient with me these last few days. I want to show you just how much I appreciate you." She licked her lips and his pelvis flexed, ready for action. "And we aren't going to use condoms tonight. I'm on a different pill." And now he was drooling. Going bare inside her was his version of heaven.

Simran started singing again with the song, "...Oh, baby, I love your stroke, 'Cause you, 'cause you get me where I'm going, yeah..." She leaned in, pushed her breasts into his face, then arched back as she came into another full-body roll. Never had he so appreciated her dance skills as he did right now while she gave him the hottest lap dance he'd ever experienced. She teased him further by coming low on his lap, gyrating erotically back and forth, but not making contact. His crotch lurched forward, looking for that touch. She stood up and turned around, pulling her hair up again and swaying those full hips side to side. He groaned aloud staring up close at the tiny material of lace that disappeared into her luscious ass cheeks. "You haven't said anything, baby." She pouted. "Don't you like what you see?"

"*Fucking hell*, Sims, you're my every wet fantasy. I want you now." He dragged her hips back, and bent her over. He shoved aside the flimsy teddy material so he could lightly sink his teeth into each ass cheek, licking the bite marks afterward. She moaned sexily, her breathing uneven.

She flipped her hair back and put some space between them, taunting over her shoulder. "Not so fast, baby. Let me work you." Her eyes were hooded and flirty, her hands on his knees with her back arched. "Let me help you with these shoes." She bent over to unlace and remove each of his shoes, and Marc could only stare slack-jawed at the tiniest sliver of material covering what he knew would be her juicy middle which he so badly couldn't wait to stroke.

He pulled her ass roughly to him again and pushed aside that material. His tongue touched her opening finding her skin on fire. She was sopping, her warm juices dripping, and he lapped them up immediately, before sliding his tongue inside her swollen lips. And holy hell, she was so hot and tight and tasted better than he remembered.

"Oh God, Marc," she moaned raggedly. "This is supposed to be a show for you," she breathed, even as she pushed herself closer to him, panting.

"Baby, this is interactive; the best fucking show a man could ask for," he murmured against her. He gripped her hips more firmly, holding her in place. "There's taste..." His tongue entered her from behind again, going deeply this time, then pulling out. "And your pussy tastes sublime. You want me to work the middle, right?" She gasped, whimpering, and he did it over and over again. Her muscles started to convulse inside; he could feel the tremors, as he fucked her with his tongue. Shit, she was going to come fast. Her hands were gripping his knees now, her back arching even more as she moved back and forth against his face while he licked and lapped what she offered.

"Yes! Oh God, Marc, *yes!*" she yelled, and her legs started to collapse, her body pitching forward as she lost control. He caught her, drawing her back to sit on his lap with her legs straddling him, her back up against his chest. Her scent was everywhere, and her taste was all over his tongue. He needed to be in her now.

"And, of course, let's not forget about touch." He undid his pants so that his hard, almost painful cock sprung out against her ass cheeks. He rubbed himself against her lower back and she shivered at the feel of his pre-cum. He snaked a hand down the front of her wet underwear and grazed the front of her swollen flesh. She sighed deeply, still coming down from her orgasm. Then he massaged that flesh, kneading her sweet little clit inside, before sliding his fingers in to find that slick bud. Her head lolled back on his shoulder as she keened, and started rolling against his hand once more, the movement making his need for her intensify. He pushed her up to standing, her legs still straddling him, and he fingered the damp crotch of her underwear.

"Baby, you ready for this? We're outside, anyone could see us," he whispered against her back, the idea of fucking her outside making him even harder—if that was possible.

"Yes," she said huskily. "Take me out here." She reached down, her hand covering his, and pushed the crotch of her underwear aside, her juiciness exposed for him.

Marc exhaled forcefully. "Then sit on me, *now*," he ordered in a growl. She complied, bending her knees until his tip grazed her entrance, and they both groaned at the contact. She circled her hips as he guided his thick length into her, her wetness making her opening slippery. She wiggled side to side to take him in entirety, her flesh hugging him snuggly. He closed his eyes at the sensation; he thought he'd died and gone to a better place. "*Fuck*, this touch is so tight." He barely got the words out. Her grip on his cock enveloped him in warmth and comfort, pushing him to a

primal need. An animalistic sound escaped him, as he rested
his forehead on her back. He was taking deep breaths in an
attempt to calm himself. It had been way too long without her
and his body wanted to move at a racing speed to the finish
line.

"Kiss me, kitten," he commanded, and she turned her
head to receive his lips, her hand coming up to grasp the back
of his head as their tongues collided. His hands roamed up
the sides of her waist to her full breasts, fondling them,
pushing them together, and massaging. Then he squeezed her
sharp nipples, plucking as she arched into his hands. Her
moans transformed into groans and her lips went slack
against him.

She tore away from him, her breath ragged. "Marc, this is
too much. You're so deep—filling me up. I need to move *now!*"
She whined breathlessly. He grinned at her bossiness, and her
inability to even kiss him at this point.

"You sure, kitten? I've been so hard on; I don't think I can
be gentle."

"Oh my God, forget gentle. *Fuck me, now!*" Her voice was
shrill at her impatience.

"Yes, ma'am." He kissed her hard one last time then
grabbed her hair, making her back arch again, while the other
gripped her hip moving her up and down on him at a brutally
rapid speed. And damn it was insane perfection. Her own legs
pumped her body up and down on him, meeting his quick
pace, so he started to push her back and forth on him,
grinding into her clit. They both moaned and writhed, taking

what they needed from each other, Simran clutching his knees for anchor once more.

"I'm—I'm coming again," she shrieked, as she threw her head back, her body shuddering around him, and her panting becoming hiccup-like squeals. He felt her contractions along his length, squeezing him tighter and tighter as she fell apart. He grabbed her hips with both hands and ground up into her harder, as he came closer to his own release. She was leaning against his chest and her hands covered his own on her hips as she rode him, coasting high, her moans a sweet call for him to join her.

"Come to me, baby," she coaxed and he felt it explode, starting from the bottom of his spine up through his length, shooting hotly into her, his thighs tensing. He held her close as he continued to jerk his release forcefully up into her. Each grunt into the back of her velvety neck only magnified a pleasure that consumed him in a way he'd never experienced before—the connection both physically and emotionally to this woman overtaking his mind and his senses.

They were both gasping for air, the sweat on his forehead dampening her shoulder. "Fuck, baby, what *was* that?" Marc asked, his eyes starting to clear up from the bright stars that had pelted the inside of his eyelids only moments ago, his breathing still ragged. Her arms were wrapped over, holding them both.

"You don't know?" she asked breathy, laughing softly. He softly kissed her shoulder, nuzzling her neck. He knew. He just wanted to hear her say it. "Um, that was us losing control with each other, like we always do, *duh*."

"Ok, wise-ass." He chuckled, dropping more kisses along her shoulder. "Sims, sweetie, I really wanted to take our time and make love the first time we came together again."

She leaned back to kiss his cheek softly. "Oh, baby, this *is* how we make love." He shifted, pulling out of her, and maneuvered her so that she was still in his lap with her legs dangling over one side of him. She wrapped her arms around his neck and gave him a tender smile. "I'm sorry, but I wouldn't have it any other way." She rained soft kisses all over his face.

"You do not need to apologize for what we just did. I wouldn't have it any other way either," he murmured into her hair.

೧೨೧೨

Suddenly he spanked her thigh lightly. "Up," he said firmly. *Huh?* What was happening here?

"Marc—"

"Up, Sims." His tone held no argument to it. She scrambled to stand, her hands on her hips as she squinted at him. What was he doing ruining their incredible moment?

He stood up, placing one hand under her knees and the other around her lower back as he scooped her up, bridal style, cradling her to his body. She gasped and quickly slid her arms around his neck. He clearly had something in mind, his face taut and serious. But as he stood, his pants slipped down around his ankles. She started laughing. She couldn't help it.

"Fuck it, baby, I've got—" he stepped out of his pants, juggling her in his arms. "—A goal that I really plan on accomplishing." It was a wonder he didn't completely trip, taking them both down, while trying to get out of those pants and holding her. She gripped onto him and giggled even louder at the hilarity of it all.

"You won't be laughing when I'm done with you," he teased as he took long strides to the bedroom in just his shirt, socks, and boxer briefs, kicking the bedroom door open with purpose. She shivered in anticipation in his arms.

He moved to the bed, gently laying her down, and then just stepped back to stare, his eyes roving over her from head to toe, like he didn't even know where to begin. Obviously, she was still in her racy get-up, but no doubt with a freshly fucked look about her with hair even wilder, cheeks hot, and a light sheen of moisture covering her body.

He shook his head in wonder. "You are Goddamn *perfect.* I'm the luckiest man on the planet." Oh golly, was this his way of making love? It was a very, very good start. She started smiling, leaning up, reaching for him.

"No. Don't move a muscle. I'm making love to you if it's the last thing I ever do."

"Oh God, you're trying to kill yourself?" she asked incredulously, giggles starting to bubble up again. "Babe, you don't have to do that." The look he gave her squelched any humor in the situation. His mouth was set in a hard line of determination. So, she leaned back on her elbows to watch her own version of perfection as he finished undressing. First, he slowly unbuttoned his shirt and shrugged it off and she couldn't help licking her lips at the sight of his muscular chest with a sprinkling of hair, his wide, broad shoulders, and his six-pack that flexed under her stare. God, what a hunk of a man. She could see him already starting to harden again, the thick length pushing against his boxer briefs. What an insatiable beast. But, sheesh, he was her insatiable beast, and somehow she was becoming one, too. Her own stomach muscles clenched in response to him pulling his black boxer briefs completely off, along with his socks. He stood there eyeing her again, naked, his ice-blue eyes hooded, his hand fisting his cock, the muscles in his arm tensing as he groped himself. And she knew what he was doing—gauging if she was ready to take him again. She arched her back, her hands coming between her own legs, as she felt more wetness rush into her already sopping underwear. He lifted the corner of his mouth in that roguish one-sided grin and slowly came to kneel between her legs on the bed.

His hands caressed the undersides of her knees. "Are you ok?" She nodded. "Will you let me worship you, baby?" he pleaded lovingly. This man was her undoing. She would do anything for him, but his tenderness completely unwound her. She nodded again and he proceeded to unclip the stockings from her garter belt, kissing and licking his way down each leg as his warm hands slowly slid them off with her shoes. He kissed each toe, then licked the arches of her feet adoringly, his bright eyes watching her reaction. Her head fell back onto the pillow, her eyes closed as she enjoyed the pleasure he was bestowing.

His big, hard body moved up her own, dragging his cock along her thighs as he helped her remove her teddy, her breasts spilling out. He cupped them, squeezing firmly, holding them in the perfect position for him to lavish with attention, gently pulling a nipple into his mouth as he sucked and nipped. She bowed into him, her hands coming to thread through his silky, thick locks, holding him to her. The pleasure ignited throughout her down to between her legs. He moved to her other breast to do the same, and her hips bucked up into him. She moaned in absolute surrender, and he answered back with his own groan of appreciation.

"My goddess," he said before he moved down her body, his tongue leaving a warm trail of worship. As he started pushing her thong down, he paused, staring at her hips. She heard him inhale sharply. Oh crap, he was seeing the bruises from her surgery for the first time. She didn't love them, but they were there for good. She hoped he didn't think they were ugly. His warm fingers came up to brush the dime-sized dark spots below each hip bone, then he bent his head to kiss each one. He looked up at her, as if reading her mind, his eyes so warm, so intense. "Flawless, my sweet Sims." Emotion overcame her, tears springing to her eyes, as he kissed her belly button, dipping his tongue into the crevice. He finished sliding her underwear and garter belt off, then came to lay on top of her, his cock resting in her sensitive mound. He bent down to kiss her, his tongue sliding into her mouth as he circled his hips, and she felt his thick length teasing her. He continued kissing her, and grinding sensually into her pelvis, and she reciprocated, the slow pace building her arousal even further. She swept her hands along his warm skin, up his sides, over his muscular buttocks, and up his back, finally holding him to her as she arched her body up to his, needing there to be no space between them.

"I'm the lucky one," she whispered against his lips, shivering at the knowledge that this man was all hers. "I need you, baby." She writhed against him, opening her legs wider, giving him access to her.

He kissed the tip of her nose. "Are you ready, sweetie?" He asked gently, positioning himself so he could start sliding into her wetness. She nodded, and he gradually entered her until he could go no further. He paused so they could feel the sensation, the completeness of being connected. He stared down at her tenderly.

"This is my favorite place to be, Sims." Good God, the man was taking no prisoners with his love-making. She reached up and cupped his face, pulling his lips down to hers. He rested his body on both of his elbows on either side of her, their bodies flush, and started pumping into her unhurriedly, pulling almost all the way out, then pushing all the way back in, over and over again.

It was a gliding pleasure that was putting her into an erotic, love trance, her body relaxed, but the intensity building in her core. Her moans were starting to turn into heavy pants, as his length slid smoothly in and out, hitting her in just the right way. Her hips moved up to meet his, gyrating slowly in sync, and his tongue moved to the same rhythm in and out of her mouth.

They continued like this for moments, lost in languidly making love to each other, their hands stroking each other's bodies. He put an arm under her and lifted her ass off the mattress, adjusting his position so he could drive her crazy, but kept his pace slow. And, holy Krishna, the new position bumped and caressed that spot that drove her bonkers. Her breathing turned into high-pitch whimpers now, while their bodies suctioned together in stickiness. She gripped his shoulders tight while she wrapped her legs around his torso and writhed even more quickly against him. She was going to come hard again.

"Baby, that's it. Fall apart in my arms, I've got you." He exhaled, as he sensed her impending release, and he continued to thrust, while she lunged her hips up to him more forcefully.

Their pace started to quicken, and her body started to quiver, as he buried his face into her neck. All of a sudden her muscles shuddered forcefully inside and around him, and she detonated like a love bomb, her eyes widening, then closing. "Yes!," she screamed. "Holy Durga, mother of the fucking universe, I love you, I love you, I *love you!*" she yelled at the top of her lungs, the rawness of her passion for this man making her tears fall freely down her face. His lips were on her cheeks, tenderly kissing her, as he continued to pump in and out of her then she heard that sexy animal-like growl of his in her ear as he started to gain speed. She could still feel the aftershocks of her pleasure as wave after wave washed over her and she pulsed deliciously around him, moaning. Then his arms tensed, his body stiffened, and his hot release poured into her as he continued to grind into her, as if he wanted to impale her all the way through with his dick. She held him tight and hugged him close as he finally collapsed on top of her, his breathing hot and heavy in her neck. She felt whole with this man inside her, her body around his.

"Marc, that was ... I have no words," she breathed, her brain a complete fog.

He lifted his head to look at her, his forehead sweaty, and his eyes moist, clearly as overcome as she was. "I want to hear you shout you love me from the rooftops every single day, my sweet Sims."

"Hm, you'll get tired of it—"

"No. It'll never get old." He chuckled a little bashfully as he uttered this, while a tear escaped onto his cheek.

Surprised, her hand shook as it came up to swipe away the wetness lovingly. Then she felt his own fingers wipe her own, which she'd forgotten had rolled down her cheeks into her ears while lost in ecstasy a few moments ago.

"Oh my God, look at us. We're a bunch of crying cheeseballs in love," she laughed, feeling like her heart was going to burst. Was there any better feeling than this?

Marc pulled out of her carefully and adjusted them so that he was on his back with her snuggled next to him, one of her legs firmly wrapped over him. "Listen, if it's wrong to be a bunch of cheeseballs in love, then I don't ever intend to be right." His tone was gentle, but firm. "Now, kitten," he asked with extreme seriousness, "tell me about this mother of the universe. Is she aware that you yell out her name when my dick is inside you?" His fingers were grazing the side of her waist before they danced into her armpit starting to tickle her.

"You've ruined the love-making moment with your big dick talk," she uttered, between laughs, when she could come up for air.

"I never said my dick was big." His grin was devilish as he wiggled his brows at her. Simran shook her head. The man was just so full of himself, and she had nothing but love for him.

They spent the night in each other's arms, alternating between talking and lovemaking. They moved from the bed to the shower, back to the bed again, only to come up for air and order room service late in the night. They snuggled by the fire in robes and sipped wine, feeding each other bites of their meals. It was passionate, romantic, and perfect—exactly how Simran wanted their first night back together to be.

But just before she could fall asleep content in his arms, she heard a ping come from her phone. She pulled out of his hold carefully so as not to disturb him and read the text message.

Anil: "Hey, Sima! Still on for brunch tomorrow? How about 11 am? Looking forward to seeing you. I've missed you."

Chapter 22

The next morning, she reluctantly left her beautiful man sleeping peacefully in bed to go shower. She needed to be up, ready and alert for when she met with Anil.

She cringed as she took one last look at Marc in bed, splayed wide on his back, muscular chest rising and falling, full lips parted as he slept peacefully. How peaceful would he be when he found out about this? Anil had texted her the previous day and they hadn't confirmed a time until late in the evening. They were meeting for brunch at his parent's condo where he was currently staying.

She came out of the shower, drying herself with a white plush towel, and she startled, her pulse racing. Leaning in the doorway was her man, wearing just his boxer briefs and an adorable grin. Light and dark blond hair was a floppy mess making him utterly boyish. That smile started to slowly turn wicked as he watched her wrap the towel around herself.

"Being a pervert again?" she teased, the butterflies swirling in her stomach, making her cheeks heat up. This would never get old would it; when you flirted with the person you were in love with?

His grin widened. "Only you make me a pervert. Now the real question is," and he came in, backing her against the counter, "why are you getting so cleaned up, sweetcheeks? I'm only going to dirty you up again." His hands landed on either side of her, trapping her. Her heart more than fluttered, and her loins woke up ready to get busy as her pelvis instinctively met his. She looked up at his handsome face, fingering his dimpled chin as his mouth came down swiftly on hers, gently coaxing hers open so his tongue could find hers.

When they broke apart for air a few moments later, she realized her towel had slipped so that her bare breasts were pressed into his chest. Crap, it felt good and she tried to hide the moan that escaped her. Shouldn't she be a little uncomfortable today? They'd went at it like bunnies last night, and considering she hadn't been with this sex god in months, her nether regions should need a rest. But right now, she actually ached for him to fill her up again; she could feel the pulse beating between her legs. Discipline, Simran, she scolded herself. You can have your way with him when you get this Anil conversation over with.

Marc's hand roamed up to cup a breast while the other slid underneath her towel to grab her ass, making her gasp and arch against him.

"See what I mean, sweetcheeks?" he asked, his eyes hooded now with lust while she felt him start to harden against her stomach.

"Marc, wait. I have to tell you something." She adjusted her towel, pulling it back over her breasts, trying to dampen the growing desire.

"What's that, sweetie?" He leaned down to kiss her neck gently, dropping feathery kisses along her collar bone. "Was I too rough last night? Are you ok?" Now he was concerned and he pushed himself away to arm's length, examining her from head to toe with a sharp eye.

"No. Oh my God, no, nothing like that." Her hand came up to finger his chest. "Um, I have to go. I have an appointment this morning."

He cocked his head to one side, an eyebrow quirked. "So, no breakfast on the veranda?" His face had fallen as if he was a little boy whose balloon had flown away. Eating breakfast on the balcony had become their morning ritual while here and one they were getting comfortable with in the past week.

"So, what is it?" Now he was really looking at her with alarm, his eyebrows climbing his forehead and he was trying to reach for her again.

"I'm meeting Anil for breakfast." His arms dropped; his mouth open, speechless. "I'm sorry, babe, I didn't get a chance to tell you last night. We were texting before you got home and ... given the direction the night went—" She caught the stoniness of his face before he turned sharply away, adjusting the waistband of his underwear.

"You were texting with him before I got back? Before we made love?" Although he appeared stone cold, the hurt in his voice was unmistakable.

"Babe..." She tried to wrap her arms around his stiffened body. He didn't reciprocate. Her arms fell away, giving him space. "Well, not *right* before, but, yesterday, yes. I had that sexy surprise for you and I didn't want to screw it up with talks of my ex-boyfriend." Ugh, what a mistake. She should've found a way to mention it.

"And you're just telling me now?" he asked coolly. He started to leave the bathroom, and she grasped his arm.

"Hey, wait. Where are you going? You're mad."

He turned back to her, his hand running through his hair, his jaw ticking. "Yeah, I'm mad." His voice was stiff. Gone was playful Marc.

"Why? When would I have told you last night? Between our incredible love-making, or in between bites of chocolate-covered strawberries in front of the fire? That would have messed up the mood—"

"Shit, Sims. I don't know, I just would have appreciated a heads up at a time other than right before you're about to leave to see him." His arms were crossed over his chest now. "What time are you meeting him?"

"In about an hour."

"All right, give me some time to dress. I'll come with you." He moved past her to start the shower.

Now she was dumbfounded. "Wait, what? No, you're not. I need to do this on my own." What was he thinking? She saw his jaw clench again.

"Simran, I'm not letting you go talk with your ex-boyfriend by yourself; the man your dad wants you to marry; the man who probably thinks you're meeting him to throw yourself at him and say 'yes' to his proposal." Her mouth dropped open. *Was he being serious!?*

"First of all, 'let'? I don't need your permission to see an old friend. Second, I would never throw myself at anyone, not even *you*," she said in exasperation, trying her hardest not to roll her eyes at him. She knew he was hurt about this. "And third," she softened her tone, "it'll be better this way, Marc. Don't you think your presence would be like pouring salt into an open wound?" She met his eyes, hers pleading, his icy. But she noticed that he must be working out what she'd just said, as his hardened look started to defrost.

With pursed lips, he reached over to shut off the water. Then he came to lean his backside up against the counter beside her while she reached for her hair products. He watched her rake her fingers through her hair and distribute the creams throughout the strands.

"What?" she finally asked, breaking the silence.

"You're right, Sims. I'm sorry. I just ... well, after last night, I can't even think of you seeing your ex. It makes me want to punch something." Simran smiled in understanding. She'd be jealous, too, if he was going to see a past lover.

"Noted. A punching bag is on your Christmas list. Heck, Diwali is starting soon, I'll get you one then."

His grin was lopsided. "Listen, I just want you to know that I'm here for you. I could go with you if you like—" He put his hands up in surrender before she could protest again. "But I respect that this is something you have to do on your own."

"Thank you," she said quietly, reaching for her toothbrush.

He continued, "I know you have a lot going on, Sims. But I wanted to ask you something over breakfast and seeing as how we aren't going to enjoy each other's company this morning, well, here goes. I want you to think about moving in with me when we get back to New York."

She stopped mid brush, her toothpaste-filled mouth agape, her eyes big. The man was off his rocker, there was no other explanation.

"I have plenty of space on my yacht." He shrugged with a blinding smile. "Fuck, let's 'Rock the Boat' every single day."

"Marc!" she wailed around the burning spearmint. She quickly spit and rinsed. "What the hell? You can't just spring this on me right now!"

"Why not? I didn't know you were meeting your *ex-boyfriend* today. I'd planned on asking you this morning." He crossed one ankle over the other, continuing to lean on the counter, his blinding smile down a few wattages now.

She huffed out a big sigh. "Ok, he has a name. Let's be grown-ups, shall we, and just start using it from now on. And I already told you I didn't have time to tell you yesterday. We got caught up in our beautiful night. I didn't mean for this to be such a surprise. But you can't just ask me to move in as a reaction to me going to see Anil."

His huff of exasperation filled the room. "As I said, I was planning on asking you before I knew you were meeting *Anil.*" He pulled her to him, holding her close. "Simran, I promise I'm not asking you because I feel doubtful about how you'll be with him. I trust you. I'm asking you because I want to be able to come home to you, sleep in your arms, wake up next to you, sometimes in you." She chuckled. "This short time here in India has been a peek into something in our future that I can't wait to get started. I don't want to be separated from you again when we get back to NY. I love you, baby." Simran melted into him, his words wrapping around her heart, and she hugged him, while her brain started listing off every reason to be wary of this. He was moving quickly, especially for a man who lacked commitment in the past.

"I love you, too," she said softly against him. "And I've also loved our time here in India. It's been so special. But are we really ready for that next step?" She looked up at him. His lips pursed, thinking, and then he frowned, obviously thrown by her answer.

"Why did I think you would say 'yes'?" he asked, his brow furrowed. "Nothing is ever easy with you, is it?" He was teasing, but they both knew there was some truth there.

She reached up to smooth his brows. "I didn't say 'no,' did I? Let's just see how we feel when we get to New York. I don't like the idea of being apart from you either but we just reconnected," she reminded him. She hated being the "level-headed" one in the relationship. Why *couldn't* they just throw caution to the wind and jump into living together? Because, although he'd freely admitted he trusted her, she still needed time to completely trust him again, a small part of her admitted in the furthest corner of her brain. "And anyway, who says I want to live on your boat? *If* we move in together, we'd have to find a new place," she said, trying to ease the sting of not saying 'yes' immediately.

"Hmm, we'll see," he said, seemingly satisfied with her answer and kissing the top of her head. He backed out of the bathroom grinning, heading straight back to bed, the lucky bastard.

Chapter 23

Simran slid into the backseat of Marc's car which had been waiting for her outside of Anil's condo for the past two hours. That meeting went exactly the opposite of what she was expecting. She motioned for Akash to return to the hotel and stared out the window blindly, a little shook.

When she'd arrived at Anil's family's condo, in the same neighborhood of Bandra West where her dad's home was, she was nervous and she didn't know why. Maybe it was because Anil always reminded her of her father and she felt like a truant child telling him she didn't want to marry him, wanting the chance to choose her own life. Her stomach grumbled loudly on the way up to the thirtieth floor where their floor-length duplex was. Oh God, shut up, she told it. She needed her brain to be on point and it usually took a backseat when her stomach monster emerged.

She rang the doorbell and he immediately opened the door in a wide flourish, a humongous grin on his face. She forgot how cute he was. He was tall for the average Indian man, standing at about five feet, ten inches. He'd always had a stocky build, but after all these years, she could tell he'd filled out with more well-defined muscles. His thick, almost black hair was buzzed on the sides, with longer waves on top. He was attractive with what one might call a babyface, his rounded cheeks puffing up with whatever emotion he was feeling, and expressive hazel eyes fringed with thick, long lashes. Though good-looking on the outside, she knew there was an ugliness lurking beneath the surface; his cheating side. And to her, that would always affect how she viewed him; the attractiveness forever marred.

"*Sima*! My God! You are as beautiful as ever! How are you, my sweet?" he asked, engulfing her in a bear hug. He let go and took his time sizing her up in her casual white, off-the-shoulder t-shirt, tucked into faded wide leg jeans and wedge sandals. She hadn't put too much make-up on, nor fussed too much with her hair. She wanted to ensure she appeared like she wasn't trying anything with him.

"Hungry, Anil. Hungry," she said smiling, trying to keep things light. "You promised me brunch."

He threw his head back, laughing boisterously. "You're right. Come along, I have a veritable feast waiting for you." He led her into the spacious apartment, through the luxurious dining room that could easily seat twenty, toward the intimate breakfast nook tucked in the corner of the living room. She remembered having numerous meals here with his parents when they were together years ago.

He pulled a chair out for her, and then went over to the other side. "Please, go on. I know your stomach is going to start yelling soon if you don't," he commented smiling. He started serving himself from the numerous platters of Belgian waffles, bacon, eggs, toast, fruit, and coffee. No traditional Indian breakfast item in sight, Simran thought a little sadly.

She remembered their cook made a mean masala omelet, which was one of her favorite dishes. She helped herself to a waffle and fruit anyway, while he poured them coffee. They ate in silence for a while, and when her stomach was satiated, she put her fork down and cleared her throat.

"Anil, we need to talk, remember?"

He smiled around his full mouth, swallowing, then took a long sip of his coffee. "Yes, *Shona*, we do," he answered gently, calling her by his pet name from so long ago. It meant 'lovely one' in Hindi. Simran inwardly cringed. *Oh Jeez.* Was this going to be harder than she initially thought? What had she expected? Dumping someone was always difficult unless you were a cold-hearted snake.

He wiped his mouth with his napkin and cleared his throat before saying, "So, we can't do this."

At the same time, she said, "Anil, I can't marry you." His hazel eyes went round in surprise, and she saw his full, almost feminine lips, make a perfect "O."

They eyed each other warily, trying to decipher if they'd heard the other correctly. Then they both started laughing.

"Oh, thank God," Anil said, with a relieved smile.

"Wait, wasn't this also your idea? Didn't you want to get married to me?" Simran was absolutely confused right now. She'd been under the impression that this scheme was something her father *and* Anil cooked up together.

"*Shona*, I..." He fiddled with his coffee mug, and stroked one of his sideburns, a nervous tick of his. "I'm actually..." he looked up and his eyes met hers, "already married."

Simran sat back in her chair in amazement, completely at a loss for words.

"I'm sorry, Sima. The woman I met years ago—her name is Marlene—I loved her then and I love her now. We got married in a private ceremony last year in Berlin before I moved back to Mumbai to work for your father again."

Simran started to splutter.

Anil continued quickly, oblivious to the relief that Simran was feeling, likely worried that her reaction was because she might still feel slighted. "My parents know nothing about it. They think I've been a bachelor, sowing my wild oats in Europe before your dad offered me this incredible opportunity last year to rejoin his company. She and I have been doing long-distance these past months and it's been awful. I miss her like crazy. I need to tell my parents, and your father, because I pain her every day with the knowledge that she's a secret to my family." He frowned, with his round cheeks drooping sadly.

Simran sat forward. "Oh my God, Anil. I am so freaking relieved. You have no idea," she said grinning wide and grabbing his hand to squeeze it.

Now he looked confused. "You are?"

"Yes!" She breathed out. "I mean, not because you're upset about keeping your wife a secret. That totally sucks. But I'm completely in love with someone else, too."

"You are?" he asked again, his face perking up, his cheeks bubbling out as he started to smile. "Wait, is this with that playboy, Marcus Lehigh?" he asked suspiciously.

Simran rolled her eyes.

"Don't roll your eyes at me, *Shona*," Anil said firmly. Simran sat back flabbergasted again. It was funny how she'd never noticed before, but his intonation with her nickname was more like a big brother to a little sister, rather than lover to lover. When had that happened? Things about their past together were starting to click firmly in her head. "Will he treat you like you deserve?" Anil asked, interrupting her thoughts. "I worked with him in India, you know. Great guy, successful businessman, but his attitude with women…" Anil trailed off and looked away embarrassed, his hand waving at some unspoken notion in the air.

"He's changed, Anil. But, how did you know about us?" was all she could muster, even though she still had one million questions she needed answered.

Anil started chuckling and served her another waffle and topped off her coffee. "That man makes it into worldwide news no matter how great his PR team thinks they are. And you know my dirty habit of reading the rag mags. You showed up a few times in there, too, you know."

"I heard, from Tina," she commented dryly.

"Ah, Bettina. How is she?"

"Don't change the subject, Anil. We need to figure this out." She put her forehead in her hands. "My dad thinks that you're on his side about this marriage, which is to say that your parents are of the same mind, correct?"

"Yes, correct," he said a little morosely. "Sima, I don't need to figure this out. I'm going to tell them outright that this is a fucking—pardon my language—joke. You and I, we've never been like some of these other Indians, needing our parents to not only guide us, but force-feed us our life decisions—"

"Excuse me, Anil, but I think you've had it a little better than me, a female—a daughter—that my dad thinks too silly to run my own business or make my own choices."

"That's not true, *Shona*," he said vehemently.

She leaned her chin in her hand on the table. "Ok, tell me then, how hard did the firstborn son have it where his parents thought he could do no wrong, even when he cheated on his almost fiancé years ago."

Anil looked up sharply. "You have it all wrong, Sima. I never promised you marriage, did I? I never said those words. I had to be in Germany for a few years working, and I didn't expect you to wait for me. Regardless of that, toward the end, you were more like a sister to me. Surely, you felt it at some point, too? I didn't fully see it until I met Marlene. I realized there was no hunger between us for each other in that manner."

Shit, even though there had clearly been some miscommunication between them, Simran knew Anil was right. Even though she'd thought she was in love, it'd been her first real relationship, and her father had played a huge role in pushing them together. And compared to what she and Marc had now? Well ... there was no comparison. Nothing came close to the connection and passion she held for Marc. They just fit; two halves coming together who now knew they were meant to be from the moment they met.

She didn't want to argue about the past and Anil went on, shaking his head. "And you don't think I had it hard? I was the first-born son. I *had* to be perfect. I *had* to get high marks in school and then university." He wagged his pointer finger in the air, mimicking the deep tone and accent of his father perfectly. "No son of mine will major in the theater! What kind of BS is this? You will work for your Kumar Uncle, as we've discussed since you were young," he huffed out angrily, his puffed-up cheeks scarlet. "Do you see? I didn't think I had a choice with my career. *Bas.* Let them make that decision." His hand waved in finality. "Working for your father hasn't been bad at all for me. I actually enjoy it and the travel. But choosing my bride, my future? No." He banged his hand on the small breakfast table, making the dishes clatter loudly and Simran hopped in her seat. She never knew he felt this way.

"I'm sorry, Anil. I had no idea. But ... theater? Really?"

Anil smiled shyly. "Yes. I really fell in love with it during Senior Secondary School. I needed to fill a social arts requirement and theater was the only thing available. It was one of the best classes I took that year. I even acted in a few plays." Why hadn't she known about any of this? She and Anil hadn't really known each other at all. He'd taken her to a few plays in Mumbai but she'd never known he'd wanted to actually act, too.

With breakfast finished now, and their older servant clearing the table, giving Simran a toothy grin in recognition, they moved to the living room and sat on the overstuffed sofa.

"Well, Anil, I have to say, I'm surprised as hell at how this conversation is going." His brow furrowed. He'd never liked her cursing. "So, what do we do, now?"

"How about we talk about things that are a little lighter and we'll circle back to this topic?"

"Good idea."

She filled him in on her business, her friends, and her love of NY. And she learned about what he'd been up to in Germany after they parted, how his career had him move around and finally end up back in Mumbai. He talked about his wife, his eyes distant and soft, the love and admiration for her apparent. And she told him about Marc and how they'd recently reunited after some time apart, aware that they had a special love and connection. She explained how he was not just the successful, powerful man he seemed to the public. He had a warm, empathetic side and he really understood her, pushed her to continue to be who she was. She knew deep down he was her future, but she was still wrapping her head around how that was going to look.

"Ah, yes." Anil nodded in agreement. "Women still fall all over him, don't they?" He looked at Simran curiously. "Have you really not seen posts about him on the internet or social media sites? The fact that he's in India alone has 'Mumbai Stud Alert Sighting' blowing up."

"Are you serious?" Simran's mouth was agape. "You know I was never one for gossip like that ... but how do *you* know about that?" Why was Anil following such a sleazy gossip site?

"Ah Sima, when you're in the entertainment business, you have to be smart about where you can locate new client leads. You know I already read the rag mags, but sometimes you have to delve into even deeper, more sordid places. Did you know that I sniffed out Marcus and his partner as prospective clients on that specific site years ago? They were a major success story for us, so I keep my eyes on it."

"Well, sheesh. Thanks for the tip. I usually leave that kind of client hunting to my staff."

"Absolutely," Anil agreed. "So, what are your plans this evening? Would you and Marcus like to come with me to try a new street vendor I just heard about? He's doing his own version of *vada paav* (spiced potato patty on a bun) and is actually putting yellow mustard and ketchup and an American-style special sauce on it, sweet relish and all. What will they think of next?" he said, throwing his hands up, laughing hysterically.

Simran smiled, remembering Anil's love of strange mash-ups in the food world. She shook her head. "Maybe next time, Anil. We have plans to meet with some friends at Club Sundar Social tonight. Maybe we can get together one day, you, your wife, me and Marc?"

"Ah, Marcus' club. Beautiful space, for beautiful people." He smiled warmly at her. "Yes, I would really like that. And no problem about tonight." He gave her a serious look now. "Ok, now, about our parents ... Sima, I have to be truthful, we need to tell them. I'm going to do it, perhaps even tonight." He gave that South Asian head bob. "You should tell Uncle soon, too. Don't hide it from him. The quicker it's done, the quicker everyone can gossip amongst themselves and then come to terms with it."

"I do plan on telling him, I'm just not sure when," she said, anxious even thinking about approaching her dad. All arrows led to telling him, she just didn't know if she was ready.

"Soon, *Shona*. Do it soon, before you lose your nerve."

Chapter 24

As soon as the door closed behind Simran, Marc got out of bed. He couldn't just lie there thinking about her with her ex. He threw some workout shorts on and a t-shirt. He put on his running shoes and went down to the gym. He needed to pound out his frustrations on the treadmill. He couldn't believe Simran had kept this from him. Did she still not trust him? Weren't they an official couple now? He knew last night had been momentous for both of them. He'd never felt such a connection, something so real, almost tangible with another person. But she could have mentioned something so poignant to him at some point.

He entered the gym, grabbed a towel, and headed straight for the treadmills. He hit the button at a high speed and just ran. He'd forgotten his music in his hurry, which irritated him further because now he was alone with his thoughts and the pounding of his feet on the hard surface.

Had he been trying to throw her when he asked her to move in with him? A small part of him acknowledged some truth to that. But even if his timing stunk, he still wanted it, so it couldn't be all bad, could it?

After almost an hour of nonstop running—his mind also sprinting in circles—he cooled off and headed over to the coffee bar to grab a bite to eat, water, and some caffeine. The sweat ran down his neck and made his shirt cling to his torso. People stared as he waited at the counter for his to-go black coffee, and egg sandwich, drumming his fingers anxiously, but shit, he didn't care. When his food was ready, he decided to sit at one of the bistro tables and eat, not ready to go back to their suite. He grabbed a stack of international papers to peruse, really trying to keep the idea of Simran with Anil off his mind.

He got back to the suite a little later and just stood there, not sure what to do with himself now. He moved to the desk with his laptop to check his emails. Work was always a good distractor.

Unexpectedly, the door opened swiftly, banging the wall behind it and Simran bustled in. She caught sight of him, dropped her purse, and ran to him, throwing herself into his arms. He caught her, and her legs straddled around his waist, her arms around his neck, where her face was buried. She inhaled deeply making him chuckle. What was she smelling so enthusiastically, he wondered? He was sweaty and probably reeked from his hard run.

"What?" she asked, her face peering up at him, beaming.

"Sims, I'm as sweaty as a pig, and you're inhaling me like I'm a bouquet of spring flowers." She smiled radiantly and the anxiety he felt previously began to trickle away.

"I like pigs," she teased. "You'll always smell good to me, Marc. Like home, like I belong here." And she put her face back in his neck, inhaling deeply again, not giving a shit that his sweat was soaking her shirt. He carried her to the bedroom and gently laid her down on her back, rolling to his side, propped up on an elbow.

"You do belong here." He took her hand and placed it over his heart where its beat picked up speed just being with her. She clutched his shirt and her eyes teared up. "Hell, Simran, what's going on? Are you ok? Did Anil say something to hurt you?" Now he was getting more than anxious again; he was getting fucking angry. She cupped his face with her cool hands, smiling tearfully.

"No. Nothing like that. I'm really just thankful that things turned out the way they have," she said, her voice wobbly. Was she going to start crying? He saw her swallow hard. "You'll never guess what happened in a million years, though." She yawned loudly. He wordlessly gathered her into his arms and held her to him, inhaling her floral, spicy scent that he loved so much.

"Tell me then," he murmured into her hair. What the fuck had happened with her ex?

"Anil is already married. He fell in love with the German chick and secretly married her," she said sleepily.

Marc pushed back from her to see if she was serious. Her eyes were closed, and she had a dreamy smile on her lips. "I'm sorry, babe; I'm just so tired. Someone kept me up all night with his wicked ways..." She poked him in the chest.

"Seriously, Sims?!" Nothing could hide the elation in his voice. He grinned ear to ear as her eyes popped open, then slowly started to droop again. But he needed more information, stat. He shook her lightly.

"Seriously, Marc. You boinked me bad last night." She sighed and rolled over, fully knowing that wasn't what he was asking. "Now let me get some rest so we can do it all over again tonight." He leaned in and kissed her forehead, noticing that she was already fast asleep. He could relate. He was mentally exhausted, too, but he felt at ease, knowing that Anil Patel wouldn't stand in their way. Now Kumar Khan ... what was that conversation going to look like?

⁂

He left her napping, having helped her pull her shoes and jeans off, and tucking her in. She wore a sleepy smile on her face and just turned over, burying herself further into the sheets. She didn't seem to show any signs of anxiety or melancholy. Her emotional state about the miscarriage had been a worry for him since he'd found out days ago. He even called his mom for some advice. She'd recommended ensuring there weren't any other stressors in Simran's life and watching for any deep downward mood spirals. Her going to speak with Anil could have gone very badly if the guy had been expecting her to be his wife.

He showered and got dressed, poking his head into the bedroom to check on her. She was still asleep, snoring softly. Good. He went out to the living room looking for his phone. Something had caught his attention in the papers earlier and he needed to speak with Bruce.

His friend didn't pick up immediately. Marc was in the process of texting him when he called him back.

"There he is! How's life, Romeo?" Bruce's cheerful voice boomed before Marc could even say hello. He broke into a smile. It was good to hear his friend's voice.

"Pretty great, actually. I got my girl back." And his smile got wider. His whole chest expanded at the thought of having Simran back. And hell, the woman was right in the next room, and yet he missed her, tamping down the urge to go jump into bed with her. He shook his head with a goofy grin on his face.

"Fuck yeah! That's what I'm talking about and thank God, too, because that sad sack act was getting *really* sad," Bruce chuckled over the phone.

"Well, don't go celebrating yet. We still have her dad to contend with."

"Ah, the captain of *Unified Entertainment Solutions*. What are the fucking odds that the company we worked with to open Club Sundar Social belongs to her dad? And that dude, what's his name, something Patel was her ex-boyfriend!? The world is hella smaller than we think."

"I know. And get this, her dad wants her to marry him."

"What!? Talk to me. How is that possible? They haven't been together in years."

He explained everything to Bruce; the whole arranged marriage, transferring of finances, tying-the-families-together-for-the-security-of-everyone-involved kind of thing that still happened in India.

"Yeah. Things are still done like that in some parts of Latin America (Bruce's father was Salvadorian). Shit, what're you going to do?"

"Well, she just went to talk with Anil this morning to explain that her dad's wishes aren't her own. But, get this, she found out he's already married to the girl he cheated on her with. Fell in love while working in Germany."

"No shit? That romantic little turd. At least you don't have to worry about him."

"Exactly. Now the father ... I'm still trying to convince Sims to be honest with him, talk to him while here."

"Be patient with her, brother. She's been through a lot." Marc was surprised at Bruce's empathy, fully expecting a sexual innuendo which was his modus operandi when things got serious. "But she's also fucking exhausted. You've been doing a shit ton of make-up banging, am I right?" There it was.

"Man, I swear, if some woman ever stoops low enough to give you a shot, your brain needs an enema. Why are you always such a fucking horn dog?" Marc asked exasperated.

Bruce blustered loudly. "If a woman gives me a shot? You gotta be kidding me. I'll never enter into that kind of emotional bullshit. You're a head trip enough for the both of us." Bruce had a point, but he wouldn't trade the fullness he felt with Simran back in his life for anything. The head trip moments were preferential to not having her at all. He'd already tried that before and it sucked balls.

Marc caught himself utilizing Simran's trademark eyeroll. Yep, he was whipped. "Whatever, man. It'll hit you over the head when you least expect it and you'll have no choice, I repeat, NO CHOICE, but to go with it because you won't even be able to function."

There was a long pause. Finally, Bruce commented, "Sure, man," absolutely unconvinced.

March changed the subject because he didn't want to discuss how crazy he felt these days. "So, how's your bride? Read in the papers that you have that situation figured out, finally." The headline he'd read earlier alluded to a previous mess of Bruce's (just one of many), from last year, where he'd had an affair with a South American woman who just happened to be the one and only child and heiress to the wealthiest, most ruthless mob boss in South America. Bruce, unaware of it at the time—because the guy never took anything seriously—had been drunk on her sensuality, no doubt, along with Cointreau the entire time he was with her. The two managed to party their way across the continent, then somehow ended up married. Of course, when vacation time was over, Bruce wanted a divorce. He'd served her papers, but her father was very determined in getting involved with Bruce's American business dealings. He'd made things very difficult for him, including scaring the shit out of Bruce one night with his goons. Marc was not only concerned for their business, but was worried that Bruce would get hurt, if not murdered if he couldn't get out of this mess. Somehow Bruce did get himself out, his lawyers and a boatload of money obviously involved.

"Eh, we finally agreed on a settlement. *Fuck*, that was legit a shit-show."

"Well, I'm glad to hear that. I'm relieved for you, man. That was pretty intense and could have ended badly. Can we both agree that you need to cool it with the playboy lifestyle?"

"Don't worry, *LC Enterprises* is safe and sound."

"No man. I don't want you hurt, or worse, getting your head blown off. You seriously had me worried there."

Silence again from Bruce. "Thanks, brother," he said a little sheepishly. Good. Bruce needed to feel like an idiot at times because he sure the hell acted like one.

He cleared his throat and filled Marc in on updates of their Vancouver club—things were finally looking up. And then he mentioned that he stopped by Marc's Lower East Side gallery.

"The space is incredible, Marc. Simran has excellent taste."

"Hey, thanks, and yeah, she does," Marc said surprised. "I really couldn't have pulled it off without her."

"Sure, yeah." There was a pause on the other end and some throat clearing. "By the way, what's the woman's name who's running things there?"

Marc wracked his brain. Simran had initially been over-seeing things. Then put someone else in charge temporarily when she needed to recuperate from surgery and come to India. If Marc remembered correctly, the woman was a childhood friend of Simran's, from her Connecticut South Asian community.

"I can't remember. Why?" Marc asked cautiously.

"Well, she was giving off these vibes, and shit, I couldn't help it. I banged her in the bathroom. It was hot as fuck. Actually, come to think of it, she banged me... Gorgeous bathroom by the way," Bruce said cheekily.

"*Jesus Christ*, Bruce, can't you keep it in your pants?" Marc did not need to hear this right now. He pinched the bridge of his nose. "How many times?"

"Shit, Marc, I don't really like to kiss and tell—"

"No, you bonehead. Was it just the time in the gallery bathroom, or have you seen her again?" Simran was already dealing with a lot. She didn't need to know that a good friend of hers had ridden the Bruce rail, hard. Her opinion of his best friend and the way he discarded women was already low.

"Just the one time, I swear. But it was … well fuck, I don't know … different but in an exceptional way," he guffawed. "And I tried, brother, I really did try to stay away from her." There was a pause as Marc waited for him to go on. "Ok, I didn't," he said chuckling. "She was on fire and needed it bad. You know how I get with women who are just begging for it. Señor Canyon takes over and I have no choice but to let him take the lead. And, come on, don't tell me you wouldn't have done the same thing not too long ago. How about the time you met your fine lady?" Bruce said pointedly. True; by the time Marc met Simran, he'd already toned his playboy behavior down by many notches, but he'd absolutely wanted her immediately. He could tell she needed it bad, and, honestly, *he* needed her bad.

"Well, just keep it to the one time. And no more screwing in my gallery's bathroom." He chuckled inwardly. The fact that Bruce actually wanted to find out the woman's name was interesting, and completely out of character. But he didn't want to get into it with him right now. "Listen, I'm hanging up now. Just be good. It's probably not the best idea to go sniffing around in dangerous terrain given your track record." And he hung up before Bruce could say anything further on the matter.

Chapter 25

Simran looked herself over in the full-length mirror, taking a peek at her exposed back. She was wearing her hot, new, black number and felt on top of the world. On her feet were her super high, gold braided stilettos with flirty tassels on them, which she'd purchased for just this look. She moved her feet around, loving the shimmer and how the woven straps hugged her feet and up around her ankles. Were shoes sexy? Hell yes, and she felt like Dorothy in a sensual kind of Oz. She'd pulled her hair back into a messy half French braid, with the bottom gathered in a low, wild ponytail that trailed down her bare back. She teased some of her hair on top, giving her a glam, bouffant look. Long, multi-string diamond earrings dangled in each ear, the ends just brushing her shoulders, and she roped some gorgeous thick gold chains around her neck. She finished her look with some sexy makeup including black liner in a thick cat-eye shape, bronzed eye shadow on her lids, and deep red lipstick. She turned this way and that, now loving what she was seeing, hoping Marc would, too. She was looking forward to tonight and the surprises he had planned.

Just then, the man himself entered the bedroom, tucking a blush pink button-down shirt into grey suit pants, and then adjusting his cufflinks. He was dressed dapper and business-like in order to fulfill his role as club co-owner. But even though he had the responsibility of schmoozing regular clientele, he assured Simran he was out to have fun with her and her friends tonight, too.

Simran bit her lip as she looked at his reflection in the mirror, more than appreciating what she saw. Gone was the facial hair, his jaw smooth so that his chin cleft was prominent. She sighed at that little dimple, as her gaze glided down his body. He wore his suit like a second skin; a fit that only an expensive tailor could master. The close cut of those pants hugged his long muscular legs and his shirt accentuated his shoulders and chest. She got a little light-headed as she turned away from the mirror, wearing a giddy smile. She walked up to him, moving aside his hands so she could help him finish buttoning his shirt.

"Now, I'm not sure what's going on here, but don't go getting *too* sexy," Marc said admirably, looking her up and down.

"Mm, right back at you," she murmured, gliding a hand down the crisp smoothness of his shirt while he grabbed her hips, rubbing the taught, black material between his fingers. Oh god, were they not going to make it out the door?

"You're gorgeous," he said, his eyes starting to darken. He leaned down to kiss her and she quickly ducked, his kiss landing on the top of her head.

"Marcus Lehigh," she said sternly, "you are A) going to make us late and B) ruin my look." She stepped away and did a full spin for him. "So, you like?" she asked cheekily.

His eyes roved slowly over her again. "I love," he replied, low and gruff. But then his eyes slit, and his hand came to stroke his clean-shaven chin in thought. "It's missing something though." *What?* She'd thought of everything to complete this look. He moved toward her while reaching into his back pocket, where a long, black velvet box was half tucked in. "I think this could only add to your perfection. In fact, I'm pretty sure of it." He held the box for her to take. She was a bit fazed by his words, her cheeks heating up and she was slow to take the box and open it. Inside was a round pendant, a little larger than a quarter, with a smattering of deep blue sapphires in varying sizes set together. Brilliant diamonds were encrusted randomly in between. The pendant was set on a beautifully smooth, gold-linked chain that could be adjusted in length. She held it up to look at the light, completely at a loss for words. It was lovely and the most unique piece of jewelry she'd ever seen.

"Now, do *you* like?" he asked, a little worry line creasing his forehead at her silence as she studied the piece of jewelry.

"No." His mouth started to turn down. "Oh my God, I love it, Marc! It's beautiful. It's, well, it's also too much," she said, a little anxious. Would he be spoiling her like this from now on? She was a little uncomfortable with it. He'd purchased her trinkets in the past, but this seemed over the top.

"Too much? I don't think so." He scoffed, taking the jewelry from her and placing it around her neck. She turned around so he could fasten the clasp and it lay nestled at the base of her neck, just above the other gold ropes she was wearing, making it the focal piece. "Not for my love, so get used to it," he said definitively. "There. It looks perfect on you, baby. It was meant for you." His voice was soft, his warm hands coming to rest on her waist as they stared at her reflection.

Simran fingered the piece, the weight heavy on her neck, similar to when she wore Indian jewelry. She had to admit it looked incredible. The blue of the sapphires shown bright, and the diamonds winked back at her in sparkling little starbursts.

"Wow," she breathed.

"Yeah. Wow," he said, kissing her neck and holding her close. He started to hum a melody in her ear while swaying their bodies, and she recognized it as "Sky Full of Stars" by Coldplay. "When I saw it, I had to get it. It reminded me of our song and that night at my club in London. You looked all stunning and sexy, just waiting for me to give you what you needed." She giggled and sighed. He held that night as such a momentous event in his mind. And it *was* a magical and unforgettable moment. She just couldn't believe how sentimental he could be.

"*Our song?*" She arched an eyebrow upward.

"Come on, it's totally us, don't you think?"

She met his eyes in the mirror, and their sparkle almost fought with the brightness of the necklace. Simran melted, her legs going gooey as she leaned back into him. "Really?" she whispered, knowing the answer already.

"Really," he confirmed, that roguish grin of his, complete with dimples, made an appearance, now making her insides liquefy, her heart bubbling and wanting to burst. "And here's a secret—I saw this necklace in Vancouver when we weren't together. I had to have it anyway. I had no idea if I would see you again, but I wanted a reminder of you."

Simran turned to him dumbfounded. "*Really!!!?*" she squeaked. He nodded. She shook her head all words unavailable in her brain because it was being resuscitated from a heart-attack.

"I love you," was all she could muster. She kissed him with all she had. She had a feeling it was going to be an incredible night.

⋐⋑⋐⋑

THE NEXT DAY

Simran awoke alone in the giant hotel room bed, with a powerful staccato beating forcefully in her temples. Her hair was stuck to her face with drool and she slowly peeled it off. When she managed to open her eyes, she closed them immediately to the harsh sunlight filling the room as it physically pained her more. She groaned, heaving herself out of bed, and stumbled over to the windows, drawing the curtains closed. As she made her way back to the bed, she noticed clothes strewn haphazardly around the room. Her dress was crumpled in the middle of the floor with her sparkling golden shoes dumped next to them. She looked down at herself and realized she was stark naked. She glanced over to the nightstand and recognized her pile of jewelry, taken off in a drunken haze no doubt. On top was her new sapphire and diamond necklace glinting faintly back at her in the now darkened room.

That's when she noticed a bottle of water, two Advil tablets, and a note next to her pile of jewelry.

"Sweetie, drink this, and take these. You'll feel better." – Marc

Ok, what the freak happened last night?

She sat on the bed, popping the pills, and opened the water. She sipped gingerly at first, worried that she might not be able to keep it down, but then closed her eyes as the cool liquid hit her dry mouth, sliding down her throat. She started to gulp, the water dribbling down her chin onto her bare chest until the bottle was empty. She was about to lay her head back down on the pillow when she glanced at the clock and saw it was almost noon. How long had she been asleep, and where was Marc?

She grabbed her phone and saw about a dozen missed calls from late last night, all from him. Then she swiped her texts open and saw he'd texted her at around 1:30 am asking if she was ok.

She saw two missed calls from Tina as well as a long text from her. She clicked it open.

Tina: "Hey, Chick-lit. How're you feeling? Suffering the wrath of grapes, yet? You did NOT need those extra helpings of champagne when we got back to your suite. You wouldn't let up about that crazy minger back at the club and you were raving mad about Marcus and his insane life, paps, stalkers and all. Then you started stripping. Thank God Raj was still back at the club with Marcus! You passed out in bed, with just your shoes on. I helped you with those, by the way, and left a trash bin by your head in case you had a spell of the technicolor yawn. Hope you didn't too much."

Honestly, what in the hell was Tina even texting? She couldn't understand half of the British slang with her headache making her eyes cross. She blinked and stared back at the dissertation Tina had written.

Tina: "Look, last night was fun, until that c*nt crashed the party. But come on, your life won't be that nuts all the time. Was that twat a one off? Who knows? Understand that life with a public persona like Marcus will be something quite different from what you're used to. All sorts of crazies will come out of the wood-work. But he'll protect you, Sima. Dude took a punch for you last night … and some scratches, too! I don't know. Just talk with him before you put your angry cap back on. Love you, lady. Call me soon. XXXX"

Sometimes Simran didn't know what she'd done to deserve a friend like Tina. Someone who honestly cared for her, and took the time to give her the pep talks she so needed in so many difficult instances of her life, even if she couldn't understand her anymore. This time was no different.

Again, Simran tried to recall what happened the night before. It was still hazy, images of Marc's incredible club flitted through her head. Then having a fantastic time with Tina and Raj, and Marc's hands all over her (and she loved that). Then an angry face flashed before her, but darted away so quickly she couldn't grasp the memory just yet. Her head was pounding too hard. Then she remembered the tequila. The yummy drink special had been almost toxic. Tequila and sugar were a bad combo for her and then the added mixture of champagne made it worse.

She sighed, got up from the bed, and went into the bathroom. Thankfully, she didn't feel the need to hurl just yet. Then she started laughing at Tina's words—"technicolor yawn" for sure. She winced at how hoarse her laugh sounded and how it vibrated her entire body. Then she cringed when she got a good look at herself in the mirror. She looked awful. Her hair was worse than a rat's nest, and her makeup was smeared all over, making her eyes look like large raccoon circles where the mascara and liner had run together, smudging in her sleep.

Her mother's voice flashed through her head. "Always wash your face before you go to bed, *beta*. You need to respect your skin." Simran snorted at the memory. If *Amma* could only see her now.

She quickly went over to the sink to wash away last night's makeup, brush her teeth, and finally make some semblance of the tangled mess of her hair. The last part was turning out to be uber painful as she had knot upon knot to get through before she could run a brush through it comfortably.

Then she went looking for some comfy clothes, putting on an NYU tank top, a pair of Marc's boxer briefs, and fluffy slippers. Now, she needed to find him.

She walked over to the door and opened it, listening for any sign of life out in the living room. She could hear him speaking to someone. She left the bedroom, making her way down the hallway toward the sound of his voice. He was standing in front of the wall of windows with his broad, back to her, in a white cotton t-shirt and grey sweat pants. He didn't hear her at first and continued his conversation.

"Yeah, make sure to redact that statement." He paused. "No, absolutely not. I don't want to address that part." He sounded annoyed. "No, Rose, I don't want to press charges. I want to settle this amicably," he said decisively to the head of his PR team, his voice all business. He must have heard the rustle of Simran's feet on the rug because he peered over his shoulder at her. "Rose, let's finish this in a few. I'll call you right back." He hung up, turning around and Simran almost tripped over the carpet. An ugly purplish-black bruise darkened one beautiful eye, which was swollen shut. A railroad track of stained red was on his cheek below his closed eye; three small bandages affixed in succession. Her hands came to cover her horrified mouth. "*Holy Shitballs!*" she squeaked, as the night's events suddenly hit her very clearly. She moved to the sofa, sitting down before her legs gave out.

২৬

Chapter 26

THE NIGHT BEFORE

They arrived at his club around nine in the evening. Marc sought to show Simran and her friends the space before it got too crowded, followed by a private dinner in the VIP lounge before things really came alive at Club Sundar Social.

The tall double doors to the club's entrance stood below a neon green light that screamed 'CLUB' with an arrow pointing to the doors, also in blinking green. The big wooden doors themselves were complicatedly carved in swirls and grooves, and while everyone stepped over the threshold, Simran held back, staring up.

"You coming, or you going to stand here all night?" Tina asked, popping back outside to see what Simran's hold-up was.

Marc realized he'd lost half of their party and went back outside, too.

"Your ladybird is totally "nerding" out, Marcus," Tina murmured dryly and went in to find her husband.

Simran was staring in awe at the carved wood, taking in how the cuts lovingly created beautiful trees on each door. He gazed down at her, the neon green of the sign flashing in the dark of her eyes, and he kind of felt like Gatsby at that moment, staring at a beacon that was his love, his home.

"Marc, this is stunning," she responded. His chest filled with heat. This woman got him, and he got her. They were perfectly "nerding" in harmony in their appreciation of all things architecture and design.

"Wait 'til you see inside," he murmured in her ear and escorted her in.

Two burly bouncers stood on each side of the entrance inside and Marc greeted them warmly, introducing them to Simran, Tina, and Raj. Vijay and Sanjay looked intimidating in their black button-down shirts and dark slacks, all muscles and brawn, not a hint of even an ounce of fat on them. But their faces became relaxed and friendly when they chatted with Marc and met Simran and the others.

Marc led everyone through a dim hallway which was painted with a bold chartreuse green jungle design over black walls. The vines appeared alive, dancing under the effect of black lighting installed overhead. Simran's eyes glimmered as she looked all around. He didn't realize until that moment, that he was just as eager, viewing the place in her eyes, as if for the first time. It was by far one of his favorite venues in their portfolio and much thought had gone into coming up with the theme and décor. He was actually a little nervous (Him! *The* Marcus Lehigh, who exuded confidence in every business decision) about her reaction and if she appreciated the design scheme as much as he did.

The constant babble came from the back of the group as Tina and Raj "oohed" and "aahed," especially when they emerged into the main lounge where the black lighting continued with exotic plants painted on the walls over black in yellow, fuchsia, and green swirling and mingling together with what looked like slivering burgundy snakes. A long bar covered the expanse of one wall and monkeys were depicted along the counter's front panel in bright blue. They were done in a caricature-like style, chattering amongst each other in the colorful room. Tiny lights lined the ceiling in circular formations across the expanse of the ceiling, alternating between purple and neon green, creating the illusion of movement in the paintings. Leather loungers in varying sizes were strategically spaced about with tables in between, their color a subdued metallic grey which played off the pops of light almost dramatically at intervals. It was truly a beautiful and bold look—a neon jungle—that put one immediately in a peppy mood. It was a perfect place for guests to energetically socialize and those already there were doing just that. Some swiveled their gaze to their attractive group, and Marc felt a swell of pride with Simran on his arm.

"Wow, Marc," Simran breathed, turning 360 degrees, trying to see everything at once. "This is truly magnificent." Tina and Raj murmured in agreement as they followed Marc to the bar where a round of top-quality champagne was waiting for them. Drinks in hand, he clasped Simran's hand, linking his fingers through hers as he led them to another hallway, which looked like a tunnel of trees, their branches hanging low creating a lush canopy.

"So, you don't get lost," he whispered in her ear. One corner of her mouth lifted in an impish smile, and she squeezed his hand in her own.

The tunnel was indeed made of trees—large potted palms. It led to a spacious dance floor, where even taller potted palms and mangrove trees dotted the floor, the fan-like fronds and distinctive broad, flat mangrove leaves creating an awning high up overhead. It was remarkable, and Marc heard Simran's breath hitch as she took in the space and the explosion of colors must have overtaken her senses once more. Beautiful burnt orange Bengal tigers were painted on the walls lurking behind large leaves, and bright fuchsia and turmeric yellow macaws were drawn to appear like they were sitting on branches. Everything again was lit up by black lighting. Marc's intention was to create a surreal, scintillating atmosphere where one could get lost in the mesmerizing, wild scene surrounding them. Simran turned to him.

"Marc, I have no words." She shook her head.

"Well, there's a first," Tina said wryly, taking a sip of her drink, nudging Raj in the arm. They both started laughing.

Simran ignored them, only giving her trademark eye-roll, and went on, "I have to ask but I think I know the answer ... is everything hand-painted? They have an artisan's touch to them," she said a little contemplatively, taking a sip of her drink and looking around again in wonder, the pendant he'd just gifted her glittering rainbow bursts in the florescent lighting.

Marc squeezed her hand. "You bet, baby. I hired local artists to add their touch to the place, while providing them the opportunity to showcase their work. So, what do you think? Do you like it?" he asked, not able to keep a little bit of hopefulness out of his voice. He really wanted her approval on this.

"Oh my God, are you kidding? It's phenomenal and so sexy. No wonder all the Aunties want to get into your pants," she said, grinning sweetly at him.

Marc hooted out a loud laugh, making her also giggle. "They got nothing on you, sweet kitten." He leaned in, planting a kiss on those luscious red lips.

"Hello, what's that now?" Raj asked, a curious smile hovering over his wide mouth. Marc had only just met Raj a few days ago, but he'd liked him immediately. The man was reserved at first, had a dry, British sense of humor, but could handle Tina's outlandish behavior. He was tall and thin, but well-built, and had a surprising love of American football which he and Marc had started bonding over immediately. Marc could also appreciate his confident sense of style. Tonight he was dressed in a deep maroon suit jacket and matching slim-cut pants with a finely cut, dark blue shirt underneath. His wrists flashed stunning gold and ruby cufflinks and he had effortlessly but elegantly popped a mustard yellow and blue handkerchief into his suit pocket. He finished the whole look off with black- and whiskey-colored wingtips. His entire appearance was 'funky aristocrat' and he carried it well.

He turned his long face and hawk-like nose to Tina, who was equally tall. "Eh, Tins. You know about this?" Marc and Simran proceeded to explain to them about last summer's party at Pinky Aunty's house and how all the aunties wanted a piece of him. "I can't believe you got out alive. I hear they go absolutely mad over new meat," Raj said chuckling again. Tina batted him in the arm, laughing, too, and he grabbed her baby pink, leather-clad body around the waist in adoration while winking at Marc.

"But really, Marc, what *was* the inspiration for this club," Raj asked curiously. "I'm guessing it has something to do with the Sundarbans given the name and the very hip and energetic jungle-like décor." The lights glinted off his gelled back hair as he nodded his head in approval.

"That's correct, Raj," Marc said appreciatively, liking the guy even more. "This," he said, sweeping his arm, "is like an ode to the Sundarbans." They were referring to the huge, lush mangrove forest bordering India and Bangladesh, which was also a natural preserve with numerous wildlife sanctuaries. "I have to say, the inspiration in this country is astounding. There's so much history, so much natural beauty." He looked down at Simran when he said this and she glanced away embarrassed, tucking some stray hair behind her ear. "Bruce and I had the opportunity to visit some of India's wonders and the Sundarbans were one of them. It was so inspiring that we decided to use it as our design concept with Club Sundar Social, but we took it to the next level. And not only that, but we agreed to donate a percentage of all club proceeds to the Sundarbans."

"These trees though ... how are you managing to keep them alive?" Raj asked.

"All fake. We had them specially commissioned by artisans here in India. *LC Enterprises* might be a big dog in the entertainment industry, but we're committed to helping locals in whatever country we're staked in."

"Marc, I had no idea the Sundarbans inspired you," Simran said in admiration. Her praise made him puff up with pride. She pressed her lush body against his. "You truly are one of the most inspiring, creative, and kind individuals I know. How did I get so lucky?" Her voice was husky and his dick stiffened. He wrapped an arm around her and his hand glided down her warm, bare spine, to her ass as he pulled her pelvis even closer. She moaned very softly under her breath, loud enough for only him to hear. Holy fuck, the way his body reacted to her, and she was just referring to his charity work.

"Ok, you two, keep your clothes on," Tina drawled, tossing her chin-length bob. Her baby pink leather mini dress creaked and shone in the light as she started moving to the beats the DJ was spinning. "So, what else have you to show us, Marcus?" Marc smiled. Tina was warming up to him, but he still had a way to go to gain Simran's closest friend's complete trust.

"One more thing." He led them off the dance floor back to the lounge to a roped-off area. One of the bouncers from before was standing there now and lifted the end of the rope for them to enter. They passed through another hallway also lined with low palms. Then they entered the VIP lounge. This space was still electrified with color, but Marc had imagined a more tranquil, relaxed vibe. It was lit up in soft blue and purple lighting lining the ceiling, with bright white lights projecting intricate rangoli designs all throughout the black floor. White curtains swathed along the walls and on either side of the numerous private sitting areas that lined the perimeter of three of the four walls. Colorful images of large animals, the same paintings from the other club areas, were projected faintly onto the curtains that backed each sitting space. The fourth wall of the lounge had the full-length bar that sat under a multitude of silver, palm-like chandeliers. The bar itself was a sleek black, a simple contrast to the beautiful décor surrounding it.

Marc ushered them with their astounded faces to one of the private sitting areas. Bottle service was already waiting for them, as were some covered silver dishes, plates, and cutlery. Marc lifted them up with a flourish and they saw it was their dinner—an assortment of tasty, innovative bites that the chef had put together, especially for them. Everyone dug in and remarked on how delicious the food was.

⁓⁓⁓⁓⁓

The VIP lounge started to fill up, and Marc excused himself to go and speak with some of the regular clientele.

"Oh my God! Sima, look!" Tina grabbed her hand, squeezing hard. Simran glanced over to where Tina was staring and she almost choked on her champagne. A well-known, beautiful Bollywood star, one who'd recently become very popular in America and who had also married an American musician, was there, with said husband.

"No f'ing way!" Simran squealed. They gawked at them for a bit, taking in what the actress was wearing and how much smaller she was in person.

"All right, kids. Calm yourselves," Raj said drily. "They're just working stiffs trying to enjoy themselves like the rest of us—oy! Is that who I think it is!?" And his own eyes widened at seeing an older Bollywood film star, one who was now known as a much-admired director, with his two well-known actress daughters flanking either side of him. "*Whoa!* Must be a family affair. Shit, Simran, Marcus knows *all* of the who's who around here!" And he sat back ogling the good-looking, famous family.

"I know," Simran said a little sullenly. This part of Marc still made her edgy, the lifestyle he led, the people he knew. He loved her and wanted her, but she remained self-conscious at times, like she would never measure up.

"Why so glum, lady?" Tina asked, bumping her shoulder with her own. "You look hot as hell. You're about to make Marc cream his pants in that get-up. Look how he can't keep his eyes off you." It was true, Marc couldn't take his eyes off of her, and would smile every time he caught her eye. At one point he even mouthed a sexy "hi" to her, like that first time they met back in London. Her whole stomach did a belly flop. She sighed, leaning back, letting the champagne bubbles go to her head, and the love bubbles go to her heart as she watched his handsome figure in that grey suit meet and greet his clientele. She could see the looks of admiration from the men, and the lusty, tongues-almost-wagging-out-of-their-mouths stares from the women. But his bright eyes kept coming back to her.

"You're so his turtle dove," Tina cooed. Simran burst into giggles at Tina's continued trial of cockney rhyming slang, not to mention the endearing, more recent slight slur of her words, like she was going native with the Brits now that she lived there.

"All right, my 'trouble and strife'," Raj said air-quoting the cockney rhyming slang for the word 'wife' while rolling his eyes. "I think that's enough practice for one day. You're really squashing it all into one conversation, which I think is a bit of overkill." Raj shook his head, chuckling. Tina's face fell.

"Well, I think it's super cute *and* sweet of Tina to try. She only wants to make you look good, Raj, and impress the other financiers and their wives," Simran said, hugging Tina.

Raj leaned forward, engulfing Tina in a bear hug, and Tina relaxed into him. Simran smiled and turned to the center of the room where the lights had just dimmed, and then the entire VIP lounge went dark. She realized a performance was about to begin as figures appeared in the shadows. The lights came on in a swath of gleaming white, and beautiful men and women dressed in gold unitards, with Indian-inspired detailing, started moving their feet in a *kathak*-like beat, no music accompanying them. Their feet created the percussive, staccato rhythm similar to the stamping of Flamenco dancing (which *kathak* dance was very similar to). Then the music began in an upbeat mix of *sitar* (an Indian string instrument), *tabla* drums (Indian hand drums), a synthesizer, and saxophone. The dancers moved sensually to the jazzy Indian fusion and Simran couldn't take her eyes off of them. All of a sudden someone pulled her from her seat, sat in her spot, then tugged her onto their lap.

"This is a new dance troupe I wanted to try out as the VIP entertainment this weekend," Marc whispered gruffly in her ear. His hands roamed up her behind and skimmed her bareback. "What do you think of the performance? I have no idea how it's going because you're all I see, baby. You're driving me crazy. I don't even know what I said to some of my regular clientele." His mouth met the back of her neck, his lips grazing her skin. Simran shivered, wriggling on his lap.

"Marc," she protested faintly, leaning into his mouth, rubbing her behind on his groin. His big, warm hands moved to her thighs and stroked them, inching the material of her dress slowly up in the darkened room so that she was almost obscenely exposed.

"I want to show you another special place." His voice was low and gravelly in her ear and a burst of moisture came between her legs as her nipples pebbled up hard, almost painfully, against the snug material of her dress.

"What about the performance, and Tina and Raj." She was breathless now, arching her back, her head leaning on his shoulder. She was pulsing between her thighs now, and his hands were so close to relieving her.

"Lucky for you I own the joint. You can see them another time. And Tina and Raj won't notice." Truth be told, the two were snuggled in the corner, completely entranced with the dancers on stage.

Marc pushed her off and grabbed her hand, leading her to a doorway hidden behind the bar. He opened it and practically shoved her into the room, shutting the door behind them and locking it. When he flipped on the light, Simran burst into laughter.

"A broom closet!? You wanted to show me a broom closet?" She turned to face him and saw absolute desire written all over his face, his eyes darkened. "Well, well, well. And what's so special about this closet, Marcus Lehigh?" She stood with her hands on her hips, surveying the space.

"God, I love it when you use my entire name. It's like I've been a naughty kid or something." He groaned, pushing her up against the wall, possessing her mouth in a drugging kiss. Simran was already feeling carefree from the champagne, the show, the club, and this only made her feel lighter, dizzier. She wrapped her arms around his neck and pulled him even closer, rubbing her body against his hard one. She felt his stiffened length pressing into her belly and she whimpered, widening her legs as far as her tight dress would let her.

"You certainly are a naughty boy, Marcus Lehigh. Dragging me from the show, having me all to yourself," she taunted, while his lips drew down her neck, nipping and pulling at his favorite spot where her pulse was beating fast butterfly wings underneath her skin. He couldn't go any further because of the high neckline of her dress, and she heard him growl in frustration, his face motorboating her breasts over the material.

"Fuck, you'll see how bad I can be." He hiked her dress up around her waist and hoisted her up so her legs were straddling him, her back against the wall. She yelped in delight, as her legs wrapped around him, and she rubbed herself against his hardness. "Hold on, kitten," he murmured, holding her up with his body while he undid his pants, jerking his thick, rigid length out. He pushed aside her underwear and plunged into her without hesitation, his hands gripping her thighs. "*Holy hell*, always so hot and wet for me, aren't you, baby?" She moaned long and loud at how good he felt inside her, filling her up all the way, and how he just took possession of her body like it was his and he knew exactly what it needed. He started grinding into her hard, and she held on tight for the ride.

"Oh God," she gasped, the intensity building inside, moving fast in a river of lava, as he hit all the right spots, his grunts muffled into her neck where his face was buried. "Yes, do it, fuck my brains out," she panted. She didn't know what she was saying, she just knew it felt out of this world, and the fact that they were in his club, right behind the bar and stage only turned her on more. He started moving faster, with more pressure, and she couldn't take it anymore. She shattered fast all around him, wave after wave of pleasure consuming her as her head lolled back on the wall, and she was boneless. She continued clenching him inside as he held her up, jack-hammering until she felt him stiffen. He grunted a warm exclamation of release into her neck as his hot cum shot into her, his body jerking until he was finished.

He was breathing hard as he held her close and felt her soft breasts rapidly rising and falling against his chest. He kissed the top of her head as he slowly pulled out, and let go of first one leg, then her other, making sure she could stand. She swayed a bit as she stood, a loopy grin on her face, her eyes closed. Her hair was mussed, and her dress was still hiked up around her waist and, sweet Jesus, she was so beautiful. He would never get enough of her.

He'd been staring all night, watching her with her friends. He noticed many, many other men doing the same, and couldn't help the jealousy that ripped through him. A few times she and Tina were approached by groups of male guests, but Raj sent them away—good man. She was his. It took everything in him not to leave his clientele as he noticed her red mouth opened with that husky laugh of hers, making his tongue thick every time. He wanted to be by her side, chuckling in on her joke, too. He wanted to slide his hands along her shiny, copper legs, which went on forever in that little dress. She kept crossing and uncrossing them, making her shoes glitter and he was transfixed, wanting nothing more than to have those legs wrapped around him. And that dress, so help him, he'd restrained himself from ripping that thing off her earlier in the evening. Sure, it had long sleeves and a high neckline, but the fabric left nothing to the imagination, and shit, the back of it, or lack thereof, had him hard all night. He hadn't been kidding when he told her he had no idea what he'd conversed with his guests about. She occupied his mind, body, and soul now.

He helped her fix her clothes, while she helped him adjust his pants. She smoothed her hair back.

"Do I look ok?" she asked, a little worriedly. She looked like she'd just been thoroughly fucked and she looked perfect.

"You look more than ok." He pulled her to him hugging her, inhaling her scent, then he nuzzled her nose. "Let's get back before your friends miss us." He gave her a final kiss then opened the door in a wide flourish. "I'm glad you enjoyed the private tour of the broom closet." They went out and back into the VIP lounge where the dancers had already finished and exited the stage. Now, only the musicians remained and were playing jazzy, Indian, and reggae fused tunes.

When they returned to their sitting area, Tina scooted over toward Simran and he heard her ask under her breath, "Coat closet?"

Simran picked up her drink and smiled like the cat that got the cream. "Broom closet," she answered a little smugly, wiggling her shoulders as she took a sip of her champagne.

Tina nodded, a half-smile on her bright pink lips. "Nice." She tapped her glass with Simran's in a small salute.

Marc chuckled, shaking his head.

"Guys, let's hit the dance floor and show everyone how it's done," Tina said excitedly, bouncing in her seat. "The music is awesome in here, but I need to move my body!" She stood up, wriggling her hips. "Raj?" she asked, holding her hand out to him expectantly. He put his drink down and stood up with her.

"You know, I think I've had enough to want to cut a rug now. You guys coming?" His eyes were slit as he looked at them, absolutely knowing what they'd been up to when they'd disappeared. Then he gave Marc a good-natured grin. "Totally ok if you don't, mate." He nodded his head in Simran's direction.

Marc turned to Simran and she had an eager look on her face. "Sweetie, you go start warming up out there. I'll just check in with my staff and then come meet you in a bit."

Simran stood up, smoothing the skirt of her dress down. She leaned in and kissed him on the cheek. "I'm already warmed up." She tossed him a cheeky wink before she followed the other two out of the VIP lounge to the dance floor.

२९

Chapter 27

Marc found them later in the middle of the dance floor, having a great time. He leaned on the bar to watch them. A tumbler of his favorite whiskey appeared before him, neat, and he thanked the bartender. He grinned, seeing Simran with her arms in the air, jumping up and down and shaking her hips, and started laughing at Raj and Tina as they went over the top mimicking the infamous dance moves from *Pulp Fiction*. They were dancing to some innovative Indian and hip-hop mix-up by the DJ. Simran and Tina were mouthing the Hindi and English words to each other dramatically, "My name is Sheila, Sheila Ki Jawani," and something about this Sheila woman being too sexy. Both of them were shaking their hips sharply now, body rolling, and waving their hair around, completely over the top. Raj was somewhere in the background, trying to keep up. Even though Simran was hamming it up on the dance floor, Marc still thought she was the most stunning woman out there, and his eyes followed her. She flicked her ponytail side to side with attitude, her hand on her chest as she gave Tina and Raj big eyes, mouthing, "What's my name? What's my name?" along with the song.

The track ended and the new melody the DJ faded into made everyone on the dance floor groan. It was an uber popular and overplayed Punjabi dance remix by Punjabi MC. And yet, everyone still started dancing to the hyped-up music, bopping to the beats.

"Nice to see you, Marcus," a voice said behind him. He turned around to find a young woman standing at the bar. Pretty, long brown hair, and petite. She was wearing a seafoam green jumper so short that it looked more like a bathing suit than a proper outfit. He recognized her, but couldn't place her name.

She obviously realized he couldn't recall her name so she reminded him. She put her hand on his chest and leaned up, her lips close to his. "Eulalia, remember?" And she met his lips with her own.

He drew away quickly, almost in shock as he realized it was the young woman from Vancouver; the major investor's daughter. He bumped into a clubgoer behind him, trying to put space between himself and Eulalia.

"Sorry," he apologized over his shoulder. He turned back around to face her. "Eulalia. That's right. Nice to see you, too," he said trying to act nonchalant. He took a sip of his drink to calm his nerves. Why was he so anxious all of a sudden? Nothing happened between them except for that damn kiss. "How's school?" He remembered she was finishing her last year of university.

She pulled an annoyed look. "School? We didn't talk about school last time I saw you." She tried to put her hand on his chest again.

He grabbed it and pulled it away from him. "Eulalia, I'm pretty sure I made it clear that anything between us is a bad idea. And I'm back with my girlfriend, now."

He glanced over to where Simran was still enthusiastically dancing, thankfully too preoccupied to notice him with Eulalia.

"Where is she?" She glanced in the same direction as his eyes. "Is that her?" By this point, Simran had a sheen of sweat on her forehead and her sleeves were rolled up to her elbows. "Oh," Eulalia said, unimpressed. "She should be here with you. Anyone could come up and snatch you away," she said flirting with him as her fingers edged onto his shoulder.

Marc counted to three with his eyes closed. He was starting to get irritated with this girl. He pulled her fingers off of him again. "What makes you think I'm snatch-able? I freely belong to someone else and prefer her company right now, actually," he said, taking off his suit jacket and folding it, passing it to the bartender. "Enjoy yourself tonight and be careful," he tossed over his shoulder as he turned to the mass of dancers on the floor, looking for Simran.

The song turned to a popular Weeknd track as he spotted her at the exact same moment she saw him. She grinned and curled her finger in a come-hither motion. And hither he did, moving between the sweaty bodies, toward that smile, a warm guiding light.

The beams overhead started throwing soft yellows and pinks and the beats continued, toned down to a lower key song. The Weeknd crooned, "I feel it coming, I feel it coming, baby," and he was coming to his baby.

He reached her and encircled her waist, as she sensually wrapped her arms around his neck. Their bodies moved together to the upbeat sultry tune; their eyes locked. "Just a simple touch, and it could set you free," she mouthed with the song, as she closed her eyes and swayed her head side to side, lost to the moment, making it feel like they were the only ones on the dance floor.

He put his face into her sticky neck and inhaled, letting the music take him over, too, as he pulled her even closer. He felt her pulse race as her arms clutched him tighter.

It was a heady combination with the crowd around them, but the two of them were lost in their own world together. Admittedly, it put his usual sharp mind in a haze. His guard was down and he didn't have a moment to even comprehend what happened next.

He felt hands behind him and he lifted his head, confused. A body was up against his backside trying to dance with them. Hands covered his eyes, trying to tease him. He let go of Simran to pull the unknown hands off. When he had his vision back he noticed the uncertainty on Simran's face, too.

"Marcus, darling!!!" a high, whiny voice drawled, competing with the Weeknd's sweet voice. "Introduce me to your girlfriend." It was Eulalia.

Fuck. He looked down at the smaller woman and saw only viciousness in the squint of her eyes and the upturn of her lips.

"Marc, who is this?" Simran asked, her hands still on him as her look bounced between the two of them. Marc was trying to come up with something and in that moment of hesitation, her hands dropped from him.

Before he could speak, Eulalia answered, "Oh, you didn't tell her, Marcus?" She batted her eyes at Simran. "Marcus and I got to know each other *very* well while he was in Vancouver working." Her tone turned girlish. "Most of his time was taken up working with my daddy." She curled her lips up. "But when Marcus and I could find the time, we couldn't keep our hands off each other. It's actually good to see you with your pants on, darling," she quipped at him, before laughing hysterically.

"She's lying," Marcus finally uttered, stunned at the lies coming out of this little witch's mouth. He watched as Simran's confusion grew, the 'v' between her brows deepening. What the hell was wrong with him? Why couldn't he react fast enough?

"I'm actually really thirsty, babe. I'm going to the bar to get something to drink." Simran shrugged and whispered something to Tina, who whispered something to Raj, and they started toward the bar. She looked over her shoulder. "You guys coming? I'd love to hear more about how you two got to know each other very well," she said with a sharpness that belied any of the heat they shared just moments ago.

"Love to." Eulalia smirked, joining the group as they headed to the bar.

⁂

Simran didn't know what to think. She trusted Marc, but this missy was talking about a time when they'd been apart.

Did she even have a reason to be upset? Probably not, but then why did it still hurt so much? Marc had maintained that nothing had happened between him and this tartlet. Oh, and she knew who this was. She recognized the whiny voice as the bitch in the background of his voice message. Had he been lying? Did they hook up? Did they have sex!?

She swallowed hard and squared her shoulders, approaching the bar. Tina signaled that she'd already ordered for all of them.

She turned to Marc, who stood beside her, his hands shoved in his pockets. He sure was acting a little guilty. He stared at her intensely, almost as if trying to convey a message to her.

Simran knew one thing for sure: innocent until proven guilty.

"I'm Simran," she said without any malice toward the much younger woman. She didn't look like she was even out of college yet. She put her hand out to her.

"Eulalia." She barely shook Simran's hand. "My father works with Marcus. He's funding the Vancouver project," she said, smugly, as if she was in on something that Simran wasn't.

"That's … interesting." She turned to Marc expectantly. Was he going to jump in; say anything to save his ass here?

He cleared his throat. "That's right. Eulalia—"

"Marcus, call me Lala, remember? All my friends do, and we're more than friends, aren't we?" the younger woman said smoothly, eyeing him up and down.

Simran turned again to Marc, but she remained calm. "Are you good friends?" She cocked her head and waited.

"Only if being the daughter of a main investor in Vancouver means we're good friends, though, I'm not sure it does…" He put his arm around Simran and squeezed. She leaned into him understanding, her apprehension dissolving. This woman was nothing to him.

"Oh, come on, Marcus." Eulalia looked up at the ceiling, shaking her head. "You didn't say that when you sucked my face outside of the restaurant that one night. And when it turned into much, much more…" She shrugged suggestively, twirling her hair.

"Hey yo! What did we miss?" Tina came up with two drinks in hand, Raj followed behind with three more and they distributed them to everyone.

"We're trying to figure out if Marc and Eulalia, here, are good friends or not," Simran said as carefully as she could. What she really wanted to do was toss her drink in this young twat's face. She casually took a sip of her drink then started swirling the sugar cane stick it came with. "This is good. What is it?"

"A Sundar Tropical Storm. A mixture of lime juice, tamarind paste, sugar, and tequila," Marc said absently, as he stared down at the young woman, anger making his jaw taut. "What kind of BS are you spouting, Eulalia?" he asked with gritted teeth, his stance rigid. His upper body was leaning down as if he was going to strike the smaller woman.

The young woman brandished him with slit eyes, before turning large, doe-eyes to Simran.

"You obviously know nothing about Marcus Lehigh," Eulalia sneered, tossing her thick wavy hair over her shoulder. She bent down to adjust the buckle on her towering shoes, and her ass cheeks hung out, while her boobs almost spilled over. She put a hand to her chest as if realizing how exposed she was, drawing attention to them. She stood up. "The man's a two-timing, sometimes three-timing player." She swung to look at Marc again, a malicious smile on her shiny lips. Simran heard Marc's sharp inhale.

"Oh ho!" Tina spat out behind Simran. "What a *frigger*."

"Not now, Tins," Simran commented absentmindedly.

"I think she actually used that term properly. This person is a terrible nuisance. Well done, my lady-love." Raj kissed a beaming Tina.

"Oh yeah? What does it mean exactly—" Simran turned her attention to them.

"Are you listening to me, Simran, is it? You're with a player. He'll never change, you know." She crossed her arms over her chest, her breasts ballooning up almost comically on her small frame, and Simran realized that they were fake. The red varnish on her nails flashed brightly in the light. "Are you ok with that? Or maybe we could team up and take him on together?" She leaned her head back and cackled. She had a wild-eyed look about her, even hyenas would run in fear.

"Sims, she's full of bullshit," Marc began. Simran turned to him with a small smile, only nodding. Then she glared back at Eulalia.

"Let me ask you a really important question, Eulalia." She leaned down with purpose to the girl, drilling her with a cold stare. "Does the loony bin know you've escaped?" She took another long sip from her drink—liquid courage.

"Savage!" she heard Tina exclaim admiringly behind her as Raj chuckled. She noticed Marc trying his hardest to keep a straight face.

Then Simran continued. "Marc, this drink really is delicious—" Before they knew what was happening, Eulalia swung her arm and the drink knocked out of Simran's hands, making the sticky sour and sweet concoction go flying through the air, landing on a group of club-goers standing next to them at the bar. The glass crashed to the floor, first bouncing and then spraying shiny shards everywhere that caught the dancing overhead club lights as they landed.

"Hey! What gives?" The surprised group stared angrily at them. Marc turned to calm them down and offer an apology while simultaneously catching the bartender's eye and motioning for him to get someone out to clean the mess.

From the corner of Simran's eye, she saw the movement of shiny red and she ducked.

"What the *fucking fuck!*" It was Marc yelling. She turned to see him holding a hand over his eye and trying to maneuver around the flying fists of the young woman who'd clearly gone insane. Miraculously, he was able to grab her from behind with just one arm, before she tore into Simran.

"Let me go! You asshole! Get the fuck off of me! I'll tell my father!" She was struggling, almost terrified in his arms. All Simran could do was stare at Marc's eye, which was scrunched up and the blood dripping down his cheek from torn flesh.

"She's gone bananas!" Tina cried, clutching both Simran and Raj's arms.

"Raj, go get Sanjay or Vijay, either of them," Marc ordered, while his body jerked with the woman's spastic movement. Other clubgoers had stopped what they were doing to watch the commotion and the DJ was trying his best to dispel the forming crowd. He started another upbeat track trying to encourage everyone to continue dancing.

"What can I do?" Simran asked helplessly.

"Just stand back. I think she's hyped up on drugs right now. Who knows what she's capable of?" Her wiry body was determinedly strong as she seethed in his grip. And she was spouting some of the ugliest insults to the both of them.

"—You prick! This is who you're with? What makes her so special that you'd fuck her? Is she why you didn't want me back then? I was there for you when you were moping around." Then she swiveled in his grip to Simran. "You know he'll tire of you, right? He's a man with a big dick and he needs someone with imagination—"

"That's enough, you little girl," Simran said through clenched teeth, right in the young woman's face. "Obviously imagination is the least of your worries. You've lost your goddamn mind." Simran jabbed a finger in her chest, aware that she was literally poking the bear.

Vijay appeared and took the struggling young woman, but she stomped on his foot, her elevated heel cracking a painful grimace over Vijay's otherwise stony composure. She darted through the crowd, jarring people as she stumbled. Vijay was hot on her tracks, and for some idiotic reason no one could justify, people began to shove each other around. It was, quite literally, the beginnings of a shit show, as Simran was jostled and separated from Marc. She shrieked his name in panic as she was pushed across the sea of club-goers toward the other end of the dance floor.

Somehow the other bouncer, Sanjay appeared and grabbed her arm. He had Raj and Tina with him. "My orders from Mr. Lehigh are to get you out of here." She nodded trying to ask where Marc was, but the burly man didn't wait. He barreled through the throng of scuffling people, using his big beefy arms as a shield. He made a quick path through the lounge area, where people were trying to push in the opposite direction causing a bottle-neck into the dance area entrance to watch the fights.

"Damn skulkers ..." Raj said disgustedly, referring to how many were just hurrying to observe the drama instead of actually lending a hand to help the rising situation. "Will Marcus be ok in there?" he asked the bouncer.

The bouncer only nodded.

"I think I'll stay," Raj said, stopping in his tracks. They were now at the front doors and could hear police sirens wailing. "Tina, I want to make sure Marcus is ok." Tina nodded and gave him a hug.

"Be careful, *nah*? This is supposed to be our second honeymoon, not your funeral."

"Take Simran home and make sure she's ok." That snapped Simran back into focus. What in the actual fuck happened back there? A stampede of sorts as a result of Marc rebuffing some woman from the past? How would she get through life like this? She heard the straining music of Daft

Punk's "Lose Yourself to Dance" over the din in the dance area. The DJ was not going down with the ship; if she could praise him, she would. She wanted nothing more than to lose herself to dance at that moment, the pull of loving Marc, wanting to be with him a strong contrast to the push of her anxiety in what being with him actually looked like. He'd already experienced blackmail, and now this. Would this be what it was going to look like all the time? And what about Marc, now? Was he ok? Concern was the only thing on her mind as she turned back in the direction of the dance floor but she felt the jerk on her arm. Tina shook her head furiously and dragged her in the opposite direction out the club entrance while police officers started filtering in.

Bright bulbs flashed and Simran was momentarily blinded, stumbling down the stairs.

"Ms. Khan, over here!" shouted a voice.

"No, Ms. Khan, over here! How did you and Mr. Lehigh meet?"

Huh? Why were there reporters?

"Fucking paps," Tina muttered, as she dragged Simran down the steps. "Just cover your face, Sima."

But the voices continued. "Ms. Khan, is it just a fling, or do you and Mr. Lehigh plan to get married? Do you plan on having children?"

"Ms. Khan, are you pregnant?" Holy shit, she was going to crumple into a puddle, now. She saw Marc's car and driver waiting for them out front already, the back door held open. They ducked in quickly, and as soon as Simran's butt hit the deep leather seat, she put her head in her hands and finally fell apart.

২৮

Chapter 28

Marc turned to Simran after hanging up the phone on Rose. If anyone could get *LC Enterprises* out of this sticky situation—or at least make it look less damning—then it was Rose, the head of his PR team, who worked around the clock when she needed to.

Simran collapsed onto the couch, her face in utter shock, and regardless of what happened last night, the only thing he felt at the moment was relief that she was up and that she didn't seem sick. He'd called her numerous times after last night's debacle, between the police questioning, and the press mob outside. *Fucking tabloids.* He couldn't get a hold of her so he tried Tina. When he caught her, on his third try, she said she'd just left Simran in their hotel suite safe and sound. They'd been hit with a barrage of paparazzi as they'd left the club, and by the time they got back to the hotel, Simran was fuming. She'd stubbornly had more champagne to drink, then passed out. Tina warned him that Simran wasn't her best at the moment. She was vulnerable and upset, not sure where their relationship could go if a life with him was going to be a constant soap opera. Marc had been dumbfounded. After just getting her back, was he going to lose her again? He could only respond by thanking Tina for taking care of her and that he would be back soon.

When he finally got back to the hotel suite at around three in the morning, he'd immediately headed straight to the bedroom to see her. Reassurance surged through him as he took in her sleeping form in bed in the darkened room. Her clothes were dumped haphazardly in a pile, her underwear hanging off a mirror, and she was belly-flopped on the bed, spread eagle. A blanket was laid over her naked body and a trashcan placed near her head—no doubt Tina's careful ministrations. He just stared at this mess of a woman who, no matter what, would always be perfect to him. She was snoring softly, her face muffled into a pillow. He came over and tenderly touched her back, her skin so warm and velvety under his fingers. She didn't stir. He undressed and got into bed, turning toward her, resting a hand on her waist. Sleep overtook him immediately, his consciousness needing to be suspended for a few hours before he tackled his anger and anxiety.

When he woke up only a few hours later (he'd never been one to sleep in), Simran was still out cold. He left her sleeping and pulled on some comfy clothes. He had a feeling he'd be on the phone for the better part of the day dealing with this new problem.

After requesting an ice pack from the front desk for his swollen eye (the scratches on his face had been tended to and bandaged by a medical professional when he was at the police station), and ordering room service, he called Raj first to thank him for staying by his side during last night's mayhem.

Then he called Rose, who'd already left him dozens of voice messages.

He was on his third call of the day with her when he heard Simran creep in behind him. Her face was squeaky clean, and her hair was thrown into a high messy ponytail. She was in a pair of his boxer briefs, an NYU top, and her fluffy pink slippers were on her feet. He loved her the best like this, when she was relaxed, wearing some of his clothes. He smiled at her as he watched her twist her hands in her lap, unsure of what to say.

"That's my underwear, Sims," he said, teasing her, trying to ease her tension. Her eyes got a little big, then she squinted, chuckling throatily.

"Yeah, but they look so much better on me, don't you think?" Her brows wiggled comically; two slim black caterpillars dancing on her forehead.

Marc just shook his head. "Room service came hours ago, so the food may be a little cold. You should still try to eat. I heard you had more to drink when you came back here last night." He was trying not to sound angry with her. He didn't like the fact that she'd been so upset she'd felt the need to chug more alcohol, only adding to her fragile emotional state. Even more than anything he hated that he was the cause of her irrationality.

She came up behind him, but instead of sliding into a chair, her slim arms came around to hug him from behind.

"Thank you for a wonderful evening," was all she said, then laid her head on his back.

"But ...?" he queried, the anxiety creeping back into his voice, his body becoming stiff. Was this it? Was she going to tell him that they couldn't possibly be together because of shit like last night?

"But ...?" she repeated. Her hands came up to pinch his nipples, her way of teasing him.

"That's it? You're not going to reign your anger down on me about Eulalia?" He grasped her hands to his chest, stilling them, and possibly preventing her from running away if that was her intention.

She sighed deeply, the warm air swooshing over his shoulder blades. "I don't know what you want me to say, Marc. You know I was angry. But I think I handled myself pretty well, considering the crazies you attract. The thing is, why waste my energy on that bitch? I know you love me. I trust that you're mine, and only mine." She kissed his back and laid her head against him again. "Isn't that why you came to find me here in India? Unless you were only after the frequent flyer miles..." she said sardonically.

He let out the breath he hadn't realized he'd been holding. His body lost its rigidness.

"Did you think I was going to dump you?" she asked incredulously. She turned him around to look at her. "Did you really think you were going to get rid of me *that* easily? Here's the thing, Marc. You attract crazies, and I happen to be the craziest of the bunch." She cupped his face, lovingly touching the bandages covering up the scratch marks, and then tenderly fingering his bruised eye. It stung, but he wanted her hands on him. "I'm absolutely mad about you, not at you." She cupped his face again. "Tell me, though, and be honest with me, did anything happen between you two in Vancouver?"

He could take the easy way out and lie, but felt sick to his stomach with this secret. He took both of her hands in his. "She and I shared a kiss, nothing more." She closed her eyes and nodded. "But it only happened because I wanted to forget the pain of losing you."

"And did it?" She opened her eyes and studied him. "Make you forget me and your pain?"

He shook his head vehemently. "No. It made me realize you are the only one I ever want."

She nodded again calmly. "Good." Here hands we on his cheeks once more. "I want you to always remember that moment because it was our saving grace." She paused, letting that sink in. "But let me help you forget any other contact with that girl." And she leaned up to kiss him, her lips slightly parted, claiming him, nipping and sucking sweetly. This was his home. He'd never understand what the fuck he'd ever done to deserve someone like her, but he thanked the stars above every day that she could forgive him.

She pulled away all too soon, before they could get lost in their embrace. "What's up with the paparazzi, though, Marc? I was totally not expecting that."

Marc sighed. Yes, eventually they would land on this topic. He sat down at the table, patting the seat beside him. "I'll get to that, but first, Sims, please eat something." He leaned over and pulled the silver domes off the dishes.

⁊⁊⁊⁊

Simran nodded and sat down, her stomach growling loudly at the reminder of not being fed in hours. She helped herself to some coffee, still hot in the carafe, and lukewarm eggs and toast. "Oh nice," she untwisted one of the jars that had come with breakfast. "Mango *achar* (mango pickled in flavored oil)." She then proceeded to dump some of the pickles on the side of her plate, drizzling her eggs with the pickling oil. She took a bite and chewed thoughtfully, the pungency of the pickles stinging her nostrils, followed by the creaminess of the eggs that dampened the spiciness on her tongue. It was addictive, and she took another bite, feeding some to Marc as well. He leaned back, an arm resting on the back of her chair as he chewed in thought.

"So, what do you think?" she asked, needing to continue the conversation about the reporters. How did he handle it in his life? Could she learn from him?

"It's unusual, but I like it." He opened his mouth for another bite. She rolled her eyes.

"Isn't this supposed to be *my* breakfast?" But she fed him another hefty forkful anyway. To her, these were flavor combinations she'd known since she could speak, and she was glad he liked what he called "unusual" flavors.

"I mean about the paparazzi. Marc, I don't remember them around when we were together in NY and London. Was I blind?" She buttered her toast and then spread on a thick layer of orange marmalade before she took a bite.

"Not really. I'm not *that* famous, Sims."

"You could've fooled me," she said, recalling the group of vultures hounding her outside the club last night.

"Remember the blackmail situation?" He arched his brow high, his arms crossed now. He got a little defensive talking about it because it ended up involving and subsequently hurting his mother.

"Yes." Then it dawned on her. He'd been careful after that incident, ensuring the paparazzi had no access to his personal life. She fiddled with the fork on her plate, swirling the oil around into flower-like patterns. "But how did you keep us from getting into certain news outlets?"

"I pay my PR team a lot of money to ensure I don't show up in the rag mags, Sims. And I also pay those news outlets a lot of money to leave me alone. A few we don't know about get their photos somehow though. Hence, why we ended up in a few tabloids toward the end of our time together in London, and a few times in New York. You didn't seem to mind then, or I guess, notice since that kind of gossip isn't really your thing." She nodded, admitting that she was oblivious when it came to celebrity gossip. Her staff at *Lavish Your Events* always reprimanded her for her nonchalance because to be in touch with the private affairs of anyone with even a hint of celebrity status could only widen her business to higher net worth clients. And Simran, well, she was clearly out of touch when it came to this kind of thing and was always grateful that she had a staff that was with it.

Marc went on. "And while in New York, we kind of flew under the radar at times when we took public transportation, or we'd go to hole in the wall clubs and bars..." he trailed off.

"Hey! I thought you liked those divey joints!"

"I did. I do. But it really helped my cause out, too," he said, smiling reassuringly.

"So, what's happening right now? Why are they hounding you—us?"

"Well, I haven't been active with any kind of social outings in India lately, so we've stopped paying off some of the news outlets here. We can't really control social media, though—"

"Ah yes, India's Stud Watch, or whatever it's called." She nodded remembering what Anil had told her the day before.

A smile started to crack on Marc's face. "Are you starting to keep tabs on social media?"

"Nuh uh. Anil mentioned it to me yesterday." He nodded. "So that's how that stupid girl knew you were in Mumbai? And she just hopped on over here? Doesn't she have finals or something?" Simran asked testily. These spoiled, rich socialites ... she would need to figure out how to handle herself around them.

"Probably." He shrugged. "Listen, I'm sorry if this invades your privacy. There are some things that can't be helped when you're with me." Simran remained silent, ruminating over this. She felt Marc lean into her, put his arm around her waist, and tug her onto his lap, the fork clattering onto the plate. He turned her chin so he could meet her eyes. "I'm going to ask you and tell me the truth. Is this a deal-breaker for you?" His voice was soft. His eyes held a fearful, wounded expression, and he looked even more vulnerable with the bandages and the black eye.

She shook her head, leaning her forehead onto his. "It's going to take some getting used to, Marc. But I can't deny us. It's something bigger than both of us." She fingered his bandages again, and then caressed his brow above his swollen eye. "You'll have to be ok with me needing time to figure out how to maneuver in your world again. I didn't have so much at stake back then," she admitted truthfully. Their love was strong but it would make her crazy seeing these other women throw themselves at him. "And, I might just have to take out the next person who does this to you. I would have scratched that girl's eyes out if I could have." She remembered the seething anger she felt when she saw the damage to Marc's face. She would have done something, too, if she hadn't been stunned by the events unfolding, and then carried away—literally—by the crowd.

"Would you have protected me?" he asked tenderly, the fear from his eyes replaced by sparkles.

"Hell yes, I would have protected you."

"My angry goddess." He nuzzled her hair.

"Can I be straight up with you?"

"You know you always can." His face was in her neck trailing soft kisses up and down and she had to keep herself from losing her train of thought.

"When all those famous people walked into the VIP room, I freaked out a little. Honestly, I'm not sure how to handle myself in this world of yours. Before, I just rolled with it because I didn't know where we were going, what we were doing in our relationship. But now..." She gazed up at him, the fear coming into her voice now. "I want to be that confident woman who deserves to stand by your side, but I get self-conscious because I'm not used to all this next-level glitz and glam."

"I know, sweetie, that's one of the reasons at the top of my list on why I love you so much. You get star-struck, sure, who wouldn't? But you don't aim to become like that crowd, some of whom can be selfish, snobby, even forget where they came from and who they really are. You're absolutely the most genuine, sweetest, coolest chick around. Why do you think I traveled all the way around the globe to make sure you knew that?" His smile wavered again. She was doubting his love for her and she could tell it was hurting him.

She hugged him hard. "So, *not* for the frequent flier miles?"

২৯

Chapter 29

Marc spent the better part of the day making sure *Club Sundar Social's* image wasn't too tattered. *LC Enterprises & Holdings* released a statement ensuring the club was not a danger to anyone's well-being, confirming security was ramped up, and finally, issuing a formal apology to one Eulalia Mosa, for the actions taken against her—she'd been arrested for aggravated assault and disturbing the peace. Late in the night she'd been questioned at the police station and finally released on bail. Now, all he had to do was let his PR team come up with some publicity stunt to bring wary clientele back into the club, while Marc concentrated on filling Bruce in and smoothing any issues they may have with the girl's father.

Hours later, he finally felt some tension leave his body. He leaned back at the desk in the living room where he'd set up his laptop and cracked his neck loudly. He was still livid about how that girl behaved the previous night but was thankful for Simran's trust in him.

He heard her come up behind him, placing her cool hands on his back where she started to massage the tightness in his shoulders. He groaned in appreciation, momentarily forgetting about everything but her skilled fingers.

"So tense, babe," she whispered and continued kneading the muscles with a pressure that started to relieve the tautness. "Are you ready to wind down now? I ordered room service, and drew you a bath," she said matter-of-factly, a little proud of herself.

"A bath?" He snorted. "Really, Sims? What am I, eighty-years old?" Then he got a kinky idea. "Wait, if I'm an eighty-year-old man, then you're my hot young nurse who's just aching to sponge me down." He pulled her onto his lap, and she squealed as his hands roamed down her back to her ticklish spot.

"You are so bad," she said between bursts of air as she squealed some more.

"We've already established that, sweetcheeks." He stood up with her in his arms and hefted her over his shoulder with her ass in the air. He gave it a nice, resounding slap and headed into the bathroom where the enormous tub was already filled with effervescent bubbles, the subtle smell of sandalwood and rose hitting his nostrils pleasantly.

He slid her down the front of his body, so she was standing in front of him. He was starting to get stiff, and he pushed his pelvis into her, telling her, without words, what he wanted.

"Ah, is that so, Mr. Lehigh? Do you need to be worked a little before your sponge bath, sir?" she asked innocently, looking at him from beneath her eyelashes as she batted them quickly. "All right then, we do what the patient wants around here." She sighed with feigned annoyance, and before he could even respond, she was on her knees, pulling his pants and boxer briefs down, his thick, long length springing out. She palmed his balls in one hand, and gave his dick a long slow lick while holding the base with her other hand. Then she leisurely took him into her mouth, moving all the way to meet her hand at his base, then pulled all the way off with a resounding "pop." He was fully hard now and he groaned.

"Sweet Jesus, Sims." He grabbed her ponytail, pulling it from its tie, so that her hair tumbled around her shoulders. Then he fisted her hair, pushing her forward so that she took him deep into her mouth again, the tip of his cock hitting the back of her mouth. She moaned around him, starting to swirl her tongue in his precum, around his engorged length. He was so hard; he was actually in a little pain. He needed a release soon. "Fuck. Your mouth, baby, it's incredible," he panted. "Shit, you're so sexy, even in my clothes and those fuzzy slippers." She giggled, almost choking. "Focus, sweetie. I—" he gasped, "need this." He picked up the tempo, taking control of her movements and fucking her mouth. She grabbed his ass cheeks for anchor as he rode her. It was too much; he was already there. "I'm coming," he warned and he jerked forcefully, as his cum filled her mouth. He stroked her hair, finishing, feeling her struggle to take it, but then she relaxed and swallowed. She pulled off him, giving him a few swift pats on his taut butt-cheeks, and stood up, a smug smile on her lips. He was absolutely content, feeling his eyes start to droop in relaxation. "I've got the best fucking nurse out there," and he grabbed her in a dizzying kiss, his tongue finding hers and twining in a tangling dance.

When she finally got him into the tub, the water had cooled. She sat on the edge draining some of the tepid liquid and then refilling with warmer water while he leaned his head back and soaked with his eyes closed. "You're coming around to the idea of a bath, I see," she commented, as she stood up to leave.

"Where do you think you're going?" His eyes shot open.

"I'm leaving you to it."

And as she leaned in to peck him on the forehead, he sat up quickly, pulling her into the bath, clothes and all, and onto his lap while she shrieked. "I don't think so, sweet kitten. I only do baths with my woman so that I can convince myself it's a sex thing, not just an old man thing." And he started removing her wet clothes. Simran just shook her head, laughing, helping him take her clothes off. He maneuvered her so that she was facing him, straddling his body.

"This is a huge tub, Marc," she pointed out, looking over her shoulder at the expanse of the empty side.

"What's your point?" he murmured, kissing her neck, making love to his favorite spot, then moving down to sip her nipple into his mouth. She could feel him starting to stiffen again under the water and she arched into him involuntarily. His insatiability with her was such a turn-on. Good God, he would always have control of her body, wouldn't he? "See, you feel it, too. The tub is way too damn big." And he kept teasing her nipples with his tongue while one of his hands slid between her thighs. He slipped a long finger in, pulsing in and out of her, then another. He finally added a third, making her throw her head back as she started to ride his hand and held him there with her own.

"That's it, kitten," he murmured against her encouragingly, watching her move on top of him, his eyes hooded with desire for her. "You're beautiful," he said reverently, rapt attention moving from her face to her bouncing breasts, to her wet torso. She was so close when he removed his hand and was in the middle of protesting when his hands gripped her hips, lifting her off of him and then sliding her back down onto his waiting cock. Just that one thrust had her insides trembling, and she lost it, moaning in complete surrender, as she closed her eyes and saw white light flashing behind her lids. She started to buck on him, her hands gripping the tub's edges, and he continued to thrust up into her, groaning his pleasure. The water was sloshing out, and their skin slapped together. He paused suddenly. "Open your eyes for me, Sims." She did. "Look at me when you come again," he pleaded, his bright eyes on hers. With gazes locked, they started to move again. She panted faster, her body aching for another release, and she felt him stiffen inside her, pushing hard and deep as he came, his eyes still on her own. "I love you so much, baby," he panted, continuing to move inside her, feeling her tremors as she started to convulse around him, the pleasure only intensified as she was staring into his gaze which was filled with his every emotion for her. "I love you," she cried out, her words echoing off the bathroom walls as she collapsed against him and he held her close.

Later they ate on the rug in front of the fireplace, then snuggled on the couch to watch a movie. Marc was only interrupted twice by his PR people.

"Are you going to press charges against Eulalia?" she'd asked after his last conversation. When he'd answered 'no,' that they were actually issuing a formal apology to her, that it was a misunderstanding that escalated way out of their control, and that this would be printed in the press, Simran's jaw dropped.

"But why? She acted horribly!" she'd protested. He then explained to her that it wasn't worth it. His personal issue with the girl would and should be addressed personally when they had both cooled off. And after speaking with her father, he was confident in no hard feelings from him. He'd agreed that the company and shareholders (a large one like himself) didn't need this kind of bad press.

Simran could only nod trying to wrap her brain around this, as his phone beeped and he got up to take another call. He was essentially letting that chick off the hook. Marc had every reason to leak to the press that the entire misunderstanding had all been started by the crazy girl. The details didn't have to be there, but the blame could be, and rightfully so. And, yet, Marc was taking the high road. She didn't know if she could ever be as noble as him. Sure, he had his business in mind, his partner, their shareholders, but putting the blame on Eulalia would serve her right. A spoiled and cruel socialite like that deserved to be taken down a notch or two, but he wasn't letting her bring him down and everything he'd worked so hard to create. Sheesh, she'd need to put a lot of effort into herself in order to be half as mature as Marc was. She would be more than happy to tell the world what a conniving bitch Eulalia Mosa was, ruining her social standing in the process if she was in his shoes.

He came back to sit on the sofa. "That was Bruce," he said in some exasperation. "He's giving me shit. He's usually the one in the press about some crazy antic or other. But now, here I am, splashed across the papers about my 'incident'." Marc air-quoted. He glanced at the time on his phone. "We should probably turn in soon. Remember we're meeting your father tomorrow?"

"Oh crap. Marc, do we have to?" she whined, making a pouty face at him.

"We don't have to, but don't you want to?" he asked with a seriousness that made her feel like a petulant child. Instead of bristling up, her shoulders sagged. He was right about this.

"Yeah, I do," she conceded. "But, babe, I don't know if you should come with me, considering everything that happened, and, you know, the scratches and black eye," she said meaningfully, pointing at his face.

"No way, I'm coming with you. Your dad probably already knows about the entire thing; hell, all of India knows by now. And who cares about a couple of scratches and a shiner. I don't."

Simran thought about this for a moment. She and her father had a lot to discuss, he wouldn't expect Marc with her. It could go one of two ways: maybe his wrath toward her wouldn't be so bad in front of a guest, or maybe he'd be so angry that he wouldn't even see them. Regardless, it would be freaking fantastic to have Marc there supporting her. Even if her dad was in a disowning mood, she would still be holding Marc's hand.

"Ok, fine, you and your shiner can come, scratches and all," she relinquished, huffing out a breath of relief.

૭૦

Chapter 30

This time, while his driver maneuvered up the circular drive, it was Simran who stared up at the large peach house and shuddered. Marc turned his gaze to her profile, and squeezed her hand. She could do this.

Today she was wearing her hair up in an elegant bun, and had decided to go traditional in a sweet, pea green *salwar kameez* with bright pink flowers and jewels embroidered around the short-collared, high neckline and along the body of the knee length tunic. Matching fitted pants encased her legs, and her *dupatta* (scarf) was chiffon with an ombre effect of green and pink. Marc didn't have the heart to tell her that she looked amazingly sexy to him, no matter what she wore. He wasn't her main focus today. Her father was, and she needed to be confident, but also maybe with a hint of contrition.

Marc was thankful when she decided to meet with her father a few days ago. Even if it didn't go in the direction they wanted it to, she would at least know that she tried. The ball would now be in Kumar's court.

She squeezed his hand back, her nervous eyes flying to his, the gold, fan-shaped earrings dangling in her ears, glinting to the movement. "Thank you for being here," she murmured, her voice shy, low, and husky, making Marc want to pull her onto his lap. Instead, he leaned over and quickly kissed her on the forehead, whispering he would always have her back. She smiled and took a deep breath as they got out of the car. They went up the front stairs and rang the bell.

She peered around the property and exclaimed happily, "Oh look! Dad put Babar back!" She was pointing to the elephant fountain in the lake as they waited. Marc was convinced he hadn't heard correctly.

"Um, I don't mean to teach you about your culture, but that's Ganesh, baby." A smile tugged on his lips as he looked down at Simran and her face became relaxed with a silly grin as she rolled her eyes.

"Oh, babe, you know everything, don't you?" She poked him in the stomach. "Yeah, duh, it's Ganesh. But when Sabine and I were little, we re-named him Babar because we were reading those children's books with my mom at the time." Her voice became wistful as she thought about those memories.

Marc hugged her tight, resting his chin on the top of her head. "I wish I could have had the chance to meet your mom. You don't talk about her much."

"I know. I will. Give me time." And Marc understood. He was close to his mom, too. If anything happened to her, he would have no idea how to handle it. For Simran, not talking about it was her way of managing her feelings. But he knew she would come around when she was ready.

The door opened, and the same male servant from a few days ago stood before them.

"Bilal!" Simran exclaimed, her face breaking into a huge ear-to-ear grin. She stepped forward and hugged the man tight. Clearly not expecting to see her, he embarrassingly stood there, his hands at his sides, but his face also had a huge smile on it.

"*Namaste*, Simran Madam," Bilal whispered, his eyes downcast as Simran unwound her arms from him.

"Marc, this is Bilal. He's been a part of the household since before I can even remember." She wound an arm tightly around Marc and explained something in Hindi to Bilal, which made his eyes go big. He looked Marc over again with a startled gaze, recognizing him. This time Marc wasn't disheveled like he'd been last time, having just hopped off an extremely long plane ride, and in search of Simran. He was wearing grey jeans, a burgundy polo-style shirt, and grey oxford shoes. His arm was around Simran, too, and he could tell this was a lot for Bilal to take in. "I just told him that you and I are *very* good friends and that he should treat you like one of our family," she whispered to Marc. Then she continued speaking to Bilal in Hindi as they were ushered inside. She grabbed Marc's hand and led him through the cavernous foyer to the back. A few dark heads popped up from behind columns or potted plants to peer at them curiously, and Simran called a greeting to each and every one of them, knowing them all by name.

They entered a room in the back which was more intimate. It was toned down in swirls of beiges and yellows. The heavy furniture was more modern with a huge tan leather sectional sitting along the back wall with a large flat screen tv hung up opposite and a souped-up surround sound lining the perimeter of the room, which Marc appreciated. Windows covered one wall with glass doors encased in them, leading out to a patio and pool. What had him in awe were the pictures upon pictures framed on the walls, and sitting on the various surfaces around the room. Family photos ranging from when the girls were small to when they were adults documented their growth and special milestones. Clearly, this was the part of the house that was lived in, unlike the over-showy front rooms. In one corner he noticed an elaborate altar covered in a beautiful deep blue material fringed with silver. A framed picture of a woman stood on it, along with several votive candles in gold holders. Marc had to step closer to take a better look because something in that picture caught his attention. When he got closer, he realized it was because the image so resembled Simran, he had to do a double-take. He felt her arm brushing his as she came up to stand beside him.

"My mom, Noor," she said reverently, then reached over to light the votives. The portrait depicted a young woman lounging under a tree in a brilliant, sapphire-colored sari with silver trim, the same fabric the altar was made up with. Her face was serene, and her large eyes, so like her daughter's, were playfully looking up at the camera, a look that Marc was all too familiar with. Her hair was draped over one shoulder in long, thick waves and she was wearing the same heavy, gold jewelry that Marc had seen Simran wear months ago.

"Wow, you look so much like her, Sims."

"I get that a lot," she replied, also staring closely at her mother.

The glass door slid open abruptly with a loud clang, and they heard "*Kulsom!*" being shouted by Kumar as he entered the room. He didn't see them and was bopping his head to music he was listening to through his earbuds. He started humming and then broke out into a little jig, snapping his fingers. He was wearing a tan tracksuit with matching mesh sneakers. He looked winded, his face flushed, sweat shining on his forehead. He must have been outside exercising.

Marc stared in astonishment as the man continued to wiggle and dance, absorbed with a stack of mail he'd found on the side table, and Simran started to giggle, trying to hide it behind one of her hands.

When he looked up and finally noticed them, a hand came up to his chest and he shouted, "*Orey baba!* (Oh my god), Sima! You scared the spirit out of me!" And Marc couldn't help chuckling at how similar his reaction was to his daughter's when he found her by the waterfall a few days ago.

"*Abba, Namaste—*" She started to move toward him.

"*Nah, nah, nah!* You cannot come to me as if nothing happened, after making me worry for days and days and days," he said dramatically, his voice high pitched, making her stop in her tracks. "And then I see your picture in the papers associated with some incident at a club." He pointed and turned to Marc. "Your club if I'm not mistaken? Sima, I am not happy about any of this," he finished, a hand up in the air as if he was dismissing them already.

Simran raised a brow and gave a meaningful 'I told you so'
look to Marc.

"Mr. Khan," he interjected and walked toward Kumar,
hand outstretched. Kumar eyed him warily, staring a little too
long at the exposed healing scratches on Marc's face, along
with his black eye. Then he reluctantly took his hand and
shook it. "It's so nice to see you again. I finally found Simran."
He turned to her when he said this, winking. Turning back to
her father, he continued, not revealing where she'd been. "I
know you were as worried as I was. Anyway, she and I both
came to a decision about our relationship and decided it was
a good idea to come and see you first. We wanted to clear the
air."

Kumar grunted, looking at him suspiciously before a
genuine smile finally broke out on his face. Marc heard
Simran gasp behind him, clearly taken aback.

"Marcus Lehigh. Twice in one week." He shook his head,
South Asian head bob and all.

Kulsom appeared and Kumar asked for refreshments.
Everyone sat down on the large couch as they waited.

"So, what were you listening to on your power-walk,
Abba?" Simran asked a little hesitantly, breaking the silence.

"Oh," and he fiddled with his device which was still in his
pocket, "Ariana Grande, *beta*. My God, her voice—oh, so
beautiful," he closed his eyes reverently. "And her songs—so
catchy," he said, smiling and jiggling his head side to side.

"Nice! I love her recent album! Have you heard it?" Simran
continued. Marc could tell that clearly this was where
Simran's love of music stemmed from but also that she was

doing her best—and admiringly so—to bring Kumar's tension down a few pegs. Kumar nodded enthusiastically as they discussed Ariana Grande's merits.

When the tea and snacks were set on the table before them, and each of them had settled back with their refreshments, Kumar continued with the more serious topic weighing in on the room.

"So, am I to understand, Sima, that you are with Marcus again?" He stirred then slurped his tea loudly. "Have you no respect for your father, your family, or your duty?" he asked her directly. Man, he just went right for the jugular, Marc thought, wincing. He glanced at Simran. Her face was passive, with no reaction … yet.

"*Abba*, I'm here now. That should be enough to tell you I respect you and the family. But I'm starting to think you don't respect me."

Kumar's brows went high, so stunned was he by this statement. Then he grinned, a little coolly. "You were in Lonavala visiting with your Rani Khala this whole time, weren't you?" A hand went to his forehead dramatically. "*Eeesh*. I should have known to look there."

Marc was confused. How did the lack of respect Simran felt she received from her dad lead to her aunt? Then he remembered what Simran had briefly filled him in about her aunt's history and the rift she had with Kumar because of her independence.

"I was," Simran said matter-of-factly, as she stirred her own tea and took a sip. "And thank baby Krishna, too, because

I was a mess, *Abba*. I didn't know what to do in the face of what you wanted from me for the family."

"Why should you have to think about it at all? I made the decision for you. It was all pretty simple, Sima." Kumar sucked his teeth, shaking his head.

"I don't want you making decisions for me, especially when it comes to my future. It's my life, shouldn't I be the one making the decisions?" Kumar simply shrugged, his only indication that he heard her. "And as for Anil, he's already married."

"*Bah!*" Kumar waved a hand as if the statement was a fly bothering him. "He's a bozo. Do you know he just told his parents and they almost died of broken hearts?"

"I'm sorry they feel that way, *Abba*, but he told the truth, and that deserves more respect than ever treating your child like a puppet," Simran said, raising her chin slightly.

It was like watching a tennis ball volley back and forth, this heated discussion between father and daughter. Marc doubted they even remembered he was still sitting there.

"Listen, *Abba*, I don't want a wedge between us." She put her cup down and gripped her hands, the only sign that she was struggling with this conversation, as her face and composure remained tranquil. She took a deep breath. "My duty is to be a good daughter. What that means to *me* is someone who was raised to be a good person with good values, and is true to one's self." She paused, then continued so that Kumar couldn't interject. "I'm beyond happy with my life in New York. I love my job and my friends. I have you to thank every single day for your support so that I would be confident in my decisions, and make a success of myself. The cherry on top is that I've found someone who makes me feel fulfilled." She stopped, putting a hand on Marc's knee. "So, yes, Dad, I'm here with Marc. I love him and he's it for me."

Kumar let out a hefty, passionate sigh and was silent for a while, staring back and forth between them as he continued to drink his tea. Then he gave an Indian head bob saying, "And what about your elders, Sima? What about what I want and wish for your future? I only want what is best for you; what is the most simple and easiest for you. That's what any parent wants for their child. Do you think I would lead you astray?" He sounded hurt and offended. He took a napkin from the tea tray and dabbed furiously at the sweat dripping over his brow now.

"Well, I thought about it, *Abba*, and gave it some real consideration. It's a good plan, don't get me wrong," she assured him. "For any other Indian family, with a daughter who needs guidance about her future, this would completely be the gold standard. But I'm not that girl. I don't want to disappoint you, I never have, but you're expecting too much from me. How could I, the independent woman that you pushed along to be a successful American, who lives most of my life with American values, be expected to become the Indian wife? No. It's expecting *too* freaking much." She shook her head vehemently and stood up. Her hands were clenched at her sides. "It's not going to make me happy. Do you want me to be unhappy for the rest of my life?" And Marc saw Kumar's lip pucker and his eyebrows lift in contemplation. Was he actually considering this? Simran continued. "I respect you; you know that. But you have to view me as an adult and respect *me* now, too. Or we can never have the closeness that we've been able to have." Again, Kumar's mouth pursed, thinking about what his daughter was telling him.

Simran walked over to her mother's altar. "Look at *Amma.* That's the face of a woman in love. I know you were arranged, but you fell for each other during your courtship. It was a fairy-tale, and so, so lucky. But guess what, I've found someone who makes me feel that way, without your help. Can't you understand that I want what you and *Amma* had?" she said passionately. Kumar silently took a bite of a chewy condensed milk disc dripping in its creamy sweet sauce from the bowl he was holding.

"Have you tried this *ras malai?*" he asked, chewing around the crushed pistachios on top. "I would eat it for breakfast every day if it wasn't so sugary!" Simran wordlessly stepped back to the tea tray, helped herself to some, and took a bite. Marc reached for his bowl and tried a taste, too. The chewy, chilled disc burst with the sweet, creamy syrup it'd been sitting in, and slid slowly, coolly down his throat. It was delicious.

"You know it's one of my favorites, too," she said, nodding as she licked her lips of the syrup. She put her bowl down and sat on the couch again. "Are you listening to me, *Abba?*"

"I am," Kumar said mildly.

"So, Anil is already married, and I'm genuinely happy for him. Do you know why? Because *he* is genuinely happy. Even if he hadn't already been tied to someone else, do you think he would have been the perfect son-in-law? Hear me out." She waved her hand just as her father opened his mouth. "He disappointed me back then when he left for Germany. I can't completely blame him, though, because I didn't really know him. We didn't really know each other at all. I learned more about him in the two-hour breakfast we had a few days ago than I ever did before!" She shook her head in astonishment. "We were both playing a role, pandering to our elders. But now, marriage to each other, at this stage in our lives—it would never work because we know the other side. We know what love looks and feels like." She glanced at Marc with tenderness. "It would be phony if Anil and I got married now. We might not make each other unhappy, but the situation absolutely would." She took a deep breath. "God, Dad, I would hate you for it forever. Is that really what you want?" Now her voice was getting louder, higher pitched. Her cheeks were infusing with pink. Marc put a hand on her lower back to steady her.

Kumar put his empty bowl down slowly. He wiped his mouth with his napkin, throwing it onto the table. Then he put both hands up in surrender, bobbing his head again. "*Atcha, atcha.*" His tone was calmer than it had been the entire conversation and he continued, "Ok, Sima." He sucked his teeth. "I already have a daughter I cannot talk with." He was referring to Sabine and how tense their relationship was. "I don't like this decision." He shook his head emphatically. "I don't know if I ever will. This ..." he swept his hands between them, "is unknown to me. All my life I have been taught that I am the one who takes care of my wife, my family, my in-laws, and especially my daughters. What is this between you, is this love or is this lust?" he asked her frankly, then turned his golden eyes to Marc questioning, too. "How long will this last? When you are done with my daughter, where does she go from there? I know you are a good man, Marcus, but you are not Indian. Indians do things differently. We don't date casually. Our relationships are serious and reflect our family honor. Who is your father, Marcus? Who is your mother? Where do they come from and what are their stories?"

⋐⋑⋐⋑

Simran scoffed, a little disgusted at this speech. Times were changing.

"Sima, this is our culture. You may be repulsed by it, but it is how things are done here," her father said to her.

"Not always," she shot back. "People marry for love."

"*Atcha,* but what about marrying someone who is not Indian? This is all extremely new to our family. What will people *say?*" And now he sounded timid, almost frightened by the prospect. Simran's heart defrosted, as it always did toward her dad. "And then what about your children?" He sucked his teeth hard at the prospect of half Asian and half American grandchildren and how he would explain this to all of their more traditional relatives.

"Oh my God, *Abba!*" She glanced at Marc. Here her dad was talking about marriage and children and she hadn't even given Marc an answer about moving in together. Would Marc go running for the hills if he wasn't already put off by this conversation? Marc held a sardonic half-grin on his face as he stared closely at the tea service. *Great.*

"We haven't even discussed marriage or kids, and we don't need to start now—" she said, laughing a little nervously. She turned to Marc who was staring at her now, his brain working out what he wanted to say, she could almost see it.

"We haven't discussed marriage or kids, you're right, Sims. But," he turned his focus to her father, "I could see that in our future." He swung back to Simran. "Couldn't you?" His head was cocked to the side, his look so sincere.

"I ... well ..." Simran stuttered. "Yeah." She finally said, biting her lip from smiling like a crazy person. This was new. Her heart flip-flopped and then stuck its tongue out at her brain as if to say, "I told you so."

Kumar broke their intense stare with a loud sneeze and then he blew his nose, honking garishly in the process. "*Eeesh,* these allergies," he proclaimed as if he was the unearned victim of every one of his maladies. "Could." He said the word flatly, standing up. He wagged his pointer finger at them. "That is not good enough, Marcus Lehigh. I need to know that my daughter is provided for, taken care of—"

"Dad—"

"Do not interrupt me, Sima. Let me finish. Relationships are taken seriously here, Marcus. What starts as a new marriage, with two unknown individuals, grows to trust and sometimes love, but more than anything, there is honesty in the relationship. No false promises of love and fidelity. In the end, our divorce rates are much, much lower here in India

because of that. Tell me, what is the divorce rate in America?"
He waited expectantly.

"I don't have that answer, Mr. Khan, but I do know it's high. I also know that I am not someone who will take your daughter for granted or lie to her. I love her with everything in me. I already experienced life without her and it's something I don't intend to do again. I understand her, and more importantly, I have her happiness at the forefront of my goals. If she's not happy, then I won't be either," Marc said simply, shrugging his shoulders. He stood up and moved toward Simran, putting his arm around her waist in solidarity.

Kumar stared between the two of them for what seemed like an eternity. "*Bas* (enough)," he said with a sharp head shake. "I've heard enough for today. I don't like this decision but I want you to be happy. I—" He cut himself off as he stared at the corner where his wife's altar stood. "I need time." He left the room abruptly, doors subsequently slamming throughout the house.

Chapter 31

Both Marc and Simran stared after Kumar, unsure of what to do next. Simran started to go after her father, but Marc stayed her.

"Just let him be," Marc said knowingly. "He needs space. But, Sims, I'm never letting you go again. So, he's going to have to come to terms with this one way or another." He pulled her to look at some of the other family pictures more closely, trying to break some of the strain in the air. "I think these are by far my favorite. Tell me about them." They were standing in front of a wall of memories. Simran smiled gratefully at him. The conversation with her father had been exhausting and fraught with emotions. She needed the reprieve.

The pictures were of her and Sabine as kids. Some were when they were in matching school uniforms, colorful clips in their hair, where Simran was a smaller version of herself now, but with a rounder face and toothless grin. Then even further back in time were pictures of them, not much older than toddlers, posing in matching saris on a balcony with their mother. All were smiling widely and showing off Indian dance poses, bangles snaking up their arms. They had been a tight-knit family once, Simran thought a little sadly. She hoped she hadn't completely wrecked it with her need for self-fulfillment.

When Marc saw high school pictures of both sisters, he barked out with laughter. Sabine was in all black, completely goth'ed out with black lipstick, a short pixie haircut, and even blue laced combat boots. A teenage Simran was smiling cheerily beside her, one arm around her sister, the other hand on her hip in attitude wearing a cheerleading uniform.

"What's so funny?" She punched him in the arm.

"Baby, I'm sorry, this picture ... you're so young, but it completely captures both of your personalities right now." He shook his head still chuckling.

She chuckled, too. "That was Sabine's goth phase. It was ... interesting ... and that was when I was on my school's dance team. I *loved* those days. You know how much I like to dance," she said, coming closer to the wall to stare at it more carefully. "But what was up with my hair?" she asked herself in wonder, staring at her high pigtails.

"I like it. I think you should do that hairdo again. And also look for that uniform ... I already know you love to dance," he said suggestively, his hands coming to rest on the small of her back, creeping to her ass.

"You are a dirty, dirty man." She grinned cheekily up at him. They stared at each other for a bit, lost in the moment.

"I mean it when I say I want this." His hand swept along the wall of memories. "I want a family, I want kids..." He was wistful. "It was just me and my mom growing up. Then Bruce inserted himself when we were in college." He smirked. "But growing up, I always wanted a brother or sister to play with." His hands slid to rest on her belly.

Her throat filled up suddenly, choked with tears, and her vision became blurred. "You're insane," she whispered, her bottom lip trembling.

"Wait. What's happening here?" Marc's brow creased, confused at her sudden turn of emotions, and he frowned.

"I don't know." She was confused, herself. "I just feel mixed up." She shook her head trying to clear her mind. And she knew it for what it was: the sadness about the miscarriage, triggered by the conversation of future children. *Shit.* "I just need a minute." And she turned from Marc's frowning face and hurriedly left the room to her old bedroom on the second floor.

☙☙☙

The soft knock came on her door about twenty minutes later. "Sims?" Marc's deep voice was muffled through the wood, making it even more gravelly than normal.

She was laying on her stomach on her old bed, now spent from her crying. She wiped the remnants of tears with a tissue and then blew her nose. "Come in."

Marc entered and slowly made his way to her bed, sitting down next to her as she sat up. He looked around the room, contemplating some of her old childhood posters and dolls.

"I took a few wrong turns trying to find you. I got laughed out of the kitchen by the way," he said drolly. "I'm not sure what I did to justify that, but apparently I'm hilarious." Simran smiled wryly to herself. Yes, that would happen. An American entering the servant's domain would be absolutely comical to the servants, who not only found him entertaining as he looked nothing like them (some of them had never been so close to a white person before in their lives) but because he was such a dominant, manly figure. In their old-fashioned heads, he was the furthest thing from a servant; a *sahib* (a boss) who gave orders.

He took a deep breath. "I think it's time to talk about this, Sims," he said gently. His face looked crushed and even more vulnerable again with the scars and black eye. He was genuinely concerned, making her heart tighten.

"I know." She plucked at the colorful patchwork comforter. He waited. "I may need to find a therapist when I get back to New York." That was all she could muster before she got teary-eyed again, not being able to look at him.

"All right." He scooted closer, his thigh brushing hers. "But what is it that's bothering you so much? I read miscarriages are actually quite common. Many women go on to have healthy babies after that."

She pressed her lips. Of course, he would do his research. He was a 'fixer,' and right now she needed fixing. "I feel like a failure. Why couldn't my body do what it was supposed to do?"

He sighed, gathering her up into his strong arms, and pulling her to him. "I don't think it was that. Something was wrong with the fetus, so your body did what it was supposed to do. It rejected it and stopped it from growing."

She nodded. She was aware of the science behind it, but it still didn't stop her from feeling blue. "What if I don't have healthy eggs? What if I can't give you the family you want?" She looked up at him with apprehension.

His eyes crinkled and he smiled tenderly at her. "We can cross that bridge if it happens, ok? I think we have enough to think about right now. But it's something that would never deter me from being with you."

She snorted. "It's not always about *you*."

"Ok, sweetie. Is this something that would keep you from being with me?" He was so serious, his brow wrinkled low over his bright eyes.

"Never." She reached up to kiss his jaw, then snuggled her face into his neck, comforted in his smell and the strength of his arms encircling her.

They were silent, contemplating. He stroked her back slowly, easing her.

"Should we make love in your childhood bed?" he finally asked, kissing her hair and nuzzling her.

"Pervert," she said affectionately.

"Mm," he breathed, his kisses continuing along her neck and shoulder, as he maneuvered them so they were laying on her bed. He didn't make a move to make love, though, he just continued stroking her back.

"Are you sure you're ready to take me on? You know, my crazy normal self, along with this added ... issue?"

"Watch it, that's my girlfriend you're talking about," he warned. He hugged her tight. "We'll tackle this stuff together, Sims." He put his hand behind his head, resting on his arm.

"I'd rather have a life like this, filled with these kinds of problems, than one without you. My life was lonely before you came into it. I kind of feel liberated with this love of ours if I'm being truthful with myself, and you. Like, I can tackle the world." He pumped his fist in the air.

"Me, too." Simran's heart filled up. She felt light and airy. They'd made incredible impacts on each other, and both understood that this connection was a game-changer and for good.

She pinched herself to make sure she wasn't dreaming. Then she pinched his chest with firm pressure.

"*Ow!*" he yelped, rubbing his chest, then grabbed her hand to stop her from doing it again. "Why, baby?"

"I need to make sure this is all real."

"Oh, it's real. It's as real as it gets, Sims." He flipped her onto her back, his bright eyes looking intensely into hers. "You ready for me? I can be relentless when I love someone."

"No, *really*?" she teased. "But, give me a minute. I need to think about it," she said, pretending to think about it, the smile hard to keep from her lips. Her arms snuck around his neck and pulled him in for a kiss. How they would make it work with their crazy lifestyles would be an interesting test for them. It was exciting and daunting, but Simran was surer of nothing more than this man in her arms.

৩২

Chapter 32

A FLIGHT BACK TO NEW YORK CITY

The flight back to NY from India was less fraught with emotions for both Simran and Marc than their separate trips there. They'd boarded Marc's private jet a few days after meeting with Kumar. In the time in between then, Simran called her dad numerous times, but he didn't want to speak to her. Marc even tried, but Kumar didn't relent. As they rode to the airport that morning, he finally texted Simran.

Kumar: "*Beta*, when you and Marcus reach New York, please let me know. I would like to know that you reached safely."

Simran had exhaled with relief, holding her phone up for Marc to see the message, then texted him back.

Simran: "I will, *Abba*. Happy Diwali. I'll make sure to pass the presents you sent to our hotel out to everyone in New York and Connecticut."

It was a start. Kumar had what he believed to be the true, authoritative side of the South Asian culture so ingrained in him that his youngest daughter's independence still threw him. And because her father wouldn't speak to her, Simran continued trying by sending over article links of famous

Indians who'd married foreigners. Her father had sneered at these examples, only responding that these were silly Bollywood folk. She finally gave up when a liaison between an Indian actress and Pakistani made him angry—the tumultuous history between India and Pakistan still a major point of contention for him. Saddened that she hadn't been able to make headway before she left, the relief in just that short text exchange that morning was enough for her now. He would come around at some point. It didn't hurt that he respected Marc, actually liked him, either.

Marc glanced over at Simran dozing in her seat in flight. The sunlight streaming in from the other side of the cabin danced over the curve of her cheek, down her neck, and she had a small smile on her full lips. His chest swelled at witnessing her stillness, how lovely she was. He had to refrain from getting up from his own seat across the aisle where he was working, and climbing in next to her under the blanket covering her.

He smiled, recalling how the entire time leading up to their flight, she'd tried to act as if taking a private jet was no big deal, but her eyes let on how excited she was. Big and shiny as she looked around in awe at the interior with two sets of large tan leather captain's seats at the front of the main cabin, each with their own little tables, and then the tan couches lining either side with a table set in the middle. In the back, there was a nice size bathroom with a stand-up shower and a bedroom with a double bed which was cozy, but the sparse décor led to not feeling cramped. Marc had desperately wanted to take Simran back there, make love to her, but she shyly looked at the cabin crew, accepted the flute of champagne from the flight attendant, and dropped herself in one of the large captain seats. He sat next to her, holding her hand as she fell asleep.

He looked back down at his screen, going through the emails from his PR team about the club and updates from Bruce. But he heard Simran sigh as she shifted in her seat and his glance turned to her again. Fuck work. This woman completely captured him. He felt full, more than full. He overflowed with his love for her and wanted everyone to know they were together. She teased him about wanting a future and children with him, but it was the truth, even though she still hadn't agreed to move in with him. He tried not to let that bother him. He was anxious to begin their life together, but patience was a virtue with her, as he'd experienced in the past. Simran was hard-headed, and in many respects, so like her father (something he would never admit to her, but had a feeling she already knew). She did things her way and in her time, especially when it came to allowing someone into her heart. She'd already let him in, so he could wait for this next step. And he would wait longer for her to agree to marry him if he had to.

"What are you staring at so intently?" she asked sleepily, her eyes half open, staring back at him. She smiled and stretched her arms over her head sensually. Did she even know how sexy she always was, he wondered? She stepped across the aisle, swerved his table out of the way, and plopped herself into his lap. Her arms wove around his neck. "Hi," she said huskily. She felt warmer than usual from sleep, her eyes hooded, her lips open and pouty. He felt himself start to harden, and so did she. She sighed and rubbed her round ass against him, moaning sweetly.

"Hi, yourself," he replied, wrapping his arms around her, and pressing her soft breasts against him. He leaned in to kiss her, his tongue looking for hers. She moaned softly again and pushed herself even further into his embrace. Her mouth started sucking his tongue in an animalistic tempo similar to what he wanted his dick to do to her.

The captain's announcement of cruising altitude broke them apart. She was breathing into his neck, her breath warm and feathery. Fuck he wanted her. His hand slid down to grab her ass and squeezed.

"So, what's going through that head of yours?" she asked, threading her cool fingers through the hair at the back of his neck, tickling him.

"That this might be the right time to initiate you into the mile-high club." He lifted his pelvis slightly and made closer contact with her ass.

"*Marc!*" she hissed, looking around, making sure none of the attendants were around.

"What? They work for me, sweetie. They won't tell." He started lavishing her neck, finding her soft spot that beat furiously under her skin. He grazed his teeth against the vulnerable skin and started lapping and sucking. She tasted so good, and she would feel good, too. His hand glided up under her sweater to cup her breasts, squeezing the full globes tenderly, seeking her nipples and plucking. "I want your tits in my mouth, baby." He pinched a hardened bud, making her back arch.

"*Marc!*" she whispered again and pushed his hand away. "I meant, what were you thinking when I was sleeping?"

Marc reluctantly slid his hand to her back but continued to kiss her neck. She let him, her head tilted to give him access, her fingers caressing his chest. "Well, baby, I was thinking about how I'm going to marry you one day." Her hands stilled.

"And who says I want to marry you?" she asked quietly, biting her bottom lip, a small crease between her brows. But her mouth was trying very hard not to break into a smile. "I haven't even agreed to move in with you, yet," she said primly now, her hands in her lap.

"About that," he sighed. "What can I do to make you agree to it?" Here he was pleading with her again. But he wasn't as annoyed as he thought he would be.

"You've done quite enough, Mr. Lehigh," she said decisively, as she watched her fingers unbutton then button his shirt. "I'm ready to move in with you."

Marc's heart soared. As predicted, she just needed time. He put a hand over her worried one, stopping her movements. "I'm so fucking happy to hear you say that, Sims. What made you change your mind?"

"Well, I can't go back to who I was before you, nor would I want to. It just doesn't make sense. I mean, don't get me wrong, I'm still me. I will still run my business, I intend to see my friends, and I'm still going to DJ randomly on the side, but I *do* want to wake up to you every morning and see you when

I come home, maybe throw in a few *extra special* lunch dates where ever we choose to live," she said, brushing his thick locks back from his forehead. "Marc, don't try to change me, ok? I want this, I want us, but I want my independence, too." He realized that she needed to have this conversation with him; the need to accept him as her partner, but vow to retain her identity.

"Sims, I would never dream of changing you. You're exactly who I fell for in the first place. Why would I change that?"

She shrugged. "It's been a struggle with the men in my past, so I want to put this out there front and center."

"All right. I get it. Listen, baby. I want *you* to be you." He kissed her nose. "And, I want to continue to be me. If I lavish you with 'the fancy stuff,'" he air-quoted the phrase she used for the presents he'd gifted her recently, "you're just going to have to deal with it, accept them, and love them. And, you'll have to be ok with me whisking you away on surprise vacations. And, kitten, when I grab your ass in public—not all the time, but secretly when no one is looking, I want you to own it because you're the hottest, sexiest woman and I can't help it, because you're mine."

"You're an idiot," she snorted. "I do own it, by the way, hence the private tour of the broom closet." He chuckled. "I'm looking forward to more of those, actually." She wiggled on his lap again. "But surprise vacations ... *only* if they mesh with my work schedule."

"See, this is where your staff and I agree. They're on my side about this—you're a bonafide workaholic." His eyebrows wriggled at her.

"Please." She rolled her eyes. "And what about you? Talk about double-standard."

"Fair enough," he conceded. "But, I plan on cutting back a bit from work, to focus on us. I think you should consider it, too. But," he put his hands up, "I would never be a chauvinistic pig about it. I do want you happy, you know."

಄಄಄಄

Simran cocked her head to the side, staring at him. His eyes were so bright and warm, and he didn't back down from her stare, like he was challenging her. But he was challenging her in accepting a life together filled with their incredible love. How could she ever deny that?

She pursed her lips, considering his words. "Hm ... I do like pigs ... we'll see."

He linked his hands through hers, chuckling. "And I *do* plan on marrying you one day, so get used to the idea."

She snorted again. "But, you hate marriage." Her heart was beating frantically, ecstatically right now, even though she'd only just agreed to move in with him. She was well aware of what he'd admitted in front of her father, but that was in the heat of a very tension-filled moment. He'd obviously been giving this some real thought lately.

"Not when I can see it with you." Sheesh, this man always killed her with his frank words, and what he wanted from her.

It was so freaking refreshing. She abhorred the dating games she'd played in the past, the measures some men took to keep their emotions hidden, or their agendas protected. She's used it as a protective measure in the past with this man, too. But she now knew, that this, what he was presenting to her, was real. If she was really being truthful with herself, she could see marriage in their future, too.

"Jeez, babe." She breathed, a little overcome by his simple speech. "Marc, I love you with all my heart. I'm yours. Let's just take this one step at a time, ok?"

He nodded. "I love you, too, baby. With everything I have in me." He was so tender, pushing her hair behind her ears. He leaned in to kiss her sweetly, his lips roving softly over hers.

She wrapped her arms around his neck again and murmured against his lips, "Now take me back to that bedroom and initiate me into the club." It was a command, not a request.

He pulled back to see if she was serious, then grinned at her sly smile. He stood up with her in his strong arms and marched back to the bedroom. "Yes, ma'am. I thought you'd never ask." She held on tight, secure in their love and trust for one another.

ধন্যবাদ

Thank you so much for taking the time to read my conclusion to Simran and Marcus' story. I don't know about you but I'm not ready to let them go! So stayed tuned, because there may be more of them to come in the future!

Now, if you haven't already guessed, the wild, uber lady's man, Bruce Canyon—Marc's crazy, but loveable, best friend—is next up to find love. What happens when he meets someone so like him but, refuses to succumb to his wiles? There may be a frustrating, ultra-steamy, and heart-warming story in his future, yet.

A little about me . . .

I love romance, travel, and exploring the South Asian identity. As a South Asian American woman, I write about what I know, having been brought up in the US and living from coast to coast. When I'm not taking my readers on a journey of love and self-discovery, you can find me enjoying my family, friends, crafting, and dancing, and I'd be lying if I didn't add Netflix binge-watching!

Follow me on social media, or join my newsletter to find out what I'm reading, and what I find fascinating in the South Asian American/Western/Female diaspora. Or drop me a line☺, I'd love to hear from you!

www.instagram.com/ktsromance/
www.facebook.com/KhushiT.S
Newsletter: http://subscribepage.io/PG9p3a
Dhanyabad—Thank you—and XO,

Khushi T. Saha